Arthur Murphy

The Old Maid - A Comedy in Two Acts

As it is Performed at the Theatre-Royal in Drury-Lane

Arthur Murphy

The Old Maid - A Comedy in Two Acts
As it is Performed at the Theatre-Royal in Drury-Lane

ISBN/EAN: 9783337067441

Printed in Europe, USA, Canada, Australia, Japan

Cover: Foto ©Andreas Hilbeck / pixelio.de

More available books at **www.hansebooks.com**

THE

OLD MAID.

A

COMEDY

In TWO ACTS,

As it is PERFORMED at the
THEATRE-ROYAL in DRURY-LANE.

By Mr. MURPHY.

Tempus erit, quo tu, quæ nunc excludis amantem,
Frigida Desertâ Noâe jacebis Anus.
OVID.

LONDON:

Printed for P. VAILLANT, facing Southampton-Street
in the Strand. MDCCLXI.

(Price One Shilling.)

3 ADVERTISEMENT.

AS the OLD MAID is now adventuring into the world, it would be proper to acquaint the mere Englifh reader, that the fubject of it, and part of the fable, were taken from a *little piece*, in one act, called, *L'Etourderie*, by Monfieur *Fagan*, but that the author of thefe fcenes is fenfible, how fuperfluous that information will be rendered by the affiduity of fome people, who, no doubt, will make a notable difcovery of this prodigious crime, and prefs it home with all the reproaches of *plagiarifm, pilfering, borrowing, robbing, tranflating,* &c. But while this writer can add any thing to the decent amufements of the public, he is willing to be abufed for it, in whatever manner the illiberal fhall think fit.

LINCOLN's INN,
Nov. 18, 1761.

Dramatis Personæ.

M E N.

CLERIMONT,	Mr. OBRIEN.
Capt. CAPE,	Mr. KING.
Mr. HARLOW,	Mr. KENNEDY.
Mr. HEARTWELL,	Mr. PHILLIPS.
FOOTMAN,	Mr. CASTLE.

W O M E N.

Mrs. HARLOW,	Miss HAUGHTON.
Miss HARLOW,	Miss KENNEDY.
TRIFLE,	Miss HIPPISLEY.

THE
OLD MAID.

ACT I.

Enter Mrs. HARLOW *and Miss* HARLOW.

Mrs. HARLOW.

MY dear sister, let me tell you——

Miss HARLOW.

But, my dear sister, let me tell you it is in vain ; you can say nothing that will have any effect.

Mrs. HARLOW.

Not if you won't hear me——only hear me——

B   Miss

Miſs HARLOW.

Oh! ma'am, I know you love to hear
yourſelf talk, and ſo pleaſe yourſelf;---but
I am reſolved——

Mrs. HARLOW.

Your reſolution may alter.

Miſs HARLOW.

Never.

Mrs. HARLOW.

Upon a little conſideration.

Miſs HARLOW.

Upon no conſideration.

Mrs. HARLOW.

You don't know how that may be---recol-
lect, ſiſter, that you are no chicken---you are
not now of the age that becomes giddineſs
and folly.

Miſs HARLOW.

Age, ma'am---

Mrs. HARLOW.

Do but hear me, ſiſter---do but hear me--
A perſon of your years——

Miſs HARLOW.

My years, ſiſter!—Upon my word——

Mrs. HARLOW.

Nay, no offence, ſiſter——

Miſs HARLOW.

But there is offence, ma'am :—I don't
underſtand what you mean by it---always
thwarting me with my years---my years, indeed!

deed !---when perhaps, ma'am, if I was to die of old age, some folks might have reason to look about them.

Mrs. HARLOW.

She feels it I see---oh ! I delight in mortifying her----(*aside*)--- sister, if I did not love you I am sure I should not talk to you in this manner---But how can you make so unkind a return now as to alarm me about myself ?---in some sixteen or eighteen years after you, to be sure, I own I shall begin to think of making my will---How could you be so severe ?——

Miss HARLOW.

Some sixteen or eighteen years, ma'am !--- If you would own the truth, ma'am,---I believe ma'am,---you would find, ma'am, that the disparity, ma'am, is not so very great, ma'am——

Mrs. HARLOW.

Well! I vow passion becomes you inordinately——It blends a few roses with the lillies of your cheek, and——

Miss HARLOW.

And tho' you are married to my brother, ma'am, I would have you to know, ma'am, that you are not thereby any way authorised, ma'am, to take unbecoming liberties with his sister.——I am independent of my brother, ma'am,---my fortune is in my own hands, ma'am, and ma'am——

Mrs.

Mrs. HARLOW.

Well! do you know now when your
blood circulates a little, that I think you
look mighty well ?——But you was in the
wrong not to marry at my age---ſweet three
and twenty !——you can't conceive what a
deal of good it would have done your temper and your ſpirits, if you had married
early——

Miſs HARLOW.

Inſolent !---provoking---female malice——

Mrs. HARLOW.

But to be waiting till it is almoſt too late
in the day, and force one's ſelf to ſay ſtrange
things ;——with the tongue and heart at
variance all the time——" I don't mind the
hideous men"——" I am very happy as I
am"——and all that time, my dear, dear
ſiſter——to be upon the tenter-hooks of
expectation——

Miſs HARLOW.

I upon tenter-hooks !——

Mrs. HARLOW.

And to be at this work of ſour grapes, till
one is turned of three and forty——

Miſs HARLOW.

Three and forty, ma'am !——I deſire,
ſiſter——I deſire, ma'am——three and forty,
ma'am——

Mrs. HARLOW.

Nay---nay---nay---don't be angry---don't
blame me---blame my huſband ; he is your

own

own brother, you know, and he knows your
age——He told me fo

Mifs HARLOW.

Oh! ma'am, I fee your drift——but you
need not give yourfelf thofe airs, ma'am---
the men don't fee with your eyes, ma'am---
years, indeed !---Three and forty, truly !---
I'll affure you---upon my word---hah! very
fine !——But I fee plainly, ma'am, what
you are at---Mr. Clerimont, madam !---Mr.
Clerimont, fifter ! that's what frets you——
a young hufband, ma'am——younger than
your hufband, ma'am——Mr. Clerimont,
let me tell you, ma'am——

Enter TRIFLE.

TRIFLE.

Oh ! rare news, ma'am, charming news---
we have got another letter——

Mifs HARLOW.

From whom?——from Mr. Clerimont ?——
where is it ?

TRIFLE.

Yes, ma'am——from Mr. Clerimont,
ma'am.

Mifs HARLOW.

Let me fee it——let me fee it——quick—
quick——   [*reads*

" Madam,

" The honour of a letter from you has
" fo filled my mind with joy and gratitude,
                                   " that

" that I want words of force to reach but
" half my meaning. I can only fay that
" you have revived a heart that was expiring
" for you, and now beats for you alone"—

There fifter, mind that!---years indeed!--
[reads to herself.

Mrs. HARLOW.

I wifh you joy, fifter——I wifh I had not
gone to Ranelagh with her laft week——
Who could have thought that her faded
beauties would have made fuch an impref-
fion on him? *[afide.*

Mifs HARLOW.

Mind here again, fifter.——*(reads)* " Ever
" fince I had the good fortune of feeing
" you at Ranelagh, your idea has been ever
" prefent to me; and fince you now give
" me leave, I fhall, without delay, wait
" upon your brother, and whatever terms
" he prefcribes, I fhall readily fubfcribe to;
" for to be your flave is dearer to me than
" liberty. I have the honour to remain
" The humbleft of your admirers,
" CLERIMONT."

There, fifter!——

Mrs. HARLOW.

Well! I wifh you joy again——but remember I tell you, take care what you do.--
He is young, and of courfe giddy and in-
conftant.

Mifs

Miſs HARLOW.

He is warm, paſſionate, and tender——

Mrs. HARLOW.

But you don't know how long that may
laſt——and here are you going to break off
a very ſuitable match,——which all your
friends liked and approved, a match with
captain Cape, who to be ſure——

Miſs HARLOW.

Don't name captain Cape, I beſeech you,
don't name him——

Mrs. HARLOW.

Captain Cape, let me tell you, is not to
be deſpiſed——He has acquired by his voy-
ages to India a very pretty fortune——has a
charming box of a houſe upon Hackney-
Marſh,——and is of an age every way ſuitable to you.

Miſs HARLOW.

There again now!——age! age! age!
for ever!——years—years—my years!——
But I tell you once for all, Mr. Clerimont
does not ſee with your eyes——I am determined to hear no more of captain Cape——
Odious Hackney-Marſh! —— ah! ſiſter,
you would be glad to ſee me married in a
middling way——

Mrs. HARLOW.

I, ſiſter!——I am ſure nobody will rejoice more at your preferment——I am reſolved never to viſit her if Mr. Clerimont
marries her——   [aſide.

Miſs

Miſs HARLOW.

Well! well! I tell you, Mr. Clerimont
has won my heart—young—handſome—rich
——town houſe, country houſe——equipage——To him, and only him, will I ſur-
render myſelf——Three and forty, indeed!
——ha! ha!——you ſee, my dear, dear
ſiſter, that theſe features are ſtill regular and
blooming;——that the love-darting eye has
not quite forſook me; and that I have made
a conqueſt which your boaſted youth might
be vain of——

Mrs. HARLOW.

Oh! ma'am, I beg your pardon if I have
taken too much liberty for your good——

Miſs HARLOW.

I humbly thank you for your advice, my
ſweet dear, friendly ſiſter——But don't envy
me, I beg you won't;——don't fret yourſelf; you can't conceive what a deal of good
a ſerenity of mind will do your health——
I'll go and write an anſwer directly to this
charming, charming letter—ſiſter—yours—
I ſhall be glad to ſee you, ſiſter, at my houſe
in Hill-ſtreet, when I am Mrs. Clerimont——
and remember what I tell you——that ſome
faces retain their bloom and beauty longer
than you imagine——my dear ſiſter——
Come, Trifle——let me fly this moment——
Siſter, your ſervant.   [*Exit with Trifle.*

Mrs.

Mrs. HARLOW.

Your servant, my dear!——well!—I am determined to lead the gayeft life in nature, if fhe marries Clerimont.——I'll have a new equipage, that's one thing—and I'll have greater routs than her, that's another——Pofitively, I muft outfhine her there—and I'll keep up a polite enmity with her—go and fee her, may be once or twice in a winter—— " Ma'am, I am really fo hurried with fuch a number of acquaintances, that I can't poffibly find time"——And then to provoke her, " I wifh you joy, fifter, I hear you are breeding"——ha ! ha !—that will fo mortify her——" I wifh it may be a boy, fifter"—— ha ! ha !—and then when her hufband begins to defpife her, " Really, fifter, I pity " you—had you taken my advice, and mar- " ried the India captain—your cafe is a com- " paffionate one"——Compaffion is fo infolent when a body feels none at all——ha ! ha! —it is the fineft way of infulting——

Enter Mr. HARLOW.

Mr. HARLOW.

So, my dear ; how are my fifter's affairs going on ?

Mrs. HARLOW.

Why, my dear, fhe has had another letter from Mr. Clerimont——did you ever hear of fuch an odd unaccountable thing patched up in a hurry here ?

Mr. HARLOW.

Why it is fudden, to be fure——

C   Mrs.

Mrs. H A R L O W.

Upon my word, I think you had better advife her not to break off with captain Cape——

Mr. H A R L O W.

No— not I——I wifh fhe may be married to one or other of them——for her temper is really grown fo very four, and there is fuch eternal wrangling between ye both, that I wifh to fee her in her own houfe, for the peace and quiet of mine.

Mrs. H A R L O W.

Do you know this Mr. Clerimont?

Mr. H A R L O W.

No ; but I have heard of the family---: There is a very fine fortune---I wifh he may hold his intention.

Mrs. H A R L O W.

Why, I doubt it vaftly——

Mr. H A R L O W.

And truly fo do I—for between ourfelves, I fee no charms in my fifter——

Mrs. H A R L O W.

For my part I can't comprehend it—how fhe could ftrike his fancy, is to me the moft aftonifhing thing——After this, I fhall be fur-prifed at nothing—

Mr. H A R L O W.

Well! ftrange things do happen ;——fo fhe is but married out of the way, I am fatisfied—an old maid in a houfe is the de-vil——

Enter

Enter a Servant.

SERVANT.

Mr. Clerimont, Sir, to wait on you——

Mr. HARLOW.

Shew him in (*Exit Servant*)——how comes
this visit, pray?——

Mrs. HARLOW.

My sister wrote to him to explain himself
to you——Well! it is mighty odd——but
I'll leave you to yourselves. The man must
be an ideot to think of her——

[*Aside and Exit.*

Enter Mr. CLERIMONT.

Mr. HARLOW.

Sir, I am glad to have this pleasure.

CLERIMONT.

I presume, Sir, you are no stranger to the
business that occasions this visit.

Mr. HARLOW.

Sir, the honour you do me and my family—

CLERIMONT.

Oh! Sir, to be allied to your family by so
tender a tie as a marriage with your sister, will
at once reflect a credit upon me, and conduce
to my happiness in the most essential point.--
The lady charmed me at the very first sight.

Mr. HARLOW (*aside.*)

The devil she did!

C 2   CLE-

CLERIMONT.

The fenfibility of her countenance, the elegance of her figure, the fweetnefs of her manner——

Mr. HARLOW.

Sir, you are pleafed to——compliment!

CLERIMONT.

Compliment!——not in the leaft, Sir—

Mr. HARLOW.

The fweetnefs of my fifter's manner (*afide*) ha! ha!

CLERIMONT.

The firft time I faw her was a few nights ago at Ranelagh——Though there was a crowd of beauties in the room, thronging and prefling all around, yet fhe fhone amongft them all with fuperior luftre——She was walking arm in arm with another lady—no opportunity offered for me to form an acquaintance amidft the hurry and buftle of the place, but I enquired their names as they were going into their chariot—and learned they were Mrs. and Mifs Harlow. From that moment fhe won my heart, and at one glance I became the willing captive of her beauty—

Mr. HARLOW.

A very candid declaration, Sir!——how can this be? The bloom has been off the peach any time thefe fifteen years, to my

know-

knowlege——(*aside*)—You see my sister with
a favourable eye, Sir.

CLERIMONT.

A favourable eye !——He must greatly
want discernment, who has not a quick per-
ception of her merit.

Mr. HARLOW.

You do her a great deal of honour—but
this affair—is it not somewhat sudden, Sir ?—

CLERIMONT.

I grant it---you may indeed be surprised
at it, Sir ; nor should I have been hardy
enough to make any overtures to you,---at
least yet a while,---if she herself had not
condescended to listen to my passion, and authorised me under her own fair hand to apply to her brother for his consent——

Mr. HARLOW.

I shall be very ready, Sir, to give my ap-
probation to my sister's happiness——

CLERIMONT.

No doubt you will——but let me not
cherish an unavailing flame, a flame that already lights up all my tenderest passions.

Mr. HARLOW.

To you, Sir, there can be no exception--
I am not altogether a stranger to your family and fortune——His language is warm,
considering my sister's age---but I won't
hurt her preferment——(*aside*)——you will
pardon me, Sir, one thing----you are very
young——   CLE-

CLERIMONT.

Sir,---I am almoſt three and twenty.

Mr. HARLOW.

But have you conſulted your friends?

CLERIMONT.

I have——my uncle, Mr. Heartwell, who propoſes to leave me a very handſome addition to my fortune, which is conſiderable already——He, Sir——

Mr. HARLOW.

Well! Sir, if he has no objection, I can have none——

CLERIMONT.

He has none, Sir; he has given his conſent; he deſires me to loſe no time---I will bring him to pay you a viſit——He rejoices in my choice---you ſhall have it out of his own mouth——name your hour, and he ſhall attend you——

Mr. HARLOW.

Any time to-day——I ſhall ſtay at home on purpoſe——

CLERIMONT.

In the evening I will conduct him hither-- in the mean time I feel an attachment here-- The lady, Sir——

Mr. HARLOW.

Oh! you want to ſee my ſiſter——I will ſend her to you, Sir, this inſtant——I beg your pardon for leaving you alone——ha! ha!——who could have thought of her making a conqueſt at laſt——   *Exit.*

CLERIMONT (*alone.*)

Sir, your moſt obedient---now, Clerimont, now your heart may reſt content——your doubts and fears may all ſubſide, and joy and rapture take their place——Miſs Harlow ſhall be mine---ſhe receives my vows; ſhe approves my paſſion,——(*ſings and dances*) Soft! here ſhe comes----Her very appearance controuls my wildeſt hopes, and huſhes my proud heart into reſpect and ſilent admiration——

Enter Mrs. HARLOW.

Mrs. HARLOW.

Sir, your ſervant——

CLERIMONT.

Madam (*bows reſpectfully*)

Mrs. HARLOW.

I thought Mr. Harlow was here, Sir.

CLERIMONT.

Madam, he is but juſt gone——how a ſingle glance of her eye over-awes me!
                                    [*Aſide.*

Mrs. HARLOW.

I wonder he would leave you alone, Sir--- that is not ſo polite in his own houſe——

CLERIMONT.

How her modeſty throws a veil over her inclinations!——my tongue faulters!——I can't ſpeak to her.   [*Aſide.*

                                    Mrs.

Mrs. HARLOW.

He seems in confusion---a pretty man too!
----That this should be my sister's luck!---

[*Aside.*

CLERIMONT.

Madam !----(*Embarrassed.*)

Mrs. HARLOW.

I imagine you have been talking to him
on the subject of the letter you sent this
morning.----

CLERIMONT.

Madam, I have presumed to ----

Mrs. HARLOW.

Well! Sir, and he has no objection, I
hope----

CLERIMONT.

She hopes! Heavens bless her for the
word ----(*Aside.*)----Madam, he has frankly
consented, if his sister will do me that ho-
nour----

Mrs. HARLOW.

For his sister, I think I may venture to
answer, Sir----

CLERIMONT.

Generous! generous creature!

Mrs. HARLOW.

You are sure, Sir, of Miss Harlow's admiration, and the whole family hold themselves much obliged to you----

CLERIMONT.

Madam, this extreme condescension has
added rapture to the sentiments I felt before;

and

and it shall be the endeavour of my life to
prove deserving of the amiable object I have
dared to aspire to.——

Mrs. HARLOW.

Sir, I make no doubt of your sincerity—
I have already declared my sentiments—you
know Mr. Harlow's——and if my sister is
willing,——nothing will be wanting to conclude this business—If no difficulties arise
from her—for her temper is uncertain—as
to my consent, Sir, your air, your manner
have commanded it——Sir your most obedient—I'll send my sister to you— [*Exit*.

CLERIMONT.

Madam, (*bowing*) I shall endeavour to repay this goodness with excess of gratitude—
Oh! she is an angel!—and yet, stupid that
I am, I could not give vent to the tenderness
I have within---it is ever so with sincere and
generous love; it fills the heart with rapture, and then denies the power of uttering
what we so exquisitely feel—Generous Miss
Harlow! who could thus see thro' my confusion, interpret all appearances favourably,
and with a dignity superior to her sex's little arts, forego the idle ceremonies of co-
quetting, teazing, and tormenting her admirer—I hear somebody.—Oh! here comes
mistress Harlow—what a gloom sits upon her
features!---She assumes authority here I find
---but I'll endeavour by insinuation and respect——

D *Enter*

Enter Miss HARLOW.

Miss HARLOW.

My sister has told me, Sir——

CLERIMONT.

Ma'am——(*bowing chearfully.*)

Miss HARLOW.

He is a sweet figure.   [*Aside.*

CLERIMONT.

She rather looks like Miss Harlow's mother than her sister-in-law——   [*Aside.*

Miss HARLOW.

He seems abashed——his respect is the cause——(*Aside*)——My sister told me, Sir, that you was here—I beg pardon for making you wait so long——

CLERIMONT.

Oh, ma'am (*bows*) the gloom disappears from her face, but the lines of ill-nature remain——   [*Aside.*

Miss HARLOW.

I see he loves me by his confusion;—I'll cheer him with affability—(*Aside*)—Sir, the letter you was pleased to send, my sister has seen——and——

CLERIMONT.

And has assured me that she has no objection——

Miss HARLOW.

I am glad of that, Sir---I was afraid——

CLE-

CLERIMONT.

No, ma'am, she has none——and Mr.
Harlow, I have seen him too——he has honoured me with his consent——Now, madam, the only doubt remains with you ;——
may I be permitted to hope——

Miss HARLOW.

Sir, you appear like a gentleman,--and--

CLERIMONT.

Madam, believe me, never was love more
sincere, more justly founded on esteem, or
kindled into higher admiration.

Miss HARLOW.

Sir, with the rest of the family I hold myself much obliged to you, and——

CLERIMONT.

Obliged !—'tis I that am obliged—there
is no merit on my side—it is the conse-
quence of impressions made upon my heart ;
and what heart can resist such beauty, such
various graces !——

Miss HARLOW.

Sir, I am afraid—I wish my sister heard
him (*aside*)——Sir, I am afraid you are la-
vish of your praise ; and the short date of
your love, Sir——

CLERIMONT.

It will burn with unabating ardor——the
same charms that first inspired it, will for
ever cherish it, and add new fuel——But I

prefume you hold this ftile to try my fince-
rity—I fee that's your aim—but could you
read the feelings of my heart, you would
not thus cruelly keep me in fufpenfe.

Mifs H A R L O W.

Heavens ! if my fifter faw my power over
him—(*afide*)——A little fufpenfe cannot be
deemed unreafonable—Marriage is an important affair——an affair for life——and fome
caution you will allow neceffary——

C L E R I M O N T.

Madam !—(*difconcerted*)——oh ! I dread
the fournefs of her look !——   [*Afide.*

Mifs H A R L O W.

I can't help obferving, Sir, that you dwell
chiefly on articles of external and fuperficial
merit ; whereas the more valuable qualities
of the mind, prudence, good fenfe, a well-
regulated conduct——

C L E R I M O N T.

Oh ! ma'am, I am not inattentive to thofe
matters——oh ! fhe has a notable houfehold
underftanding, I warrant her—(*afide*)——but
let me intreat you, madam, to do juftice to
my principles, and believe me a fincere, a
generous lover——

Mifs H A R L O W.

Sir, I will frankly own that I have been
trying you all this time, and from henceforth all doubts are banifhed.

CLE-

CLERIMONT.

Your words recal me to new life—I fhall for ever ftudy to merit this goodnefs——But your fair fifter---do you think I can depend upon her confent ?——May I flatter myfelf fhe will not change her mind ?——

Mifs HARLOW.

My fifter cannot be infenfible of the honour you do us all——and, Sir, as far as I can act with propriety in the affair, I will endeavour to keep them all inclined to favour you——

CLERIMONT.

Madam---(*bows.*)

Mifs HARLOW.

You have an intereft in my breaft that will be bufy for you——

CLERIMONT.

I am eternally devoted to you, madam—

[*bows.*

Mifs HARLOW.

How modeft, and yet how expreffive he is!

[*Afide.*

CLERIMONT.

Madam, I fhall be for ever fenfible of this extreme condefcenfion, and fhall think no pains too great to prove the gratitude and efteem I bear you—I beg my compliments to Mr. Harlow, and I fhall be here with my uncle in the evening——as early as poffible I fhall come—my refpects to your fifter, ma'am —and

——and pray, madam, keep her in my interest——Madam, your moſt obedient—I have managed the motherly lady finely, I think *(aſide)* Madam [*Bows, and Exit.*

Miſs HARLOW.

What will my ſiſter ſay now?——I ſhall hear no more of her taunts——A malicious thing!——I fancy ſhe now ſees that your giddy flirts are not always the higheſt beauties—Set her up, indeed!——Had ſhe but heard him, the dear man!——what ſweet things he ſaid! and what ſweet things he looked——

Enter Mrs. HARLOW.

Mrs. HARLOW.

Well, ſiſter!—how!—what does he ſay?—

Miſs HARLOW.

Say, ſiſter!——Every thing that is charming——he is the prettieſt man!——

Mrs. HARLOW.

Well! I am glad of it—but all's well that ends well——

Miſs HARLOW.

Envy, ſiſter!——Envy, and downright malice!——Oh! had you heard all the tender things he uttered, and with that extaſy too! that tenderneſs! that delight reſtrained by modeſty!——

Mrs. HARLOW.

I don't know tho'; there is ſomething odd in it ſtill—— 2 Miſs

Miss HARLOW.

Oh! I don't doubt but you will say so—
but you will find I have beauty enough left
to make some noise in the world still——The
men, sister, are the best judges of female
beauty——Don't concern yourself about it,
sister—Leave it all to them——

Mrs. HARLOW.

But only think of a lover you never saw
but once at Ranelagh——

Miss HARLOW.

Very true!——but even then I saw what
work I made in his heart—Oh! I am in raptures with him, and he is in raptures with
me—(*Sings*) Yes, I'll have a husband, ay!
marry, &c.

Enter Mr. HARLOW.

Mr. HARLOW.

So, sister! how stand matters now?

Miss HARLOW.

As I could wish——I shall no more be a
trouble to you—he has declared himself in
the most warm and vehement manner—Tho'
my sister has her doubts—she is a good friend
—she is afraid of my success——

Mrs. HARLOW.

Pray, sister, don't think so meanly of me.—
I understand that sneer, ma'am.

Miss HARLOW.

And I understand you too, ma'am—

Mr.

Mr. HARLOW.

Come, come, I deſire we may have no quarrelling—you two are always wrangling; but when you are ſeparated, it is to be hoped you will then be more amicable. Things are now in a fair way—Tho', ſiſter, let me tell you I am afraid our India friend will think himſelf ill-treated.

Mrs. HARLOW.

That's what I fear too—that's my reaſon for ſpeaking——

Miſs HARLOW.

Oh! never throw away a thought on him. ——Mr. Clerimont has my heart; and now I think I am ſettled for life—Siſter, I love to plague her—now I think I am ſettled for life—for life,—for life, my dear ſiſter—

Enter Servant.

SERVANT.

Dinner is ſerved, Sir.

Mr. HARLOW.

Very well! come, ſiſter, I give you joy— let us in to dinner.

Miſs HARLOW.

Oh! vulgar!—I can't eat—I muſt go and dreſs my head over again, and do a thouſand things;—for I am determined I'll look this afternoon as well as ever I can.—— [*Exit*

Mrs.

Mrs. HARLOW.

Is not all this amazing, my dear?———her head is turned———

Mr. HARLOW.

Well, let it all pafs—don't you mind it—don't you fay any thing—let her get married if fhe can—I am fure I fhall rejoice at it.

Mrs. HARLOW.

And upon my word, my dear, fo fhall I ———and if I interfere, it is purely out of friendfhip.—

Mr. HARLOW.

But be advifed by me,—fay no more to her.—If the affair goes on, we fhall fairly get rid of her—Her peevifh humours, and her maiden temper, are become infupporta-ble.—Come, let us in to dinner.—If Mr. Clerimont marries her, which indeed will be odd enough,—we fhall then enjoy a little peace and quiet.   [*Exit.*

Mrs. HARLOW.

What in the world could the man fee in her?—Oh! he will repent his bargain in a week or a fortnight; that I am fure he will —fhe is gone to drefs now!—ha! ha!—

Oh! how fhe rolls her pretty eyes in fpite,
And looks delightfully with all her might!

Ha! ha! delightfully fhe will look indeed!--
          [*Exit.*

END of the FIRST ACT.

E   ACT

ACT II.

Enter a Servant, and Capt. C A P E.

SERVANT.

Y ES, Sir, my master is at home—he has just done dinner, Sir—

Capt. C A P E.

Very well then; tell him I would speak a word with him.

SERVANT.

I beg pardon, Sir ; I am but a stranger in the family—who shall I say ?—

Capt. C A P E.

Capt. Cape, tell him—

SERVANT.

Yes, Sir.　　　　　　　　　　　[*Exit.*

Capt. C A P E.

I can hardly believe my own eyes————s'death ! I am almost inclined to think this letter, signed with Miss Harlow's name, a mere forgery by some enemy, to drive me into an excess of passion, and so injure us both—I don't know what to say to it—

Enter Mr. H A R L O W.

Capt. C A P E.

Sir, I have waited on you about an extra-ordinary affair—I can't comprehend it, Sir--
Here

Here is a letter with your fister's name—
Look at it, Sir,—is that her hand-writing?--

Mr. HARLOW.

Yes, Sir—I take it to be her writing—

Capt. CAPE.

And do you know the contents?—

Mr. HARLOW.

I can't fay I have read it—but—

Capt. CAPE.

But you know the purport of it?

Mr. HARLOW.

Partly.

Capt. CAPE.

You do?—and is not it bafe treatment,
Sir?—is it not unwarrantable?—can you
juftify her?

Mr. HARLOW.

For my part, I leave women to manage
their own affairs—I am not fond of inter-
meddling——

Capt. CAPE.

But, Sir—let me afk you,—Was not every
thing agreed upon?—Are not the writings
now in lawyers hands?—Was not next week
fixed for our wedding?—

Mr. HARLOW.

I underftood it fo.

Capt. CAPE.

Very well then, and fee how fhe treats
me—She writes me here in a contemptuous

E 2   manner,

manner, that she recals her promise;—it was rashly given;—she has thought better of it; she will listen to me no more;—she is going to dispose of herself to a gentleman with whom she can be happy for life—and " I desire to see you no more, Sir"—There, that's free and easy, is not it?—What do you say to that?—

Mr. HARLOW.

Why really, Sir, it is not my affair—I have nothing to say to it.—

Capt. CAPE.

Nothing to say to it!—Sir, I imagined I was dealing with people of honour.

Mr. HARLOW.

You have been dealing with a woman, and you know—

Capt. CAPE.

Yes, I know—I know the treachery of the sex—Who is this gentleman, pray?

Mr. HARLOW.

His name is Clerimont—they have fixed the affair among themselves, and amongst them be it for me.—

Capt. CAPE.

Very fine! mighty fine!—is Miss Harlow at home, Sir?—

Mr. HARLOW.

She is; and here she comes too—

Capt.

Capt. C A P E.

Very well !—let me hear it from herself, that's all—I defire to hear her fpeak for herfelf—

Mr. H A R L O W.

With all my heart.—I'll leave you together—you know, captain, I was never fond of being concerned in thofe things— [*Exit.*

Enter Mifs H A R L O W.

Mifs H A R L O W.

Capt. Cape, this is mighty odd——I thought, Sir, I defired—

Capt. C A P E.

Madam, I acknowledge the receipt of your letter, and, madam, the ufage is fo extraordinary, that I hold myfelf excufable if I refufe to comply with the terms you impofe upon me.——

Mifs H A R L O W.

Sir, I really wonder what you can mean——

Capt. C A P E.

Miftake me not, madam; I am not come to whimper or to whine, and to make a puppy of myfelf again—Madam that is all blown over.——

Mifs H A R L O W.

Well then, there is no harm done, and you will furvive this I hope.

Capt.

Capt. CAPE.

Survive it!——

Miss HARLOW.

Yes;—you won't grow desperate I hope—
suppose you were to order somebody to take
care of you, because you know fits of despair
are sudden, and you may rashly do yourself
a mischief—don't do any such thing, I beg
you won't——

Capt. CAPE.

This insult, madam!—Do myself a mischief!—Madam, don't flatter yourself that
it is in your power to make me unhappy—
it is not vexation brings me hither, I assure
you——

Miss HARLOW.

Then let vexation take you away;—we
were never designed for one another.——

Capt. CAPE.

My amazement brings me hither—amazement that any woman can behave—but I
don't want to upbraid—I only come to ask—
for I can hardly as yet believe it—I only
come to ask if I am to credit this pretty
epistle?——

Miss HARLOW.

Every syllable—therefore take your answer, Sir, and truce with your importu-
nity.——

Capt. CAPE.

Very well, ma'am, very well—your humble
servant, madam—I promise you, ma'am, I
can

can repay this fcorn with fcorn—with tenfold fcorn, madam, fuch as this treatment deferves—that's all—I fay no more—your fervant ma'am—but let me afk you—is this a juft return for all the attendance I have paid you thefe three years paft?——

Mifs HARLOW.

Perfectly juft, Sir,—three years!—how could you be a dangler fo long?—I told you what it would come to—can you think that raifing a woman's expectation, and tiring her out of all patience, is the way to make fure of her at laft?—you ought to have been a brifker lover, you ought indeed, Sir,—I am now contracted to another, and fo there is an end of every thing between us.——

Capt. CAPE.

Very well, madam,—and yet I can't bear to be defpifed by her—and can you, Mifs Harlow, can you find it in your heart to treat me with this difdain?—have you no compaffion?——

Mifs HARLOW.

No, pofitively none, Sir,—none—none—

Capt. CAPE.

Your own Capt. Cape,—whom you——

Mifs HARLOW.

Whom I defpife.——

Capt. CAPE.

Whom you have fo often encouraged to adore you.——

Mifs

Miſs HARLOW.

Pray, Sir, don't touch my hand—I am now the property of another——

Capt. CAPE.

Can't you ſtill break off with him?

Miſs HARLOW.

No Sir, I can't; I won't; I love him, and Sir, if you are a man of honour, you will ſpeak to me no more; deſiſt, Sir, for if you don't, my brother ſhall tell you of it, Sir, and to-morrow Mr. Clerimont ſhall tell you of it.——

Capt. CAPE.

Mr. Clerimont, madam, ſhall fight me, for daring——

Miſs. HARLOW.

And muſt I fight you too, moſt noble, valiant captain?——

Capt. CAPE.

Laughed at too!——

Miſs HARLOW.

What a paſſion you are in!—I can't bear to ſee a man in ſuch a paſſion—Oh! I have a happy riddance, of you—the violence of your temper is dreadful—I won't ſtay a moment longer with you—you frighten me— you have your anſwer,—and ſo your ſervant Sir——   *[Exit.*

Capt. CAPE.

Ay! ſhe is gone off like a fury, and the furies catch her, ſay I—I will never put up

with

with this—I will find out this Mr. Clerimont, and he shall be accountable to me—
Mr. Harlow too shall be accountable to
me.——

Enter Mr. and Mrs. HARLOW.

Capt. CAPE.

Mr. Harlow—I am used very ill here,
Sir, by all of you, and Sir, let me tell you——

Mr. HARLOW.

Nay; don't be angry with me, Sir,—I
was not to marry you——

Capt. CAPE.

But Sir, I can't help being angry—I must
be angry—and let me tell you, you don't
behave like a gentleman.

Mrs. HARLOW.

How can Mr. Harlow help it, Sir, if my
sister——

Mr. HARLOW.

You are too warm; you are indeed, Sir,—
let us both talk this matter over a bottle——

Capt. CAPE.

No, Sir—no bottle—over a cannon, if you
will——

Mrs. HARLOW.

Mercy on me, Sir,—I beg you wont talk
in that terrible manner—you frighten me,
Sir.——

F   Mr.

Mr. HARLOW.

Be you quiet, my dear,—Capt. Cape, I
beg you will juſt ſtep into that room with
me; and if, in the diſpatching one bottle, I
don't acquit myſelf of all ſiniſter dealing,
why then—come, come, be a little moderate—you ſhall ſtep with me—I'll take it as
a favour—come, come, you muſt——

Capt. CAPE.

I always found you a gentleman, Mr. Harlow, and ſo with all my heart,—I don't care
if I do talk the matter over with you—

Mr. HARLOW.

Sir, I am obliged to you—I'll ſhew you
the way——　　　　　　　　　　　[Exeunt.

Mrs. HARLOW.

It is juſt as I foreſaw—my ſiſter was ſure
of him, and now is ſhe going to break off
for a young man that will deſpiſe her in a
little time—I wiſh ſhe would have Capt.
Cape.

Enter Miſs HARLOW.

Miſs HARLOW.

Is he gone, ſiſter?——

Mrs. HARLOW.

No; and here is the deuce and all to do—
he is for fighting every body—upon my
word you are wrong—you don't behave genteelly in the affair.——

　　　　　　　　　　　　　　　　Miſs

Mifs HARLOW.

Genteelly!—I like that notion prodigi-
oufly—an't I going to marry genteelly?

Mrs. HARLOW.

Well, follow your own inclinations——I
won't intermeddle any more, I promife you
—I'll ftep into the parlour, and fee what they
are about.   [*Exit*.

Mifs HARLOW.

As you pleafe, ma'am—I fee plainly the
ill-natured thing can't bear my fuccefs——
Heavens! here comes Mr. Clerimont——

Enter Mr. CLERIMONT.

Mifs HARLOW.

You are earlier than I expected, Sir.

CLERIMONT.

I have flown, madam, upon the wings of
love—I have feen my uncle, and he will be
here within this half hour—every thing fuc-
ceeds to my wifhes with him—I hope there is
no alteration here, madam, fince I faw you—

Mifs HARLOW.

Nothing that fignifies, Sir—

CLERIMONT.

You alarm me——Mr. Harlow has not
changed his mind, I hope.

Mifs HARLOW.

No, Sir—he continues in the fame mind.

CLERIMONT.

And your fister—I tremble with doubt and fear—fhe does not furely recede from the fentiments fhe flattered me with.

Mifs HARLOW.

Why there, indeed, I can't fay much— fhe—

CLERIMONT.

How!

Mifs HARLOW.

She—I don't know what to make of her—

CLERIMONT.

Oh! I am on the rack—in pity, do not torture me—

Mifs HARLOW.

How tremblingly folicitous he is—Oh! I have made a fure conqueft (*afide*.)——Why, fhe, Sir—

CLERIMONT.

Ay,—(*difconcerted*.)

Mifs HARLOW.

She does not feem entirely to approve—

CLERIMONT.

You kill me with defpair—

Mifs HARLOW.

Oh! he is deeply fmitten, (*afide*)—She thinks another match would fuit better—

CLERIMONT.

Another match!

Mifs

Miſs HARLOW.

Yes, another; an India captain, who has made his propoſals; but I ſhall take care to ſee him diſmiſſed.

CLERIMONT.

Will you?

Miſs HARLOW.

I promiſe you I will—tho' he runs much in my ſiſter's head, and ſhe has taken pains to bring my other relations over to her opinion.

CLERIMONT.

Oh! cruel, cruel!—I could not have expected that from her—but has ſhe fixed her heart upon a match with this other gentleman?

Miſs HARLOW.

Why, truly I think ſhe has—but my will in this affair muſt be, and ſhall be conſulted.

CLERIMONT.

And ſo it ought, ma'am—your long acquaintance with the world, madam—

Miſs HARLOW.

Long acquaintance, Sir! I have but a few years experience only—

CLERIMONT.

That is, your good ſenſe, ma'am—oh! confound my tongue! how that ſlipt from me (aſide)—your good ſenſe,—your early good ſenſe,—and—and—inclination ſhould be conſulted.

Miſs

Miſs HARLOW.

And they ſhall, Sir—hark!—I hear her—
I'll tell you what—I'll leave you this opportunity to ſpeak to her once more, and try to
win her over by perſuaſion—It will make
things eaſy if you can——I am gone, Sir.
　　　　　　[*Curtſies affectedly, and Exit.*

CLERIMONT.

The happineſs of my life will be owing
to you, Madam.—The woman is really better natured than I thought ſhe was——ſhe
comes, the lovely tyrant comes——

Enter Mrs. HARLOW.

CLERIMONT.

She triumphs in her cruelty, and I am
ruined——　　　　　　　　　　[*Aſide.*

Mrs. HARLOW.

You ſeem afflicted, Sir—I hope no misfortune—

CLERIMONT.

The ſevereſt misfortune!——you have
broke my heart——

Mrs. HARLOW.

I break your heart, Sir ?—

CLERIMONT.

Yes, cruel fair—you,—you have undone
me.

Mrs. HARLOW.

You amaze me, Sir, pray how can I—

CLERIMONT.

And you can ſeem unconſcious of the mischief you have made——　　　　　Mrs.

Mrs. HARLOW.

Pray unriddle, Sir——

CLERIMONT.

Madam, your fifter has told me all——

Mrs. HARLOW.

Ha! ha! what has fhe told you, Sir?

CLERIMONT.

It may be fport to you—but to me 'tis death——

Mrs. HARLOW.

What is death?

CLERIMONT.

The gentleman from India, madam—I have heard it all—you can give him a preference—you can blaft my hopes—my fond delighted hopes, which you yourfelf had cherifhed.

Mrs. HARLOW.

The gentleman is a very good fort of man.

CLERIMONT.

Oh! fhe loves him, I fee—(*afide*)—Madam, I perceive my doom is fixed, and fixed by you——

Mrs. HARLOW.

How have I fixed your doom?—if I fpeak favourably of captain Cape,—he deferves it, Sir.

CLERIMONT.

Oh! heavens! I cannot bear this—[*afide*.

Mrs. HARLOW.

I believe there is nobody that knows the gentleman, but will give him his due praife--

CLE-

CLERIMONT.

Love! love! love!—— [aside,

Mrs. HARLOW.

And besides, his claim is in fact prior to yours.

CLERIMONT.

And must love be governed, like the business of mechanics, by the laws of tyrant custom?—Can you think so, madam?

Mrs. HARLOW.

Why, Sir, you know I am not in love.

CLERIMONT.

Oh! cruel!—no, madam, I see you are not.

Mrs. HARLOW.

And really now, Sir, reasonably speaking, my sister is for treating captain Cape very ill——He has been dancing attendance here these three years.——

CLERIMONT.

Yet that you know, when you were pleased to fan the rising flame, that matchless beauty had kindled in my heart.

Mrs. HARLOW.

Matchless beauty!—ha! ha!—I cannot but laugh at that—— [aside.

CLERIMONT.

Laugh, madam, if you will at the pangs you yourself occasion—yes, triumph, if you will—I am resigned to my fate, since you will have it so——

Mrs.

Mrs. HARLOW.

I have it fo!—you feem to frighten yourfelf without caufe,—If I fpeak favourably
of any body elfe, Sir,—what then?—I
am not to marry him, you know.

CLERIMONT.

An't you?

Mrs. HARLOW.

I!——no, truly—thank heaven!——

CLERIMONT.

She revives me. [afide.

Mrs. HARLOW.

That muft be as my fifter pleafes.

CLERIMONT.

Muft it?

Mrs. HARLOW.

Muft it?—to be fure it muft?

CLERIMONT.

And may I hope fome intereft in your
heart.

Mrs. HARLOW.

My heart, Sir!

CLERIMONT.

While it is divided, while another has poffeffion of but part of it.——

Mrs. HARLOW.

I don't underftand him!—Why, it has been
given away long ago.

CLERIMONT.

I pray you do not tyrannize me thus with
alternate doubts and fears—if you will but
blefs me with the leaft kind return——

G   Mrs.

Mrs. HARLOW.

Kind return ! what, would you have me
fall in love with you ?

CLERIMONT.

It will be generous to him who adores
you.

Mrs. HARLOW.

Adore me !

CLERIMONT.

Even to idolatry.

Mrs. HARLOW.

What can he mean ?—I thought my sister
was the object of your adoration.

CLERIMONT.

Your sister, ma'am ! I shall ever respect
her as my friend on this occasion, but love—
no—no—she is no object for that—

Mrs. HARLOW.

No !

CLERIMONT.

She may have been handsome in her time,
—but that has been all over long ago—

Mrs. HARLOW.

Well ! this is charming—I wish she heard
him now, with her new-fangled airs, (*aside.*)
—But let me understand you, Sir—adore
me !—

CLERIMONT.

You !—you !—and only you !—by this fair
hand—(*kisses it.*)

Mrs. HARLOW.

Hold, hold—this is going too far—but
pray, Sir, have you really conceived a passion for me ? CLE-

CLERIMONT.

You know I have—a paſſion of the ten-dereſt nature.

Mrs. HARLOW.

And was that your drift in coming hither?

CLERIMONT.

What elſe could induce me?

Mrs. HARLOW.

And introduced yourſelf here, to have an opportunity of ſpeaking to me?

CLERIMONT.

My angel! don't torment me thus—

Mrs. HARLOW.

Angel! and pray, Sir, what do you ſup-poſe Mr. Harlow will ſay to this?

CLERIMONT.

Oh! ma'am—he! he approves my paſſion.

Mrs. HARLOW.

Does he really?—I muſt ſpeak to him about that—

CLERIMONT.

Do ſo, ma'am, you will find I am a man of more honour than to deceive you—

Mrs. HARLOW.

Well! it will be whimſical if he does—and my ſiſter too, this will be a charming diſcovery for her, (aſide.)—Ha! ha! well! really Sir, this is mighty odd—I'll ſpeak to Mr. Harlow about this matter this very moment——(going.)

CLERIMONT.

Oh! you will find it all true—and may I then flatter myſelf—

G 2

Mrs.

Mrs. HARLOW.

Oh! to be sure—such an honourable pro-
ject—l'll step to him this moment—and then,
sister, I shall make such a piece of work for
you—   [*Exit.*

CLERIMONT.

Very well, ma'am—see Mr. Harlow immediately—he will confirm it to you—while
there is life there is hope—such matchless
beauty!—

Enter Miss HARLOW.

Miss HARLOW.

I beg your pardon, Sir, for leaving you
all this time—Well, what says my sister?

CLERIMONT.

She has given me some glimmering hopes.

Miss HARLOW.

Well, don't be uneasy about her—it shall
be as I please—

CLERIMONT.

But with her own free consent it would be
better—however, to you I am bound by every tie, and thus let me seal a vow—(*kisses her
hand.*)

Miss HARLOW.

He certainly is a very passionate lover—
Lord! he is ready to eat my hand up with
kisses—I wish my sister saw this—(*aside.*)—
Hush! I hear Capt. Cape's voice—the hi-
deous Tramontane!--he is coming this way—
I would not see him again for the world—
I'll withdraw a moment, Sir—you'll excuse
me—

me—Mr. Clerimont—(*kiſſes her hand and curtſies very low*) your ſervant Sir—Oh! he is a charming man.   [*Curtſeys, and Exit.*

Enter Capt. C A P E.

Capt. C A P E.

There ſhe goes, the perfidious! Sir, I underſtand your name is Clerimont——

CLERIMONT.

At your ſervice, Sir.

Capt. C A P E.

Then, Sir, draw this moment.

CLERIMONT.

Draw, Sir! for what?

Capt. C A P E.

No evaſion, Sir.

CLERIMONT.

Explain the cauſe.

Capt. C A P E.

The cauſe is too plain—your making love to that lady who went out there this moment——

CLERIMONT.

That lady! not I, upon my honour, Sir.

Capt. C A P E.

No ſhuffling, Sir—draw——

CLERIMONT.

Sir, I can repel an injury like this—but your quarrel is groundleſs,—and, Sir, if ever I made love to that lady, I will lay my boſom naked to your ſword,—That lady!—I reſign all manner of pretenſion to her——

Capt.

Capt. C A P E.

You refign her, Sir.

CLERIMONT.

Entirely.

Capt. C A P E.

Then I am pacified—(*puts up his fword.*)

CLERIMONT.

Upon my word, Sir, I never fo much as thought of the lady.

Enter Mr. H A R L O W.

Mr. H A R L O W.

So, Sir—fine doings you have been carrying on here——

CLERIMONT.

Sir!

Mr. H A R L O W.

You have been attempting my wife, I find——

CLERIMONT.

Upon my word, Mr Harlow——

Mr. H A R L O W.

You have behaved in a very bafe manner, and I infift upon fatisfaction; draw, Sir—

CLERIMONT.

This is the ftrangeft accident!—I affure you, Sir,—only give me leave—

Mr. H A R L O W.

I will not give you leave—I infift—

Capt. C A P E.

Nay, nay, Mr. Harlow—this is neither time or place—and befides, hear the gentleman; I have been over-hafty, and he has fatisfied me—only hear him—

Mr.

Mr. HARLOW.

Sir, I will believe my own wife—come on, Sir——

CLERIMONT.

I affure you, Mr. Harlow, I came into this houfe upon honourable principles—induced, Sir, by my regard for Mifs Harlow—

Capt. CAPE.

For Mifs Harlow!—zoons, draw——

CLERIMONT.

Again!—this is downright madnefs—two upon me at once—you will murder me between you—

Mr. HARLOW.

There is one too, many upon him, fure enough,—and fo, captain, put up—

Capt. CAPE.

Refign your pretenfions to Mifs Harlow—

CLERIMONT.

Refign Mifs Harlow!—not for the univerfe—in her caufe I can be as ready as any bravo of ye all—(*draws his fword.*)

Mr. HARLOW.

For heaven's fake, Capt. Cape—do moderate your anger—this is neither time or place—I have been too rafh myfelf—I beg you will be pacified—(*He puts up.*)—Mr. Clerimont, fheath your fword—

CLERIMONT.

I obey, Sir—

Mr. HARLOW.

Capt. Cape. how can you?—you promifed me you would let things take their courfe?—if my fifter will marry the gentleman, how is he to blame?—

Capt.

5

Capt. C A P E.

Very well, Sir—I have done—she is a
worthlefs woman—that's all—

CLERIMONT.

A worthlefs woman, Sir!—

Capt. C A P E.

Ay! worthlefs—

CLERIMONT.

Damnation!—Draw, Sir!

Mr. H A R L O W.

Nay, nay, Mr. Clerimont, you are too
warm—and there's a gentleman coming—
this is your uncle, I fuppofe—

CLERIMONT.

It is——

Enter Mr. HEARTWELL.

Mr. H A R L O W (*afide.*)

I'll wave all difputes now, that I may conclude my fifter's marriage.

CLERIMONT.

Mr. Heartwell, Sir—Mr. Harlow, Sir.—

HEARTWELL.

My nephew has informed me, Sir, of the
honour you have done him, and I am come
to give my confent.

Mr. H A R L O W.

I thought it neceffary, Sir, to have the advice of Mr. Clerimont's friends, as he is very
young, and my fifter not very handfome.

CLERIMONT.

She is an angel, Sir—

HEART-

HEARTWELL.

Patience, Charles, patience.——My nephew's eſtate will provide for his eldeſt born, and upon the younger branches of his marriage I mean to ſettle my fortune.

Mr. HARLOW.

Generouſly ſpoken, Sir, and ſo there is no occaſion for delay—who waits there?—tell the ladies they are wanting—

HEARTWELL.

I have ever loved my nephew, and ſince he tells me he has made a good choice, I ſhall be glad to ſee him happy.

Capt. CAPE.

But, Sir, let me tell you, that your nephew has uſed me very baſely, and Sir—

Mr. HARLOW.

Nay, nay, captain,—this is wrong now; every thing was ſettled between us in the other room—recollect yourſelf—do, I beg you will—Oh! here come the ladies.

Enter Mrs. HARLOW, and Miſs.

Miſs HARLOW.

Now, ſiſter, you ſhall ſee I have completed my conqueſt—

CLERIMONT.

Now then I am happy indeed—my lovely, charming bride—thus let me ſnatch you to my heart, and thus, and thus——(*embraces Mrs. Harlow.*)

Mr. HARLOW.

Zoons! before my face——(*puſhing him away.*)

H   CLE-

CLERIMONT.

Prithee, indulge my tranſport—my life, my angel!—

Mr. HARLOW.

I deſire you will deſiſt, Sir—

CLERIMONT.

Nay, nay, prithee be quiet—my charming, charming wife!—

Mr. HARLOW.

That lady is not your wife—

CLERIMONT.

How my wife,—not my wife!—extaſy and bliſs!—

Mr. HARLOW.

Come, come, Sir—this is too much—

CLERIMONT.

Ha! ha! you are very pleaſant, Sir.

Mr. HARLOW.

Zoons! Sir, no trifling—that lady is my wife—

CLERIMONT.

Sir!

Mr. HARLOW.

I ſay, Sir, that lady is my wife!

Capt. CAPE.

Ha! ha! I ſee through this——it is a comedy of errors, I believe—(ſings.)

HEARTWELL.

What does all this mean?

CLERIMONT.

Your wife, Sir!——

Mr. HARLOW.

Yes, my wife—and there is my ſiſter, if you pleaſe to take her—

CLE-

CLERIMONT.

Sir!—

Mr. HARLOW.

Sir, this is the lady whom you have defired in marriage.

CLERIMONT.

Who I, Sir?—I beg your pardon—that lady I took to be your wife (*pointing to Mifs Harlow,*)—and that lady (*pointing to Mrs. Harlow*) I took to be your fifter—

Capt. CAPE. *and Mrs.* HARLOW.

Ha! ha! ha!—

Mifs HARLOW.

Lord! lord! have I been made a fool of all this time!—furies! torture! murder!—

Capt. CAPE.

Ha! ha!—my lady fair is taken in, I think—

Mrs. HARLOW.

Sifter, the men don't fee with my eyes— ha! ha!

Capt. CAPE.

Ha! ha! the gentleman is no dangler, ma'am.—

Mrs. HARLOW.

This is a complete conqueft my fifter has made—

Mifs HARLOW.

I can't bear this—Sir, I defire I may not be made a jeft of—did not you follicit me? —importune me?—

CLERIMONT.

For your intereft in that lady, ma'am,— whom I took for Mifs Harlow—I beg your pardon if I am miftaken,——I hope there is no harm done.——

Mifs HARLOW.

Yes, Sir, but there is harm done—I am made fport of—expofed to derifion——Oh! I cannot bear this—I cannot bear it—*(cries.)*

Mrs. HARLOW.

Don't cry, fifter—fome faces preferve the bloom longer than others you know--ha! ha!

Capt. CAPE.

Loll toll loll—

HEARTWELL.

I don't underftand all this—is that lady your wife, Sir?

Mr. HARLOW.

She is, Sir.

HEARTWELL.

And pray, nephew—you took that lady for Mr. Harlow's fifter, I fuppofe——

CLERIMONT.

I did, Sir.—I beg pardon for the trouble I have given—I am in fuch confufion, I can hardly——

HEARTWELL.

Well, well! the thing is cleared up, and there is no harm done—but you fhould have known what ground you went upon—ha! ha! I can't help laughing neither——

Mr. HARLOW.

Why faith, nor I—ha! ha!

CLERIMONT.

Since matters have turned fo unexpected-ly, I beg pardon for my miftake, and Sir, I take my leave—*(going.)* Mifs

Miſs HARLOW.

And will you treat me in this manner, Sir?
will you draw me into ſuch a ſcrape, and not—

CLERIMONT.

Ma'am, that gentleman would cut my throat
—his claim is prior to mine—and, I dare ſay,
he will be very glad to be reconciled, madam.

Miſs HARLOW.

You are a baſe man then, and I reject
you—Capt. Cape I ſee my error, Sir, and I
reſign myſelf to you.

Capt. CAPE.

No, madam, I beg to be excuſed—I have
been a dangler too long—I ought to have
been a briſker lover—I ſhall endeavour to
ſurvive it, ma'am—I won't do myſelf a miſchief—and I have my anſwer—I am off,
madam—loll toll loll——

Mrs. HARLOW.

Ha! ha! I told you this, my dear ſiſter—

CLERIMONT.

Madam, I dare ſay the gentleman will
think better of it—Mr. Harlow, I am ſorry
for all this confuſion, and I beg pardon of
the whole company for my miſtake—Mrs.
Harlow, I wiſh you all happineſs, ma'am—
angelic creature!—what a misfortune to loſe
her!—— [Bows and exit.

Capt. CAPE.

And I will follow his example—Miſs Harlow I wiſh you all happineſs,—angelic creature! what a misfortune to loſe her!—upon
my ſoul I think you a moſt admirable jilt, and
ſo now you may go, and bewail your virgi-
nity in the mountains—loll toll loll— [Exit.

Miss HARLOW.

Oh! oh! I can't bear to be treated in this manner—I'll go and hide myself from the world for ever—Oh! oh!—the men are all savages, barbarians, monsters, and I hate the whole sex—Oh! oh!—(*cries bitterly,*) [*Exit.*

Mrs. HARLOW.

My dear sister, with her beauty and her conquests, ha! ha!——

Mr. HARLOW.

Ha! ha! very whimsical and ridiculous—

HEARTWELL.

Sir, my nephew is young—I am sorry for this scene of errors, and I hope you will ascribe the whole to his inexperience——

Mr. HARLOW.

I certainly shall, Sir——

Mrs. HARLOW.

I cautioned my sister sufficiently about this matter, but vanity got the better of her, and leaves her now a whimsical instance of folly and affectation.

In vain the FADED TOAST her mirror tries,
And counts the cruel murders of her eyes;
For ridicule, sly-peeping o'er her head,
Will point the roses and the lillies dead;
And while, fond soul! she weaves her myrtle
    chain,
She proves a subject of the comic strain.

FINIS.

THE
APPRENTICE.

A

FARCE.

IN

TWO ACTS.

As it is performed at the

THEATRE-ROYAL,

IN

DRURY-LANE.

BY MR. MURPHY.

LONDON,

Printed for P. VAILLANT. 1764.

ADVERTISEMENT.

THERE was Room to apprehend, before the
Reprefentation of the following Farce, that
the Subject might appear extravagant and merely
ideal; but the real Exiftence of it is difplayed in
fuch a lively and picturefque Manner by the Author
of the Prologue, and was at once fo univerfally
felt by the Audience, that all Neceffity of faying
any Thing farther on this Head is now entirely
fuperfeded. What at prefent remains to be feared,
is, that the APPRENTICE will not make fo
lively a Figure in the Clofet, as on the Stage,
where the Parts in general were allowed to be well
performed; where *Simon* was reprefented with a
Perfection of Folly; where the Skill of Mr. *Yates*
exhibited the Impotence of a Mind, whofe Ideas
extend very little beyond the Multiplication Table,
and whofe Paffions are ever in a crazy Conflict, unlefs when they all fubfide into a fordid Love of
Gain; and where Mr. *Woodward's* admirable comic
Genius gave fuch a Spirit to the Whole, that there
is Reafon to think, whenever he relinquifhes the
Part, the *Apprentice* may gain elope from his
Friends, without any one's defiring him to return
to his Bufinefs.

The Author has, however, endeavoured to render all its Defects as excufeable as he could; and he
wifhes no ftronger Criticifm could be brought a-
gainft him, than the two following Obfervations,
which he thinks very fingular, and fomewhat enter-
taining. " *I can't,* fays one, *give my Opinion of the*
" *Piece, till I have Time to confider the Depth of it.*"—
" *Po!* fays another, *this is not all his* OWN, *I re-*
" *member fome of it in other Plays.*"—In order to affift the former in his deep Refearches, and to enable
the latter to make good his Charge of Plagiarifm,
References are made to the feveral Plays, from
which the diftempered Hero of the Piece makes up
his

his motley, but characteriſtick Dialect. The intelligent Reader, if he thinks it worth his while to turn over theſe Leaves, will be pleaſed to remember, that a Parody does not always carry with it a Burleſque on the Lines alluded to. For (as it is judiciouſly remarked in a Note to Mr. *Pope's* Dunciad) " *It is a common, but fooliſh, Miſtake, that a* " *ludicrous Parody of a grave and celebrated Paſſage,* " *is a Ridicule of that Paſſage. A Ridicule indeed* " *there is in every Parody; but where the Image is* " *transferred from one Object to another, there the Ri-* " *dicule falls not on the Thing* imitated, *but* imitating." Thus, for Inſtance, when

₍ *Old Edward's Armour beams on Cibber's Breaſt* †,

It is without Doubt an Object ridiculous enough; but then, I think, *it falls neither on old King* Edward, *nor his* Armour, *but on his* Armour-Bearer *only.*

But this is prefacing a Farce, as if it were a Thing of Moment; I ſhall therefore diſmiſs it to the Preſs, without adding any Thing farther, except my grateful Acknowledgments for the very favourable Reception with which the Public has honoured the trifling Scenes of

Taviſtock-Row,   *Their moſt obliged,*
  5th Jan. 1756.   *and moſt obedient Servant.*

ARTHUR MURPHY.

† Line of Pope's in a ludicrous Account of the Coronation in Henry the VIIIth.

PRO-

PROLOGUE,

Written by Mr. GARRICK,

And spoken by Mr. WOODWARD.

*P*ROLOGUES *precede the* Piece——*in mournful*
   Verse;
As Undertakers——*walk before the Herse;*
Whose doleful March may strike the harden'd Mind,
And wake its Feelings——*for the Dead*——*behind.*
To Night no smuggled Scenes from France we show,
'Tis English——*English, Sirs!*——*from Top to Toe.*
Tho' coarse the Colours, and the Hand unskill'd,
From real Life our little Cloth is fill'd.
The Hero is a Youth,——*by Fate design'd*
For culling Simples,—*but whose Stage-struck Mind,*
Nor Fate could rule, nor his Indentures bind.
A Place there is where such young Quixotes meet;
'Tis call'd the SPOUTING-CLUB,—*a glorious*
   Treat!
Where 'prentic'd Kings—alarm the gaping Street!
There Brutus *starts and stares by midnight Taper;*
Who all the DAY *enacts*——*a Woollen Draper.*
There Hamlet's Ghost stalks forth with doubl'd Fist,
Cries out with hollow Voice,—" Lift, Lift, O Lift!"
And frightens Denmark's Prince—a young Tobacconist.
The Spirit too, clear'd from his deadly White,
Rises——*a Haberdasher to the Sight!*
Not young Attorneys——*have this Rage withstood,*
But change their Pens *for* TRUNCHEONS, Ink *for*
   BLOOD;
And (strange Reverse!)—die for their Country's Good.
 To check these Heroes, and their Laurels crop,
To bring 'em back to Reason,——*and their* SHOP,
Our Author wrote;—O you Tom, Dick, Jack, Will!
Who hold the Ballance, or who gild the Pill;——

          Who

Who weild the Yard, and simpering pay your Court,
And at each Flourish, snip an Inch too short!
Quit not your Shops; there Thrift and Profit call,
Whilst here young Gentlemen are apt to fall!

[Bell rings.]

But soft!—the Prompter calls!—brief let me be—
Her Groans you'll hear, and flying Apples see,
Be damn'd, perhaps;—farewell!—Remember me.

Dramatis Personæ.

Wingate, a passionate old Man, particularly fond of Money and Figures, and involuntarily uneasy about his Son,	Mr. YATES.
Dick, his Son, bound to an Apothecary, and fond of going on the Stage,	Mr. WOOWARD.
Gargle, an Apothecary,	Mr. BURTON.
Charlotte, Daughter to Gargle,	Miss MINORS.
Simon, Servant to Gargle,	Mr. H. VAUGHAN.
Scotchman,	Mr. BLAKES.
Irishman,	Mr. JEFFERSON.
Catchpole, a Bailiff,	Mr. VAUGHAN.

Spouting-Club, Watchmen, &c.

THE

THE
APPRENTICE.

ACT I. SCENE I.

Enter WINGATE *and* SIMON.

WINGATE.

NAY nay, but I tell you I am convinced—I know it is so,—and so, Friend, don't you think to trifle with me ;—I know you're in the Plot, you Scoundrel, and if you don't dif-cover all, I'll—

Simon. Dear Heart, Sir, you won't give a Body Time.

Wingate. Zookers! a whole Month mif-fing, and no Account of him far or near,—Wounds! 'tis unaccountable——Look ye, Friend,——don't you pretend——

B   *Simon.*

Simon. Lord, Sir,—you're fo main paffionate, you won't let a Body fpeak.

Wingate. Speak out then,—and don't ftand
muttering——What a lubberly Fellow you
are! ha! ha!——Why don't you fpeak out,
you Blockhead?

Simon. Lord, Sir, to be fure the Gentleman is a fine young Gentleman, and a fweet
young Gentleman—but, lack-a-day, Sir,—
how fhould I know any thing of him?

Wingate. Sirrah, I fay he could not be
'Prentice to your Mafter fo long, and you
live fo long in one Houfe with him, without
knowing his Haunts and all his Ways—and
then, Varlet, what brings you here to my
Houfe fo often?

Simon. My Mafter *Gargle* and I, Sir, are
fo uneafy about un, that I have been running all over the Town fince Morning to enquire for un;—and fo in my way, I thought
I might as well call here——

Wingate. A Villain, to give his Father all
this Trouble——And fo you have not heard
any Thing of him, Friend?

Simon. Not a Word, Sir, as I hope for
Marcy; tho', as fure as you are there, I believe I can guefs what's come on un. As fure
as any thing, Mafter, the Gypfies have got-
ten hold on un, and we fhall have un come
home as thin as a Rake,—like the young
Girl in the City,—with living upon nothing
but Crufts and Water for fix-and-twenty
Days.——

Win-

Wingate. The Gypfies have got hold of
him, ye Blockhead!—Get out of the Room
——Here, you *Simon*——

Simon. Sir,——

Wingate. Where are you going in fuch a
Hurry?——Let me fee; what muft be done?
——A ridiculous Numfkull, with his damned
Caffanders and *Cleopatra*'s and Trumpery;
with his *Romances*, and his Odyffey *Popes*, and
a Parcel of Rafcals not worth a Groat;——
wearing Stone Buckles, and cocking his Hat;
—I never wear Stone Buckles,—never cock my
Hat—but, Zookers, I'll not put myfelf in a
Paffion—*Simon*, do you ftep back to your Mafter, my Friend *Gargle*, and tell him I want to
fpeak with him—though I don't know what
I fhould fend for him for——a fly, flow, he-
fitating Blockhead!——he'll only plague me
with his Phyfical Cant and his Nonfenfe——
Why don't you go, you Booby, when I bid
you?——

Simon. Yes, Sir——   [*Exit.*

Wingate. This Fellow will be the Death of
me at laft——I can't fleep in my Bed fome-
times for him.——An abfurd infignificant
Rafcal,—to ftand in his own Light!——
Death and Fury, that we can't get Children,
without having a Love for 'em!—I have been
turmoiling for the Fellow all the Days of my
Life, and now the Scoundrel's run away——
Suppofe I advertife the Dog, and promife a
Reward to any one that can give an Account of him——well, but,——why fhould
I throw away my Money after him?——
why, as I don't fay what Reward, I may give

B 2   what

what I pleafe when they come——ay, but if the Villain fhould deceive me, and happen to be dead,——why then he tricks me out of Two Shillings——my Money's flung into the Fire——Zookers, I'll not put myfelf in a Paffion——let him follow his Nofe——'tis nothing at all to me——what care I?—— What do you come back for, Friend?——

Re-enter Simon.

Simon. As I was going out, Sir, the Poft came to the Door, and brought this Letter.

Wingate. Let me fee it——The Gypfies have got hold of him! ha! ha! what a pretty Fellow you are! ha! ha! why don't you ftep where I bid you, Sirrah!——

Simon. Yes, Sir.   [*Exit.*

Wingate. Well, well,——I'm refolved, and it fhall be fo——I'll advertife him To-morrow Morning, and promife, if he comes home, all fhall be forgiven:—And when the Block-head comes, I may do as I pleafe——ha! ha! I may do as I pleafe!——Let me fee:——He had on——a Silver-loop'd Hat:——I never liked thofe vile Silver Loops:——A Silver-loop'd Hat;——and——and——Slidikins, what fignifies what he had on?——I'll read my Letter, and think no more about him.—— Hey! what a Plague have we here? [*mutters to himfelf.*] *Briftol*——a——what's all this?—

" *Efteemed Friend,*

" Laft was 20th *ultimo,* fince none of " thine, which will occafion Brevity. The
                                        " Rea-

" Reafon of my writing to thee at prefent,
" is to inform thee that thy Son came to our
" Place with a Company of Strollers, who
" were taken up by the Magiftrate, and com-
" mitted as Vagabonds, to Jail.——

Zookers! I'm glad of it——a Villain of a
Fellow! Let him lie there——

" I am forry thy Lad fhould follow fuch pro-
" fane Courfes; but out of the Efteem I
" bear unto thee, I have taken thy Boy out
" of Confinement, and fent him off for your
" City in the Waggon, which left this four
" Days ago. He is configned to thy Ad-
" drefs, being the needful from thy Friend
" and Servant,
" *Ebeneezor Broadbrim.*"

Wounds! what did he take the Fellow out
for?——a Scoundrel, Rafcal!——turn'd Stage-
Player——I'll never fee the Villain's Face.——
Who comes there?——

Enter Simon.

Simon. I met my Mafter on the Way, Sir;
——our Cares are over:——Here he is,
Sir.——
Wingate. Let him come in——and do you
go down Stairs, you Blockhead.——
[*Exit* Simon.

Enter

Enter Gargle.

Wingate. So, Friend *Gargle,*——Here's a
fine Piece of Work——*Dick*'s turned Vagabond !——

Gargle. He muſt be put under a proper
Regimen directly, Sir——He arrived at my
Houſe within theſe ten Minutes, but in ſuch
a Trim ;—He's now below Stairs—I judged
it proper to leave him there, till I had pre-
pared you for his Reception.——

Wingate. Death and Fire! what could put
it into the Villain's Head to turn Buffoon?

Gargle. Nothing ſo eaſily accounted for :——
Why, when he ought to be reading the Dif-
penſatory, there was he conſtantly reading over
Plays, and Farces, and *Shakeſpeare.*——

Wingate. Ay, that damned *Shakeſpeare !*——
I hear the Fellow was nothing but a Deer-
ſtealer in *Warwickſhire :*——Zookers! if they
had hanged him out of the Way, he would
not now be the Ruin of honeſt Men's Children.——But what Right had he to read
Shakeſpeare !——I never read *Shakeſpeare !*——
Wounds! I caught the Raſcal, myſelf, reading that nonſenſical Play of *Hamblet,* where
the Prince is keeping Company with Strollers and Vagabonds : A fine Example, Mr.
Gargle !——

Gargle. His Diſorder is of the malignant
Kind, and my Daughter has taken the In-
fection from him——bleſs my Heart !——She
was as innocent as Water-gruel, till he ſpoilt
her :

her :——I found her, the other Night, in the very Fact.

Wingate. Zookers! you don't say so !—— caught her in the Fact !——

Gargle. Ay, in the very Fact of reading a Play-book in Bed.

Wingate. O, is that the Fact you mean ?—— Is that all ?——tho' that's bad enough.——

Gargle. But I have done for my young Madam :——I have confined her to her Room, and locked up all her Books.

Wingate. Look ye, Friend *Gargle,* I'll never see the Villain's Face :——Let him follow his Nose and bite the Bridle.——

Gargle. Lenitives, Mr. *Wingate*——Lenitives are propereft at prefent :——His Habit requires gentle Alteratives :——but leave him to my Management ;——about twenty Ounces of Blood, with a Cephalic Tincture,——and he may do very well.

Wingate. Where is the Scoundrel ?

Gargle. Dear Sir, moderate your Anger, and don't use such harfh Language.

Wingate. Harfh Language !——Why, do you think, Man, I'd call him a Scoundrel, if I had not a Regard for him ?——You don't hear me call a Stranger a Scoundrel.

Gargle. Dear Sir, he may still do very well; the Boy has very good Sentiments.——

Wingate. Sentiment !——a Fig for Sentiment ! let him get Money, and never mifs an Opportunity——I never miffed an Opportunity ; got up at Five in the Morning,—— ftruck a Light,——made my own Fire—— worked my Finger's Ends——and this Vagabond

gabond of a Fellow is going his own Way—
with all my Heart—what care I;—let him
follow his Nofe,—let him follow his Nofe—
a ridiculous——

Gargle. Ay, ridiculous indeed, Sir—Why
for a long Time paft, he could not converfe
in the Language of common Senfe.——Afk
him but a trivial Queftion, and he'd give
fome cramp Anfwer out of fome of his Plays
that had been running in his Head, and fo
there's no underftanding a Word he fays.——

Wingate. Zookers! this comes of his keeping Company with Wits, and be damned to
'em for Wits——ha!——ha!——Wits! a fine
Thing indeed——ha! ha! 'Tis the moft beggarly, rafcally,——contemptible Thing on
Earth.——

Gargle. And then, Sir, I have found out
that he went three Times a Week to a Spouting-Club.

Wingate. A Spouting-Club, Friend *Gargle!*
—What's a Spouting-Club?

Gargle. A Meeting of 'Prentices and Clerks
and giddy young Men, intoxicated with Plays;
and fo they meet in Public-Houfes to act
Speeches; there they all neglect Bufinefs, defpife the Advice of their Friends, and think of
nothing but to become Actors.——

Wingate. You don't fay fo!—a Spouting-
Club! wounds, I believe they are all mad.

Gargle. Ay, mad indeed, Sir:——Madnefs
is occafioned in a very extraordinary Manner,—
the Spirits flowing in particular Channels.——

Wingate. 'Sdeath, you're as mad yourfelf as
any of them.——

Gargle.

Gargle. And continuing to run in the fame Ducts——

Wingate. Ducks! Damn your *Ducks!*—— Who's below there?

Gargle. The Texture of the Brain becomes diforder'd, and [Wingate *walks about uneafily, and* Gargle *follows*] thus, by the Preffure on the Nerves, the Head is difturbed, and fo your Son's Malady is contracted.——

Wingate. Who's without there?—— Don't plague me fo, Man.

Gargle. But I fhall alter the morbid State of the Juices, correct his Blood, and produce laudable Chyle.——

Wingate. Zookers, Friend *Gargle,* don't teaze me fo——Don't plague me with your phyfical Nonfenfe—Who's below there?—— Tell that Fellow to come up.——

Gargle. Dear Sir, be a little cool——Inflammatories may be dangerous.—Do, pray, Sir, moderate your Paffions.——

Wingate. Prithee, be quiet, Man——I'll try what I can do——Here he comes.

Enter Dick.

Dick. Now, my good Father, what's the Matter? *

Wingate. So, Friend,——you have been upon your Travels, have you?——You have had your Frolic?—Look-ye, young Man,—— I'll not put myfelf in a Paffion:——But, Death and Fire, you Scoundrel,——what

C   Right

* Hamlet.

Right have you to plague me in this Manner?——Do you think I muſt fall in Love with your Face, becauſe I am your Father?——

Dick. A little more than Kin, and leſs than Kind.—— *

Wingate. Ha! ha!—what a pretty Figure you cut now?——ha! ha!——why don't you ſpeak, you Blockhead?——Have you nothing to ſay for yourſelf?——

Dick. Nothing to ſay for yourſelf?—— What an old Prig it is!

Wingate. Mind me, Friend——I have found you out——I ſee you'll never come to Good.——Turn Stage-player!——Wounds! you'll not have an Eye in your Head in a Month————ha! ha!——you'll have 'em knocked out of the Sockets with withered Apples——remember I tell you ſo.——

Dick. A Critic too! [*whiſtles*] Well done, old Square-toes.——

Wingate. Look-ye, young Man——take Notice of what I ſay:——I made my own Fortune, and I could do the ſame again. Wounds!——if I were placed at the Bottom of *Chancery-Lane*, with a Bruſh and Black-ball,—I'd make my own Fortune again— you read *Shakeſpeare!*——Get *Cocker's Arith-metick*—you may buy it for a Shilling on any Stall—beſt Book that ever was wrote.——

Dick. Pretty well, that;——Ingenious, Faith!——Egad, the old Fellow has a pretty Notion of Letters.

Wingate.

* Hamlet.

Wingate. Can you tell how much is *five Eighths of three Sixteenths of a Pound?*—Five Eighths of three Sixteenths of a Pound—Ay, ay, I see you're a Blockhead:——Look-ye, young Man,—if you have a Mind to thrive in this World, study Figures and make your-self useful—make yourself useful.——

Dick. *How weary, stale, flat, and unprofit-able seem to me all the Uses of this World !—

Wingate. Mind the Scoundrel now.——

Gargle. Do, Mr. *Wingate,* let me speak to him——softly, softly——I'll touch him gently :——Come, come, young Man, lay aside this sulky Humour, and speak as be-comes a Son.

Dick. † O *Jeptha,* Judge of *Israel,* what a Treasure hadst thou !——

Wingate. What does the Fellow say ?

Gargle. He relents, Sir——Come, come, young Man, he'll forgive.——

Dick. ‡ They fool me to the Top of my Bent.——Gad, I'll hum 'em, to get rid of 'em,—a truant Disposition, good my Lord :—No, no, stay, that's not right——I have a better Speech.— " ‖ It is as you say—when " we are sober, and reflect but ever so little " on our Follies, we are ashamed and sorry ; " and yet, the very next Minute, we rush " again into the very same Absurdities."——

Wingate. Well said, Lad, well said—mind me, Friend : Commanding our own Passions, and artfully taking Advantage of other People's, is the sure Road to Wealth :—Death and

C 2　　　　Fire !

* Hamlet.　† Ditto.　‡ Ditto.　‖ Suspicious Husband.

Fire!——but I won't put myself in a Paſſion:——'Tis my Regard for you makes me
ſpeak ; and if I tell you you're a Scoundrel,
'tis for your Good.

Dick. Without Doubt, Sir. [*ſtifling a Laugh.*

Wingate. If you want any Thing, you ſhall
be provided :——Have you any Money in
your Pocket ?—ha ! ha ! what a ridiculous
Numſkul you are now ?—ha ! ha !—Come,
here's ſome Money for you.—[*Pulls out his
Money and looks at it*]—I'll give it to you another Time ; and ſo you'll mind what I ſay
to you, and make yourſelf uſeful for the future.——

Dick. * Elſe, wherefore breathe I in a
Chriſtian Land !

Wingate. Zookers ! you Blockhead, you'd
better ſtick to your Buſineſs, than turn Buffoon, and get Truncheons broke upon your
Arm, and be tumbling upon Carpets.——

Dick. † I ſhall in all my beſt obey you,
Sir.——

Wingate. Very well, Friend,——very well
ſaid——you may do very well if you pleaſe ;
and ſo I'll ſay no more to you, but make
yourſelf uſeful, and ſo now go and clean
yourſelf, and make ready to go Home to
your Buſineſs——and mind me, young Man,
——let me ſee no more Play-Books, and let
me never find that you wear a lac'd Waiſtcoat——you Scoundrel, what right have
you to wear a lac'd Waiſtcoat ?——I never
wore a lac'd Waiſtcoat !——never wore one
till

---

* Richard III.　　† Hamlet.

till I was Forty——But I'll not put myself
in a Paffion——go and change your Drefs,
Friend.

Dick. I fhall, Sir——

     *I muft be cruel, only to be kind,
     Thus bad begins, but worfe remains behind.

Cocker's Arithmetick, Sir?

Wingate. Ay, *Cocker*'s Arithmetick——,
ftudy Figures, and they'll carry you through
the World——

Dick. Yes, Sir, [*ftifling a Laugh*] *Cocker*'s
Arithmetick!   [*Exit.*

Wingate *and* Gargle.

Wingate. Let him mind me, Friend *Gargle*,
and I'll make a Man of him.

Gargle. Ay, Sir, you know the World.——
the young Man will do very well——I wifh
he were out of his Time; he fhall then have
my Daughter——

Wingate. Yes, but I'll touch the Cafh——
he fhan't finger it, during my Life.——I muft
keep a tight Hand over him——[*Goes to the
Door.*]——Do ye hear, Friend!——Mind
what I fay, and go home to your Bufinefs
immediately——Friend *Gargle*, I'll make a
Man of him.——

                        Enter

* Hamlet.

Enter Dick.

Dick. † Who called on *Achmet* ?—Did not *Barbaroſſa* require me here?

Wingate. What's the Matter now?——*Baroſſa* !——Wounds !——What's *Baroſſa* ?——Does the Fellow call me Names ?——What makes the Blockhead ſtand in ſuch Confuſion?

Dick. That *Barbaroſſa* ſhould ſuſpect my Truth !——

Wingate. The Fellow's ſtark ſtaring mad ——get out of the Room, you Villain, get out of the Room.

[*Dick ſtands in a ſullen Mood.*

Gargle. Come, come, young Man, every Thing is eaſy, don't ſpoil all again——go and change your Dreſs, and come Home to your Buſineſs——nay, nay, be ruled by me

[*Thruſts him off.*

Wingate. I'm very peremptory, Friend *Gargle* ; if he vexes me once more, I'll have nothing to ſay to him——well, but, now I think of it——I have *Cocker*'s Arithmetick below Stairs in the Counting-Houſe——I'll ſtep and get it for him, and ſo he ſhall take it Home with him——Friend *Gargle*, your Servant.

Gargle. Mr. *Wingate*, a good Evening to you——you'll ſend him Home to his Buſineſs——

Wingate.

Wingate. He shall follow you Home directly. Five Eighths of three Sixteenths of a Pound !——multiply the Numerator by the Denominator; five times Sixteen is ten times Eight, ten times Eight is Eighty, and——a——a——carry One.　　　　　[*Exit.*

Enter Dick *and* Simon.

Simon. Lord love ye, Master——I'm so glad you're come back——come, we had as good e'en gang Home to my Master *Gargle's*——

Dick. No, no, *Simon*, stay a Moment—— this is but a scurvy Coat I have on——and I know my Father has always some Jemmy Thing lock'd up in his Closet——I know his Ways——He takes 'em in Pawn, for he'll never part with a Shilling without Security.

Simon. Hush ! he'll hear us——stay, I believe he's coming up Stairs.

Dick. [*Goes to the Door and listens.*] No, no,—no,—he's going down, growling and grumbling—ay,—say ye so " Scoundrel, " Rascal—Let him bite the Bridle"—" Six " times Twelve is Seventy-two"—all's safe Man, never fear him—Do you stand here— I shall dispatch this Business in a Crack.——

Simon. Blessings on him ! what is he about now ?—why the Door is locked, Master.——

Dick. Ay, but I can easily force the Lock— you shall see me do it as well as any Sir *John Brute* of 'em all—this right Leg here is the

best

beſt Lockſmith in *England*—ſo, ſo,—[*forces*
the Door and goes in.]

Simon. He's at his Plays again—Odds my
Heart, he's a rare Hand—he'll go through
with it, I'll warrant him—Old Cojer muſt
not ſmoke that I have any Concern—I muſt
be main cautious——Lord bleſs his Heart,
he's to teach me to act *Scrub.*——He begun
with me long ago, and I got as far as the
Jeſuit before a went out of Town :——
" * Scrub—Coming, Sir,—Lord, Ma'am,
" I've a whole Packet full of News—ſome
" ſay one Thing and ſome ſay another ; but,
" for my Part, Ma'am,——I believe he's a
" Jeſuit"—that's main pleaſant— " *I believe*
" *he's a Jeſuit.*"

Re-enter Dick.

Dick. † I have done the Deed—Didſt thou
not hear a Noiſe ?

Simon. No, Maſter; we're all ſnug.——

Dick. This Coat will do charmingly—I
have bilked the old Fellow nicely—— ‡ In a
dark Corner of his Cabinet, I found this Paper ; what it is the Light will ſhew.

I promiſe to pay——ha !——

I promiſe to pay to Mr. *Moneytrap*, or Order, on Demand—*'tis his Hand—a Note of*
his—yet more—The Sum of ſeven Pounds
fourteen Shillings and Seven Pence, Value
received, by me
London this 15th *June*, 1755.——'Tis wanting what ſhould follow——*his* Name ſhould

fol-

* Stratagem. † Macbeth. ‡ *Vide* the Mourning Bride.

follow—but 'tis torn off—becaufe the Note is paid.——

Simon. O Lud! Dear Sir, you'll fpoil all— I wifh we were well out of the Houfe—Our beft Way, Mafter, is to make off directly.——

Dick. I will, I will; but firft help me on with this Coat——*Simon,* you fhall be my Dreffer—you'll be fine and happy behind the Scenes.——

Simon. O Lud! it will be main pleafant—I have been behind the Scenes in the Country, when I liv'd with the Man that fhew'd wild Beaftices.——

Dick. Hark-ye, *Simon,*—when I am playing fome deep Tragedy, and * cleave the general Ear with horrid Speech, you muft ftand be-tween the Scenes and cry bitterly.[*Teaches him.*

Simon. Yes, Sir.

Dick. And when I'm playing Comedy, you muft be ready to laugh your Guts out [*Teaches him.*] for I fhall be very pleafant——Tolde-roll—[*Dances.*]

Simon. Never doubt me, Sir.——

Dick. Very well; now run down and open the Street-Door; I'll follow you in a Crack.

Simon. I am gone to ferve you, Mafter-——

Dick. † To ferve theyfelf——for, look-ye, *Simon,* when I am Manager, claim thou of me the Care o'th' Wardrobe, with all thofe Moveables, whereof the § Property-Man now ftands poffeft.——

D

Simon.

* Hamlet.   † Richard III.
§ The Property-Man, in the Play-Houfe Phrafe, is the Perfon who gives Truncheons, Daggers, &c. to the Actors, as Occafion requires.

Simon. O Lud! this is charming—Hufh! I am gone.   [*Going.*

Dick. Well, but hark-ye, *Simon,* come hither——* what Money have you about you, Mafter *Matthew?*

Simon. But a Tefter, Sir.

Dick. A Tefter!————That's fomething of the leaft, Mafter *Matthew,*——let's fee it.

Simon. You have had fifteen Sixpences now——

Dick. Never mind that——I'll pay you all at my Benefit——

Simon. I don't doubt that, Mafter—— but mum.   [*Exit.*

Dick, *folus.*

† Thus far we run before the Wind.—— An Apothecary!——make an Apothecary of me! ——‡ what, cramp my Genius over a Peftle and Mortar, or mew me up in a Shop with an Alligator ftuft, and a beggarly Account of empty Boxes!——to be culling Simples, and conftantly adding to the Bills of Mortality.————No! no! It will be much better to be pafted up in Capitals, *The Part of* Romeo *by a young Gentleman, who never appeared on any Stage before!*——My Ambition fires at the Thought————But hold, ——mayn't I run fome Chance of failing

in

---

* Every Man in his Humour.   † Richard III.
‡ *Vide* Romeo and Juliet.

in my Attempt——Hiffed,——Pelted,——
Laughed at,——Not admitted into the Green-
Room——That will never do——* Down,
bufy Devil, down, down.—Try it again.—
Loved by the Women, envied by the Men,
applauded by the Pit, clapped by the Gallery,
admired by the Boxes. " Dear Colonel, is not
" he a charming Creature ?" " My Lord,
" don't you like him of all Things ?"——
" Makes Love like an Angel !"——" What
" an Eye he has!——fine Legs !"——
" I'll certainly go to his Benefit."——Ce-
leftial Sounds!——And then I'll get in
with all the Painters, and have myfelf put
up in every Print-Shop—in the Character of
Macbeth ! " This is a forry Sight." [*ftands an
Attitude.*] In the Character of *Richard* [*Give
me another Horfe, bind up my Wounds.*]——
this will do rarely——and then I have a
Chance of getting well married———O
glorious Thought!—— † By Heaven I will
enjoy it, though but in Fancy——— But,
what's o'Clock ?——it muft be almoft Nine.
I'll away at once ; this is Club-night.——
'Egad I'll go to 'em for a while——the
Spouters are all met——little they think
I'm in Town——they'll be furprized to
fee me——Off I go, and then for my Af-
fignation with my Mafter *Gargle*'s Daughter
——Poor *Charlotte!*——fhe's lock'd up,
but I fhall find Means to fettle Matters for
her Efcape——She's a pretty Theatrical
　　　　　Genius

---

* Venice Preferv'd.　　　† Tamerlane.

Genius——If she flies to my Arms like a
Hawk to its Perch, it will be so rare an Adventure, and so Dramatic an Incident;——

* Limbs do your Office, and support me well;
Bear me but to her, then fail me if you can.

* The Orphan.

END *of the* FIRST ACT.

A C T

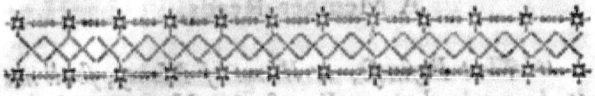

ACT II. SCENE I.

*Scene discovers the Spouting-Club, the Members
seated and roaring out* Bravo, *while one stands
at a Distance repeating——*

1st. Member. CURS'D be your Senate,
curs'd your Constitution;
The Curse of growing Factions and Divisions
Still vex your Councils.*——

2d. Memb. Don't you think his Action a
little confined?

1st. Memb. Psha! you Blockhead, don't
you know that I'm in Chains?——

2d. Memb. Blockhead, say ye?—Was not I
the first that took Compassion on you, when
you lay like a sneaking Fellow under the
Counter, and swept your Master's Shop in
a Morning? when you read nothing but the
Young Man's Pocket Companion, or the *True
Clerk's Vade Mecum,* did not I put *Chrononho-
tontbologos* in your Hand?

All. Bravo! Bravo!——

President. Come, Gentlemen, let us have
no Disputes. Consider, Gentlemen, this is the
Honourable Society of Spouters; and so, to
put an End to all Animosities, read the seventh
Rule of this Society.

A Mem-

* Venice Preserv'd.

A Member Reads,

" *That Bufinefs, or Want of Money, fhall not*
" *be received as an Excufe for Non-Attendance;*
" *nor the Anger of Parents or other Relations;*
" *nor the Complaints of our Mafters be ever heard;*
" *by which Means this Society will be able to boaft*
" *its own mimic Heroes, and be a Nurfery of*
" *Young* Actorlings *for the Stage, in Spight of*
" *the Mechanic Genius of our Friends.*"

Prefident. That is not the Rule I mean;—
but come, * we'll fill a Meafure the Table
round—now good Digeftion wait on Appetite,
and Health on both.

All. Huzza, huzza, huzza!——

Prefident. Come, Gentlemen, let us have
no Quarrels.

All. Huzza, huzza!——

Scotchman. Come now I'll gee you a Touch
of *Macbeeth.*——

1*ft. Memb.* That will be rare. Come let's
have it.——

Scotchman. What do'ft lier at Mon?—I have
had muckle Applaufe at *Edinburgh,* when I
enacted in the *Reégiceede,*—and I now intend
to do *Macbeeth*—I feed the *Degger* Yefterneet,
and I thought I fhould ha' killed every one
that came in my Way.——

Irifhman. Stand out of the way, Lads, and
you'll fee me give a Touch of *Othello,* my Dear—
[*Takes the Cork and burns it, and blacks his Face.*]
The Devil burn the Cork—it would not do it
faft enough.

1*ft. Memb.* Here, here, I'll lend you a helping Hand. [*Blacks him.*]

[*Knocking at the Door.*]

2*d. Memb.* *Open Locks, whoever knocks.—

Enter Dick.

Dick. † How now, ye Secret, Black, and Midnight Hags?—what is't ye do?

All. Ha! the Genius come to Town— Huzza! huzza!—the Genius—

Dick. How fare the honeft Partners of my Heart?—*Jack Hopeleſs,* give us your Hand— *Guilderften,* yours—Ha! *Roſencroſs*—Gentlemen, I rejoice to fee ye—But come, the News, the News of the Town!—Has any Thing been damned?—Any new Performers this Winter? —How often has *Romeo* and *Juliet* been acted? --Come, my Bucks, inform me, I want News.--

1*ft. Memb.* You shall know all in good Time—But prithee, my dear Boy, how was it?—You play'd at *Briftol,* let's hear.—

2*d. Memb.* Ay, let's have it, dear *Dick.*—

Dick. Look-ye there now—‡ Let's have it, dear Boy, and dear *Dick.*——

1*ft. Memb.* Nay, nay, but how was you receiv'd?—

Dick. Romeo was my Part——I touch'd their Souls for 'em,—every pale Face from the Wells was there, and fo on I went—but rot 'em,—never mind them—‖ What bloody Scene has *Roſcius* now to act?—

1*ft.*

* Macbeth.　　　† Ditto.　　　‡ Suſpicious Huſband.
‖ Richard III.

z

1ſt. Memb. Several Things—But, Genius, why did you come to us ſo late?—Why did not you come in the Beginning of the Night?

Dick. Why, I intended it: But who ſhould I meet in my Way but by Friend *Catcall*, a deviliſh good Critic;—and ſo he and I went together and had our Pipes, to*cloſe the Orifice of the Stomach you know;—and what do you think I learn'd of him?

1ſt. Memb. I can't ſay.

Dick. Can you tell, now, whether the Emphaſis ſhould be laid upon the *Epitaph*†, or the *Subſtantive?*

1ſt. Memb. Why, no.——

Dick. Ever, while you live, lay your Emphaſis upon the *Epitaph*.——

Iriſhman. Arrah, my Dear, but what is that ſame Epitaph now?

Dick. ‡ Arrah, my dear Couſin *Mackſhane*, won't you put a Remembrance upon me?—

Iriſhman. Ow! but is it mocking you are?—Look-ye, my Dear, if you'd be taking me off—Don't you call it taking off!—By my Shoul I'd be making you take yourſelf off——What? If you're for being obſtropolous, I would not matter you three Skips of a Flea.——

Dick. Nay, prithee, no Offence—I hope we ſhall be Brother-players.

Iriſhman. Ow! then we'd be very good Friends; for you know two of a Trade can never agree, my Dear.

Scotchman.

* Every Man in his Humour. †
† By Miſtake for *Epithet*.   ‡ Stratagem.

Scotchman. Locke is certainly reet in his Chapter aboot innate Ideas; for this Mon is born without any at all—and the other Mon yonder, I doot, is no greet Heed-piece.——

Dick. What do you intend to appear in?

Irishman. Othollo, my Dear; let me alone; you'll see how I'll *bodder* 'em—Tho' by my Shoul, myshelf does not know but I'd be frightened when every Thing is in a *Hub-bub*, and nothing to be heard, but " *Throw him* " *over*"—" *over with him*"—" *off, off, off the* " *Stage*"—" *Music*".——" *Won't y' ba' some* " *Orange-chips*"——" *won't y' ba' some Non-* " *pareills ?*"——Ow!——but may-be the dear Craturs in the Boxes will be *lucking* at my Legs—Ow! to be sure——the Devil burn the *Luck* they'll give 'em.——

Dick. I shall certainly laugh in the Fellow's Face.——

Irishman. Ow! never mind it——let me alone, my Dear——may-be I'd see a little round Face from *Dublin* in the Pit, may-be I wou'd; but then, won't I be the first Gentleman of my Name that turn'd Stage-play'r?—My Cousins would rather see me starve like a Gentleman, with Honour and Reputation—Myshelf does be asham'd when I think of it.——

Scotchman. Stay till you hear me give a Speecimen of Elocution.

Dick. What, with that Impediment, Sir?

Scotchman. Impeediment! what Impeediment? I do not leesp——do I?——I do no squeent——I am well leem'd, am I not?——

Irishman. By my Shoul, if you go to that, I am as well timber'd myself as any of them,

E   and

and ſhall make a Figure in genteel and top Comedy.——

Scotchman. I'll give you a Speecimen of *Mockbeeth.*——

Iriſhman. Make haſte, then, and I'll beg'n *Othello.*——

Scotchman. ——Is this a Dagger that I ſee be-before me, *&c.*

Iriſhman. [*collaring him.*] * Willain, be ſure you prove my Love a Whore, *&c.*

[*Another Member comes forward with his Face powdered, and a Pipe in his Hand.*]

——I am thy Father's Spirit, *Hamlet*——

Dick. Po! Prithee! you're not fat enough for a Ghoſt.——

Memb. I intend to make my firſt Appearance in it for all that, only I'm puzzled about one Thing——I want to know, when I come on firſt, whether I ſhould make a Bow to the Audience?

Another Memb. Now, Gentlemen, for the true way of dying——[*ſpreads a Blanket.*]—— now for a little Phrenzy——[*Repeats a dying Speech, and rolls himſelf up in the Blanket.*]——

[*Watch behind the Scenes; Paſt Five o'Clock, cloudy Morning.*]

Dick. Hey! paſt Five o'Clock——'Sdeath, I ſhall miſs my Appointment with *Charlotte*—— I have ſtaid too long, and ſhall loſe my Proſelyte—Come, let us adjourn.——

All. Ay, let us ſally forth.——

Iriſhman. With all my Heart; tho' I ſhould have bodder'd 'em finely if they had ſtaid.

Scotch-

* Venice Preſerv'd.

Scotchman. I fhould have fheen'd in *Mock-beeth*———but never meend it———I'll go now to my Friend the Bookfeller, and tranflate *Cornelius Tacitus,* or *Grotius de Jure Belli,*———and fo, Gentlemen, your Servant.———

All. Huzza! Huzza!

Dick. * We'll fcower the Watch———Confufion to Morality———I wifh the Conftable were married———Huzza, Huzza———

Irifhman. By my Shoul, myfhelf did not care if I had a Wife, with a good Fortune, to be hindering me from going on———But no matter———I may meet with a willing Cratur fomewhere———　　　　　[*Exit finging.*

All. Huzza, Huzza!———　　　　[*Exeunt.*

SCENE, *a Street.*

Enter a Watchman.

Paft Five o'Clock, cloudy Morning. Mercy on us———all mad I believe in this Houfe——— They're at this Trade three Nights in the Week, I think———Paft Five o'Clock, a cloudy Morning.

All. Huzza! [*without.*]

Watchman. What in the Name of Wonder are they all at?

Hurra, Hurra, without. Enter the Spouters.

Dick. † Angels and Minifters of Grace defend us!

E 2　　　　　　　1*ft. Memb.*

———————————————
* Sir John Brute.　　　† Hamlet.

1ſt. Memb. * By Heavens I'll tear you Joint by Joint, and ſtrew this hungry Church-yard with your Limbs.

Dick. † Avant, and quit my Sight—— thy Bones are marrowleſs———There's no Speculation in thoſe Eyes, that thou doſt glare withal.

Watchman. Prithee don't diſtrub the Peace——

A Member. ‡ Be ſure you write him down an Aſs.

Dick. § Be alive again, and dare me to the Deſart with thy Pole,———take any Shape but that, and my firm Nerves ſhall never tremble——

Watchman. Soho! Soho!

Enter Watchmen from all Parts, ſome drunk, ſome coughing, &c.

2d. Watchman. What's the Matter there?——

1ſt. Watchman. Here are the Diſturbers of the Peace——I charge 'em all——

Dick. ‖ Unmanner'd Slave, advance your Halbert higher than my breaſt, or by St. *Paul,* I'll ſtrike thee down, and ſpurn thee, Beggar, for this Inſolence——

[*They fight,* Dick *is knocked down.* Exeunt *Watchmen fighting the reſt.*

Dick. ** I have it; it will do;——'Egad, I'll make my Eſcape now——O I am Fortune's Fool——. [*Exit.*

Re-

---

* Romeo.   † Macbeth.   ‡ Much ado about Nothing.   § Macbeth.   ‖ Richard.
** Romeo.

Re-enter Watchmen, &c.

Watchman. Come, bring 'em along——
1*st. Memb.* * Good Ruffians, hold a while——
2*d. Memb.* † I am unfortunate, but not aſhamed of being ſo.
Watchman. Come, come, bring 'em along.
[*Exeunt.*

SCENE, *another Street.*

Enter Dick, *with a Lanthorn and a Ladder.*

All's quiet here ; the Coaſt's clear ;—now for my Adventure with *Charlotte*—this Ladder will do rarely for the Buſineſs—tho' it would be better, if it were a Ladder of Ropes—but hold ; have not I ſeen ſomething like this on the Stage ?—yes I have, in ſome of the Entertainments—Ay, ‡ I remember an Apothecary, and hereabout he dwells—this is my Maſter *Gargle*'s ;—being dark the Beggar's Shop is ſhut—what, ho ! Apothecary ! —but ſoft,—what Light breaks thro' yonder Window —It is the Eaſt, and *Juliet* is the Sun ; ariſe fair Sun, &c.
Charlotte. Who's there ? my *Romeo ?*
Dick. The ſame, my Love, if it not thee diſpleaſe.——
Charlotte. Huſh ! not ſo loud, you'll waken my Father.——
Dick. § Alas ! there's more peril in thy Eye.
Char-

___
* Revenge. † Oroonoko. ‡ Romeo. § Romec.

Charlotte. Nay, but prithee now—I tell you you'll spoil all—what made you stay so long?

Dick. * Chide not, my Fair, but let the God of Love laugh in thy Eyes, and revel in thy Heart.——

Charlotte. As I am a living Soul, you'll ruin every Thing; be but quiet, and I'll come down to you.——   [*Going.*

Dick. No, no, not so fast—*Charlotte*—let us act the Garden Scene first——

Charlotte. A Fiddlestick for the Garden Scene——

Dick. Nay, then I'll act *Ranger*—up I go, Neck or nothing.

Charlotte. Dear Heart, you're enough to frighten a Body out of one's Wits—Don't come up—I tell you there's no Occasion for the Ladder—I have settled every Thing with *Simon*, and he's to let me thro' the Shop, when he opens it.

Dick. Well, but I tell you I would not give a Farthing for it without the Ladder, and so, up I go.

Enter Simon *at the Door.*

Simon. Sir, Sir, Madam, Madam——

Dick. Prithee be quiet, *Simon*——I am ascending the high Top-gallant of my Joy—

Simon. An't please you, Master, my young Mistress may come thro' the Shop——I am going to sweep it out, and she may escape that way fast enow——

                                        Char-

* Fair Penitent.

Charlotte. That will do purely——and so do you ſtay where you are, and prepare to receive me—— [*Exit from above.*

Dick. No, no, but that won't take—you ſhan't hinder me from going thro' my Part [*goes up*] * a Woman, by all that's lucky—— neither old nor crooked———in I go——— [*goes in*] and for Fear of the Purſuit of the Family, I'll make ſure of the Ladder.

Simon. Hiſt! hiſt! Maſter——leave that there, to ſave me from being ſuſpected——

Dick. With all my Heart, *Simon*——
[*Exit from above.*

Simon alone. Lord love him, how comical he is!——it will be fine for me, when we're playing the Fool together, to call him Brother *Martin.* " † Brother *Martin.*"

Enter Charlotte.

Charlotte. O Lud! I'm frighted out of my Wits, where is he?——

Simon. He's a coming, Ma'am——[*calls to him*] " Brother *Martin.*"

Enter Dick.

Dick. ‡ Cuckold him, Ma'am, by all Means ——I'm your Man.

Charlotte. Well now, I proteſt and vow, I wonder how you can ſerve a Body ſo——— feel with what a Pit-a-pat Action my Heart beats——

Dick.

---

* Suſpicious Huſband.   † Stratagem.
‡ Suſpicious Huſband.   2

Dick. * 'Tis an Alarm to Love——quick let me snatch thee to thy *Romeo*'s Arms, *&c.*

Watchman behind the Scenes. Past Six o'Clock, and a cloudy Morning——

Charlotte. Dear Heart, don't let us stand fooling here——as I live and breathe we shall both be taken——do, for Heaven's Sake, let us make our Escape.

Watch. Past Six o'Clock, a cloudy Morning——

Charlotte. It comes nearer and nearer; let as make off——

Dick. Give us your Hand then————my pretty little Adventurer I attend you.

†Yes, my dear *Charlotte*, we will go together,

> Together to the Theatre we'll go,
> There to their ravish'd Eyes our Skill
>   we'll show,
> And point new Beauties--to the Pit below.

Simon. Heavens bless the Couple of 'em; but mum.

[*Exit, and shuts the Doors after him.*

Enter Bailiff and his Follower.

Bailiff. That's he yonder, as sure as you're alive—Ay, it is—and he has been about some Mischief here.

Follower. No, no, that an't he—that one wears a laced Coat—tho' I can't say—as sure as a Gun, it is he——

Bailiff. Ay, I smoked him at once——Do you run that Way and stop at the Bottom of

Ca-

---

* Old Batchelor.   † *Vide* Distress'd Mother.

Catherine-Street ; I'll go up *Drury-Lane*, and between us both, it will be odds if we miss him. *[Exeunt.*

Enter Watchman.

Watch. Paſt Six a Clock, and a cloudy Morning.——Hey-day ! what's here, a Ladder, at Maſter *Gargle's* Window ?——I muſt alarm the Family——Ho ! Maſter *Gargle—*
[Knocks at the Door.

Gargle, above. What's the Matter ?—How comes this Window to be open ?——ha !—— a Ladder !——Who's below there ?

1ſt. Watch. I hope you an't robbed, Maſter *Gargle ?*——As I was going my Rounds, I found your Window open.

Gargle. I fear this is ſome of that young Dog's Tricks——Take away the Ladder ; I muſt enquire into all this.—— *[Exit.*

Enter Simon, *like* Scrub.

Simon. * Thieves ! Murder ! Thieves ! Popery !—

Watch. What's the Matter with the Fellow ?

Simon. Spare all I have, and take my Life——

Watchman. Any Miſchief in the Houſe ?

Simon. They broke in with Fire and Sword ——they'll be here this Minute——Five and Forty——*This will do charmingly——* " *my young Maſter taught me this.*" *[Aſide.*

F 1ſt.

* *Vide* Stratagem.

1st. Watchman. What, are there Thieves in the House?

Simon. With Sword and Piftol, Sir,——— Five and Forty.

Watch. Nay, then 'tis Time for me to go, ———for, mayhap, I may come to ha' the worft on't——— [*Exit Watchman.*

Enter Gargle.

Gargle. Dear Heart! dear Heart———fhe's gone, fhe's gone———my Daughter! my Daughter!———what's the Fellow in fuch a Fright for?

Simon. Down on your Knees———down on your Marrowbones———(this will make him think, I know nothing of the Matter——— Blefs his Heart for teaching me)———Down on your Marrowbones.———

Gargle. Get up, you Fool, get up——— Dear Heart, I'm all in a Fermentation.

Enter Wingate *reading a News-Paper.*

" Wanted, on good Security, Five hundred
" Pounds, for which lawful Intereft will be
" given, and a good Præmium allowed:
" Whoever this may fuit, Enquire for S. T.
" at the *Crown and Rolls* in *Chancery-Lane.*"—
This may be worth looking after.—I'll have a good Præmium—If the Fellow's a Fool, I'll fix my Eye on him—Other People's Follies are an Eftate to the Man that knows how to make himfelf ufeful—So, Friend *Gargle,*——— you're up early, I fee———nothing like rifing

early

early——nothing to be got by lying in Bed,
like a lubberly Fellow—What's the Matter
with you?—ha! ha! you look like a—ha!
ha!—

Gargle. O—no Wonder—My Daughter,
my Daughter!

Wingate. Your Daughter!—what fignifies
a foolifh Girl?

Gargle. Oh dear Heart! dear Heart!——
out of the Window.

Wingate. Fallen out of the Window!——
well, fhe was a Woman, and 'tis no Matter—
if fhe's dead, fhe's provided for.——Here,
I found the Book——could not meet with
it laft Night——Here it is——there's more
Senfe in it, than in all their *Macbeths* and
their Trumpery [*reads*] *Cocker's* Arithmetick
——Look ye here now, Friend *Gargle*,——
fuppofe you have the Sixteenth Part of a
Ship, and I buy one Fifth of you, what Share
of the Ship do I buy?——

Gargle. Oh dear, Sir, 'tis a melancholy
Cafe——

Wingate. A melancholy Cafe indeed to be
fo ignorant——why fhould not a Man
know every Thing? One Fifth of one Sixteenth, what Part have I of the Whole? Let
me fee—I'll do it a fhort Way.——

Gargale. Loft beyond Redemption.——

Wingate. Zookers, be quiet Man, you put
me out—Seven times Seven is Forty-nine,
and Six times Twelve is Seventy-two,——
and—and—and—a—Here, Friend *Gargle*,
take the Book, and give it that Scoundrel of a
Fellow.——

Gargle. Lord, Sir,—He's returned to his Tricks.——

Wingate. Returned to his Tricks!—What, —broke loose again?——

Gargle. Ay, and carried off my Daughter with him.——

Wingate. Carried off your Daughter—— How did the Rascal contrive that?

Gargle. Oh, dear Sir,————the Watch alarmed us a while ago, and I found a Ladder at the Window——so I suppose my young Madam made her Escape that Way.—

Wingate. Wounds! what Business had the Fellow with your Daughter?

Gargle. I wish I had never taken him into my House—He may debauch the poor Girl—

Wingate. And suppose he does————she's a Woman, an't she?—Ha! ha! Friend *Gargle*, Ha! ha!——

Gargle. Dear Sir, how can you talk thus to a Man distracted?

Wingate. I'll never see the Fellow's Face.

Simon. Secrets! Secrets! *

Wingate. What, are you in the Secret, Friend?——

Simon. To be sure, there be Secrets in all Families——but, for my Part, I'll not speak a Word *pro* or *con*, till there's a Peace.

Wingate. You won't speak, Sirrah!—I'll make you speak——Do you know nothing of this Numskull?

Simon. Who I, Sir?——He came home last Night from your House, and went out again directly.——

Wingate.

* *Vide* Stratagem.   2

Wingate. You faw him then——

Simon. Yes, Sir——faw him to be fure, Sir——
he made me open the Shop Door for him——
he ftopp'd on the Threfhold and pointed at
one of the Clouds, and afked me if it was not
like an *Ouzel* * ?——

Wingate. Like an *Ouzel*—Wounds ! what's
an *Ouzel ?*——

Gargle. And the young Dog came back in
the Dead of Night to fteal away my Daughter.

Wingate. I'll tell you what, Friend *Gargle*——
I'll think no more of the Fellow—let him bite
the Bridle——I'll go mind my Bufinefs, and not
mifs an Opportunity.

Gargle. Good now, Mr. *Wingate*, don't leave
me in this Affliction,——confider, when the
animal Spirits are properly employed, the
whole Syftem's exhilarated, a proper Circulation in the fmaller Ducts or Capillary Vef-
fels——

Wingate. Look-ye there now—the Fellow's
at his *Ducks* again, ha ! ha !

Gargle. But when the Spirits are under Influence——

Wingate. Ha ! ha ! what a fine fellow you
are now ?—you're as mad with your phyfical
Nonfenfe, as my Son with his *Shakefpeare* and
Ben Thompfon——

Gargle. Dear Sir, let us go in queft of him
—he fhall be well phlebotomized ; and for
the future I'll keep his Solids and Fluids in
proper Balance—

Wingate. Don't tell me of your Solids—
I tell you he'll never be folid—and fo I'll go
and

* Hamlet.

and mind my Bufinefs——let me fee where
is this Chap——[*reads*] ay, ay, at the *Crown
and Rolls*——good Morning, Friend *Gar-
dle*——don't plague yourfelf about the Numfkull——ftudy Fractions Man; Vulgar Fractions will carry you through the World. Arith-
metical Proportion is when the Antecedent
and Confequent,—a—   [*going.*

Enter a Porter.

Wingate. Who are you, pray ?—what do
you want ?——

Porter. Is one Mr. *Gargle* here ?

Gargle. Yes——who wants him ?——

Porter. Here's a Letter for you ?——

Gargle. Let me fee it. O dear Heart!—
[*reads*] *To Mr.* Gargle *at the Peftle and Morter*
——'Slidikins, this is a Letter from that unfortunate young Fellow——

Wingate. Let me fee it, *Gargle*—

Gargle. A Moment's Patience, good Mr.
Wingate, and this may unravel all—[*reads*]—
Poor young Man !——his Brain is certainly
turned——I can't make Head or Tale of
it——

Wingate. Ha ! ha !—you're a pretty Fellow—give it me, Man—I'll make it out for
you—'tis his Hand fure enough [*reads*]

    To Mr. Gargle, *&c.*
" *Moft Potent, Grave** and Reverend Doctor,*
" *my very noble and approv'd good Mafter, that*
" *I have ta'en away your Daughter it is moft*
" *true, true I will marry her ;—†'tis true 'tis*
                                          " *Pity,*

————————————————————
          * Othello.   † Hamlet.

" *Pity, and Pity 'tis, 'tis true.*"——What in
the Name of Common Senfe is all this ? " * *I*
" *have done your Shop fome Service, and you*
" *know it ; no more of that——†yet I could wish,*
" *that at this Time, I had not been this Thing*
——What can the Fellow mean ?——" *For*
" *Time ‡ may have yet one fated Hour to come,*
" *which, wing'd with Liberty, may overtake Oc-*
" *cafion paft*"———overtake Occafion paft !——
Time and Tide waits for no Man——" § *I ex-*
" *pect Redrefs from thy noble Sorrows——thine*
" *and my poor Country's ever.*" R. Wingate.
Mad as a *March* Hare! I have done with
him——let him ftay till the Shoe pinches, a
crack-brained Numfkull!

Porter. An't pleafe ye, Sir, I fancys the
Gentleman is a little befide himfelf——
he took hold un me here by the Collar, and
called me Villain **, and bid me prove his Wife
a Whore——Lord help him, I never fee'd
the Gentleman's Spoufe in my born Days before.

Gargle. Is fhe with him now ?

Porter. I believe fo———There's a likely
young Woman with him, all in Tears.——

Gargle. My Daughter to be fure———

Wingate. Let the Fellow go and be hang'd
——Wounds! I would not go the Length of
my Arm to fave the Villain from the Gallows.
Where was he, Friend, when he gave you this
Letter ?——

Porter. I fancy, Mafter, the Gentleman's
                                        under

---

* Othello.   † Mourning Bride.   ‡ Ditto.
§ Venice Preferv'd.   ** Othello.

under Troubles————I brought it from a
Spunging-Houfe.

Wingate. From a Spungging-Houfe!

Porter. Yes, Sir, in *Grays-Inn-Lane.*

Wingate. Let him lie there, let him lie
there——I am glad of it——

Gargle. Do, my dear Sir, let us ftep to
him——

Wingate. No, not I, let him ftay there—
this it is to have a Genius——ha! ha!——
a Genius!——ha! ha!——a Genius is a fine
Thing indeed!——ha! ha!   [*Exit.*

Gargle. Poor Man! he has certainly a Fever
on his Spirits——do you ftep in with me, honeft
Man, till I flip on my Coat, and then I'll go
after this unfortunate Boy.

Porter. Yes, Sir,—'tis in *Grays-Inn-Lane.*
                                          [*Exeunt.*

Scene a Spunging-Houfe, Dick *and* Bailiff *at a
Table, and* Charlotte *fitting in a difconfolate
Manner by him.*

Bailiff. Here's my Service to you, young
Gentleman——Don't be uneafy——the
Debt is not much——why do you look fo
fad?——

Dick. Becaufe * Captivity has robb'd me
of a juft and dear Diverfon.

Bailiff. Never look fulky at me—I never
ufe any Body ill—Come, it has been many
a good Man's Lot——here's my Service to
you—but we've no Liquor—come we'll
have t'other Bowl——

                                          Dick.

* Mourning Bride.

Dick. * I've now not Fifty Ducats in the World—yet ftill I am in Love, and pleas'd with Ruin.——

Bailiff. What do you fay?—you've Fifty Shillings, I hope.——

Dick. † Now, thank Heaven! I'm not worth a Groat.——

Bailiff. Then there's no Credit here, I can tell you that——you muft get Bail, or go to *Newgate*——who do you think is to pay Houfe-rent for you?—You fee your Friends won't come near you——They've all an-fwered in the old Cant——" *I've promifed* " *my Wife never to be Bail for any Body;*" or, " *I've fworn not to do it*"—or, " *I'd lend* " *you the Money if I had it, but defire to be ex-* " *cufed from bailing any Man.*"—The Porter you juft now fent, will bring the fame An-fwer, I warrant.——Such Poverty-ftruck Devils as you fhan't ftay in my Houfe—— you fhall go to *Quod*, I can tell you that—
                    [*Knocking at the Door.*

Bailiff. Coming, coming, I am coming— I fhall lodge you in *Newgate*, I promife you, before Night——not worth a Groat!—— you're a fine Fellow to ftay in a Man's Houfe ——You fhall go to *Quod*.   [*Exit.*

Dick. Come, clear up, *Charlotte*, never mind this——come, now——let us act the Prifon-Scene in the *Mourning Bride*——

Charlotte. How can you think of acting Speeches, when we're in fuch Diftrefs?——

Dick. Nay, but my dear Angel——
                    G   *Enter*

———————————
* Venice Preferv'd.   † Ditto.

Enter Wingate *and* Gargle.

Gargle. Hufh! Do, dear Sir, let us liften to him—I dare fay he repents——

Wingate. Wounds!——what Cloaths are thofe the Fellow has on?——Zookers, the Scoundrel has robbed me.——

Dick. Come, now we'll practife an Attitude—How many of 'em have you?——

Charlotte. Let me fee—one—two—three— and then in the fourth Act, and then——O *Gemini*, I have ten at leaft——

Dick. That will do fwimmingly——I've a round Dozen *myfelf*—Come now begin—— you fanfy me dead, and I think the fame of you—now mind—   [*They ftand in Attitudes.*

Wingate. Only mind the Villain.—

Dick. O thou foft fleeting Form of *Lindamira* !—

Charlotte. * Illufive Shade of my beloved Lord !

Dick. † She lives, fhe fpeaks, and we fhall ftill be happy.——

Wingate. You lie, you Villain, you fhan't be happy.—   [*Knocks him down.*

Dick. [*on the Ground.*] ‡ Perdition catch your Arm, the Chance is thine.——

Gargle. So, my young Madam—I have found you again.——

Dick. ‖ *Capulet* forbear; *Paris* let loofe your Hold—She is my Wife——our Hearts are twined together.——   *Wingate.*

* Romeo and Juliet.   † Ditto.   ‡ Richard III.
‖ Romeo.   2

Wingate. Sirrah! Villain! I'll break every Bone in your Body— [*Strikes.*

Dick. * Parents have flinty Hearts, no Tears can move 'em: Children must be wretched—

Wingate. Get off the Ground, you Villain; get off the Ground.——

Dick. 'Tis a Pity there are no Scene-drawers to lift me——

Wingate. A Scoundrel, to rob your Father; you Rascal, I've a Mind to break your Head.

Dick. † What, like this? [*Takes off his Wig, and shews two Patches on his Head.*]

Wingate. 'Tis mighty well, young Man— Zookers! I made my own Fortune; and I'll take a Boy out of the *Blue-coat-Hospital,* and give him all I have.—Look-ye here, Friend *Gargle.*—You know I'm not a hard-hearted Man—The Scoundrel, you know, has robbed me; so, d'ye see, I won't hang him,——I'll only transport the Fellow——And so, Mr. *Catchpole,*—you may take him to *Newgate.*—

Gargle. Well, but, dear Sir, you know I always intended to marry my Daughter into your Family; and if you let the young Man be ruined, my Money must all go into another Chanel.——

Wingate. How's that!—into another Chanel!——Must not lose the handling of his Money——Why, I told you, Friend *Gargle,* I'm not a hard-hearted Man.——

Gargle. Why no, Sir—but your Passions— However, if you will but make the young Gentleman serve out the last Year of his Apprenticeship, you know I shall be giving over, and I may put him into all my Practice.—

Wingate.

* Romeo and Juliet.   † Barbarossa.

Wingate. Ha! ha!—Why—if the Block-head would but get as many crabbed phyſical Words from *Hyppocrites* and *Allen,* as he has from his nonſenſical Trumpery,—ha! ha;—I don't know, between you and I, but he might paſs for a very good Phyſician.—

Dick. * And muſt I leave thee, *Juliet?*—

Charlotte. Nay, but, prithee now have done with your Speeches——You ſee we are brought to the laſt Diſtreſs, and ſo you had better make it up——   [*Aſide to* Dick.

Dick. Why, for your Sake, my Dear, I could almoſt find in my Heart—

Wingate. You'll ſettle your Money on your Daughter?—

Gargle. You know it was always my Intention.—

Wingate. I muſt not let the Caſh ſlip thro' my Hands [*Aſide*]: Look-ye here, young Man——I am the beſt-natured Man in the World——How came this Debt, Friend?

Bailiff. The Gentleman gave his Note at *Briſtol,* I underſtands, where he boarded—'tis but Twenty Pounds.—

Wingate. Twenty Pounds! Well, why don't you ſend to your Friend *Shakeſpeare* now to bail you—ha! ha! I ſhould like to ſee *Shakeſpeare* give Bail—ha! ha!—Mr. *Catchpole,* will you take Bail of *Ben Thompſon,* and *Shakeſpeare* and *Odyſſy Popes?*—

Bailiff. No ſuch People have been here, Sir—are they Houſe-keepers?——

Dick. † You do not come to mock my Miſeries?——

Gargle. Huſh! young Man, you'll ſpoil all— Let me ſpeak to you—How is your Digeſtion?

                                    Dick.

* Romeo and Juliet.   † Mourning Bride.

Dick. * Throw Physic to the Dogs, I'll none of it——

Charlotte. Nay, but dear *Dick*, for my Sake--

Wingate. What says he, *Gargle?*——

Gargle. He repents, Sir——he'll reform.——

Wingate. That's right, Lad—now you're right——and if you will but serve out your Time, my Friend *Gargle* here will make a Man of you——Wounds! you'll have his Daughter and all his Money—And if I hear no more of your Trumpery, and you mind your Business, and stick to my little *Charlotte*, and make me a Grandfather in my old Days,—Egad, you shall have all mine too——that is, when I'm dead.——

Dick. Charlotte,—that will do rarely, and we may go to the Play as often as we please—

Charlotte. O *Gemini*, it will be the purest Thing in the World, and we'll see *Romeo* and *Juliet* every Time it is acted.——

Dick. Ay, and that will be a hundred Times in a Season at least——Besides, it will be like a Play, if I reform at the End——† Sir, free me so far in your most generous Thoughts, that I have shot my Arrow o'er the House, and hurt my Brother——

Wingate. What do you say, Friend?——

Charlotte. Nay, but prithee now do it in plain *English*——

Dick. Well, well, I will——He knows nothing of Metaphors——Sir, you shall find for the future, that we'll both endeavour to give you all the Satisfaction in our Power.——

Wingate. Very well, that's right——you may do very well——Friend *Gargle*, I'm overjoy'd——

Gargle.

* Macbeth.   † Hamlet.

Gargle. Chearfulneſs, Sir, is the principal Ingredient in the Compoſition of Health.——

Wingate. Wounds! Man, let's hear no more of your Phyſick——Here, young Man, put this Book in your Pocket, and let me ſee how ſoon you'll be Maſter of Vulgar Fractions.——Mr. *Catchpole*, ſtep home with me, and I'll pay you the Money——you ſeem to be a notable Sort of a Fellow, Mr. *Catchpole*, ——could you nab a Man for me?

Catchpole. Faſt enough, Sir, when I've the Writ——

Wingate. Very well, come along——I lent a young Gentleman a Hundred Pounds, ——a cool Hundred he call'd it——ha! ha!——it did not ſtay to cool with him——I had a good Præmium; but I ſha'n't wait a Moment for that——Come along, young Man;—— What Right have you to Twenty Pounds?—— give you Twenty Pounds?——I never was obliged to my Family for Twenty Pounds—— but I'll ſay no more——if you have a Mind to thrive in this World, make yourſelf uſeful, is the *Golden Rule.*

Dick. My dear *Charlotte*, as you are to be my Reward, I will be a new Man——

Charlotte. Well, now I ſhall ſee how much you love me——

Dick. It ſhall be my Study to deſerve you—— and ſince we don't go on the Stage, 'tis ſome Comfort that the World's a Stage, and all the Men and Women merely Players.

Some play the upper, ſome the under Parts,
And moſt aſſume what's foreign to their Hearts;
Thus, Life is but a Tragic-comic Jeſt,
And all is Farce and Mummery at beſt.

E P I-

EPILOGUE,

Written by a FRIEND.

Spoken by Mrs. CLIVE.

Enters reading the Play Bill.

A *Very pretty Bill,—as I'm alive!*
   The Part of—Nobody——by Mrs. Clive!
A paltry, scribling Fool——to leave me out—
He'll say, perhaps—he thought I could not Spout.
Malice and Envy to the last Degree!
And why?—I wrote a Farce as well as He.
And fairly ventur'd it, without the Aid
Of Prologue dress'd in Black, and Face in Masquerade;
O Pit—have Pity—see how I'm dismay'd!
Poor Soul!—this canting Stuff will never do,
Unless, like Bayes, he brings his Hangman too.
But granting that from these same Obsequies,
Some Pickings to our Bard in Black arise;
Should your Applause to Joy convert his Fear,
As Pallas turns to Feast—Lardella's Bier;
Yet 'twould have been a better Scheme by half
T'have thrown his Weeds aside, and learnt with me to
   laugh.
I could have shewn him, had he been inclin'd,
A spouting Junto of the Female Kind.
There dwells a Milliner in yonder Row,
Well dress'd, full voic'd, and nobly built for Shew,
Who, when in Rage, she scolds at Sue *and* Sarah,
Damn'd, Damn'd Dissembler!—thinks she's more than
   ZARA.
She has a Daughter too that deals in Lace,
And sings—O ponder well—and Chevy Chase,
And fain would fill the fair Ophelia's *Place.*

And

EPILOGUE.

And in her cock'd up Hat, and Gown of Camblet,
Presumes on something—touching the Lord Hamlet.
A Cousin too she has, with squinting Eyes,
With wadling Gait, and Voice like London Cries;
Who, for the Stage too short by half a Story,
Acts Lady Townly—thus——in all her Glory.
And, while she's traversing the scanty Room,
Cries—" Lord, my Lord, what can I do at home !"
In short, there'e Girls enough for all the Fellows, }
The Ranting, Whining, Starting, and the Jealous, }
The Hotspurs, Romeos, Hamlets, and Othellos. }
Oh ! little do those silly People know,
What dreadful Trials—Actors undergo.
Myself—who most in Harmony delight,
Am scolding here from Morning until Night.
Then take Advice from me, ye giddy Things,
Ye Royal Milliners, ye apron'd Kings;
Young Men beware, and shun our slipp'ry Ways,
Study Arithmetic, and burn your Plays ;
And you, ye Girls, let not our Tinsel Train
Enchant your Eyes, and turn your madd'ning Brain;
Be timely wise, for oh ! be sure of this !—
A Shop with Virtue is the Height of Bliss.

F I N I S.

THE

UPHOLSTERER,

O R,

What NEWS?

A

FARCE,

In TWO ACTS.

As it is Performed at the

THEATRE-ROYAL

I N

COVENT-GARDEN.

With ALTERATIONS and ADDITIONS.

———— *O Bone (nam te*
Scire, Deos quoniam propius contingis, (oportet)
Num quid de Dacis audisti? ————

By Mr. MURPHY.

The SECOND EDITION.

LONDON:
Printed for P. VAILLANT, facing *Southampton-Street,*
in the *Strand.*
MDCCLXV.
[Price One Shilling.]

PROLOGUE.

WHEN first, in falling Greece's evil Hour,
    Ambition aim'd at univerfal Pow'r;
When the fierce Man of Macedon began
Of a new Monarchy to form the Plan;
Each Greek——(as fam'd Demoſthenes relates)
Politically mad!——wou'd rave of States!
And help'd to form, where'er the Mob could meet,
An Areopagus in ev'ry Street.
What News, what News? was their eternal cry;
Is Philip ſick! *—then ſoar'd their Spirits high,—
Philip is well!——Dejeƈtion in each Eye.
Athenian Coblers join'd in deep Debate,
While Gold in ſecret undermin'd the State;
Till Wifdom's Bird the Vultur's Prey was made;
And the Sword gleam'd in Academus' Shade.

    Now modern Philips threaten this our Land,
What ſay Britannia's Sons?—along the Strand
What News? ye cry——with the ſame Paſſion ſmit;
And there at leaſt you rival Attic Wit.
A Parliament of Porters here ſhall muſe
On ſtate Affairs—"ſwall'wing a Taylor's News;"
For Ways and Means no ſtarv'd Projeƈtor ſleeps;
And ev'ry Shop ſome mighty Stateſman keeps;
He Britain's foes, like Bobadil, can kill;
Supply th' EXCHEQUER, and negleƈt his Till.
In ev'ry Ale-houſe Legiſlators meet;
And Patriots ſettle Kingdoms in the Fleet.

    • Vide the firſt Philippic.

To

PROLOGUE.

To shew this phrenzy in its genuine Light,
A modern Newsmonger appears to Night;
Trick'd out from Addison's accomplish'd Page,
Behold! th' Upholsterer ascends the Stage.

No Minister such Trials e'er hath stood;
He turns a BANKRUPT for the public Good!
Undone himself, yet full of England's Glory!
A Politician!——neither Whig nor Tory——
Nor can ye high or low the Quixote call;
" He's Knight o'th' Shire, and represents ye all."

As for the Bard,——to you he yields his Plan;
For well he knows, you're candid where ye can.
One only praise he claims,——no Party-stroke
Here turns a public Character to joke.
His Panacæa is for all Degrees,
For all have more or less of this Disease.
Whatever his Success, of this he's sure,
There's Merit even to attempt the Cure.

Dramatis Personæ.

M E N.

QUIDNUNC, the Upholsterer,	Mr. DUNSTALL.
PAMPHLET,	Mr. SHUTER
RAZOR, a Barber,	Mr. WOODWARD.
FEEBLE,	Mr. HAYES.
BELLMOUR,	Mr. WHITE.
ROVEWELL,	Mr. DAVIS.
CODICIL, a Lawyer, *	
BRISK,	
Watchman,	Mr. WELLER.

W O M E N.

HARRIET,	Miss MILLER.
TERMAGANT.	Miss ELLIOT.
Maid to FEEBLE,	Miss COCKAYNE.

* For the sake of Brevity, Codicil's Scene is omitted in the Representation, as are likewise a few passages in the second Act.

THE
UPHOLSTERER,
OR,
What News?

ACT I.

SCENE BELLMOUR'S *Lodging.*

Enter BELLMOUR *beating* BRISK.

BRISK.

MR. *Bellmour,*—let me die, Sir,—as I hope to be faved, Sir——

BELL.

Sirrah! Rogue! Villain!——I'll teach you, I will, you Rafcal, to fpeak irreverently of her I love.

BRISK.

As I am a Sinner, Sir, I only meant———

BELL.

Only meant! You could not mean it, Jackanapes,— you had no Meaning, Booby.——

BRISK.

BRISK.

Why, no, Sir,——that's the very Thing, Sir,—I had
no Meaning.

BELL.

Then Sirrah, I'll make you know your Meaning for
the future.——

BRISK.

Yes, Sir,—to be sure, Sir,—and yet upon my Word
if you would be but a little cool, Sir, you'd find I am not
much to blame—Besides Master, you can't conceive the
good it would do your Health, if you will but keep your
Temper a little.——

BELL.

Mighty well, Sir, give your Advice.

BRISK.

Why really now this same Love hath metamorphosed
us both very strangely, Master,—for to be free; here
have we been at this Work these six Weeks,——stark-
staring mad in Love with a Couple of Baggages not worth
a Groat,—and yet Heav'n help us ! they have as much
Pride as comes to the Share of a Lady of Quality before
she has been caught in the Fact with a handsome young
Fellow,—or indeed after she has been caught, for that
Matter.——

BELL.

You won't have done Rascal——

BRISK.

In short, my young Mistress and her Maid have as
much Pride and Poverty as—as—no matter what, they
have the Devil and all,—when at the same Time every
Body knows the old broken Upholsterer Miss *Harriet's*
Father, might give us all he has in the World, and not eat
the worse Pudding on a Sunday for it.

BELL.

Impious, execrable Atheist ! What detract from Heaven ! I'll reform your Notions, I will you saucy——

[*beats him.*

BRISK.

Nay, but my dear Sir !—a little Patience,—not so
hard——

Enter

Enter ROVEWELL.

ROVE.

Bellmour your Servant,—what at Loggerheads with my old Friend *Brisk*.

BELL.

Confusion! Mr. *Rovewell* your Servant,—this is your doing, Hang-dog.——*Jack Rovewell* I am glad to see thee.——

ROVE.

Brisk used to be a good Servant,—he has not been tampering with any of his Master's Girls, has he?

BELL.

Do you know *Rovewell* that he has had the Impudence to talk detractingly and profanely of my Mistress?——

BRISK.

For which Sir, I have suffered inhumanly and most un-christian-like, I assure you.

BELL.

Will you leave prating, Booby?

ROVE.

Well, but *Bellmour*, where does she live?—I'm but just arrived you know, and I'll go and beat up her Quarters.——

BELL.   [*Half aside.*]

Beat up her Quarters!—(*looks at him smilingly, then half aside.*)
Favours to none; to all she smiles extends,
Oft she rejects, but never once offends.

[*stands musing.*]

ROVE.

Hey! What, fallen into a Reverie!—Prithee *Brisk* what does all this mean?

BRISK.

Why, Sir, you must know—I am over Head and Ears in Love.——

ROVE.

But I mean your Master; what ails him?

BRISK.

That's the very Thing I'm going to tell you Sir,—as I said, Sir,—I am over Head and Ears in Love with a

B   whim-

whimſical, queer kind of a Piece, here in the Neigh-
bourhood, and ſo nothing can ſerve my Maſter, but he
muſt fall in Love with her Miſtreſs,——look at him now
Sir,——

[Bellmour *continues muſing and muttering to himſelf.*]
ROVE.

Ha, ha, ha,—Poor *Bellmour*, I pity thee with all my
Heart——

[*Strikes him on the Shoulder, then ludicrouſly repeats.*]
Ye Gods annihilate both Space and Time,—
And make two Lovers happy.——

BELL.

My dear *Rovewell*, ſuch a Girl,—ten Thouſand *Cupids*
play about her Mouth, you Rogue.——

ROVE.

Ten Thouſand Pounds had better play about her Pocket.—What Fortune has ſhe?

BRISK.

Heaven help us, not much to crack of.——

BELL.

Not much to crack of Mr. *Brazen*,—prithee *Rovewell*,
how can you be ſo ungenerous as to aſk ſuch a Queſtion?
You know I don't mind Fortune, though by the way ſhe
has an Uncle who is determined to ſettle very handſome-
ly upon her; and on the Strength of that, does ſhe give
herſelf innumerable Airs.——

ROVE.

Fortune not to be minded!—I'll tell you what *Bellmour*,
tho' you have a good one already, there's no kind of In-
convenience in a little more.—I'm ſure if I had not
minded Fortune, I might have been in *Jamaica* ſtill, not
worth a Sugar-Cane; but the Widow *Moloſſes* took a
Fancy to me;—Heaven, or a worſe Deſtiny has taken a
Fancy to her, and ſo after ten Years Exile, and being
turn'd a-drift by my Father, here am I again a warm
Planter, and a Widower, moſt woefully tired of Matrimony;—but my dear *Bellmour* we were both ſo overjoy'd to meet one another yeſterday Evening, juſt as I arrived in Town, that I did not hear a Syllable from you of
your Love Fit: How, when, and where did this happen?

BELL.

B E L L.

Oh!—by the moſt fortunate Accident that ever was,
—I'll tell thee *Rovewell*: I was going one Night from
theTavern about ſix Weeks ago,—I had been there with
a Parcel of Blades whoſe only Joy is center'd in their
Bottle, and faith till this Accident I was no better myſelf,—but ever ſince I am grown quite a new Man.

R O V E.

Ay, a new Man indeed!—Who in the Name of Wonder would take thee, ſunk as thou art into a muſing,
moping, melancholy Lover, for the gay *Charles Bellmour*
whom I knew in the *Weſt-Indies?*

B E L L.

Poh, that is not mentioned!—you know my Father
took me againſt my Will from the Univerſity, and con-
ſigned me over to the academic Diſcipline of a Man of
War; ſo that to prevent a Dejection of Spirits, I was
oblig'd to run into the oppoſite Extreme,—as you yourſelf were wont to do.

R O V E.

Why, yes, I had my Moments of Reflection, and was
glad to diſſipate them—You know I always told you there
was ſomething extraordinary in my Story; and ſo there
is ſtill, I ſuppoſe it muſt be cleared up in a few Days now
—I'm in no hurry about it tho'; I muſt ſee the town a
little this Evening, and have my Frolick firſt. But to the
Point *Bellmour*, you was going from the Tavern you ſay.—

B E L L.

Yes, Sir, about two in the Morning, and I perceived
an unuſual Blaze in the Air,—I was in a rambling Humour, and ſo reſolved to know what it was.

B R I S K.

I and my Maſter went together, Sir.———

B E L L.

Oh! *Rovewell!* my better Stars ordain'd it to light me
on to Happineſs;—by ſure Attraction led, I came to the
very Street where a Houſe was on Fire; Water-Engines
playing, Flames aſcending, all Hurry, Confuſion, and
Diſtreſs; when on a ſudden the Voice of Deſpair, Silver ſweet, came thrilling down to my very Heart;—poor

        dear,

dear, little Soul, what can she do, cried the Neighbours? Again she scream'd, the Fire gathering Force, and gaining upon her every Instant;—here Ma'am said I, leap into my Arms, I'll be sure to receive you;—and wou'd you think it?—down she came,—my dear *Rovewell*, such a Girl! I caught her in my Arms you Rogue, safe, without Harm.—The dear naked *Venus*, just risen from her Bed, my Boy,—her slender Waist *Rovewell*, the downy Smoothness of her whole Person, and her Limbs " harmonious, swell'd by Nature's softest Hand."——

ROVE.

Raptures, and Paradise!—What Seraglio in *Covent-Garden* did you carry her to?

BELL.

There again now! Do, prithee correct your Way of Thinking, take a *quantum sufficit* of virtuous Love, and purify your Ideas.—Her lovely Bashfulness, her delicate Fears,—her Beauty heighten'd and endear'd by Distress, dispers'd my wildest Thoughts, and melted me into Tenderness and Respect.——

ROVE.

But *Bellmour*, surely she has not the Impudence to be modest after you have had Possession of her Person,——

BELL.

My Views are honourable I assure you, Sir; but her Father is so absurdly positive——The Man's distracted about the Balance of Power, and will give his Daughter to none but a Politician—When there was an Execution in his House, he thought of nothing but the Camp at *Pyrna*, and now he's a Bankrupt, his Head runs upon the Ways and Means, and Schemes for paying off the national Debt: The Affairs of *Europe* engross all his Attention, while the Distresses of his lovely Daughter pass unnoticed.

ROVE.

Ridiculous enough!——But why do you mind him? Why don't you go to Bed to the Wench at once?— Take her into Keeping Man.——

BELL.

How can you talk so affrontingly of her?—Have not I
told

told you tho' her Father is ruin'd, still she has great Expectancies from a rich Relation?————

R o v e.

Then what do you stand watering at the Mouth for? If she is to have Money enough to pay for her China, her Gaming Debts, her Dogs, and her Monkeys, marry her then, if you needs must be ensnar'd; be in a Fool's Paradise for a Honey-Moon, then come to yourself, wonder at what you've done, and mix with honest Fellows again ;—carry her off I say, and never stand whining for the Father's Consent.————

B e l l.

Carry her off!—I like the Scheme,—will you assist me?

R o v e.

No, no, there I beg to be excus'd. Don't you remember what the Satyrist says,—" Never marry while " there's a Halter to be had for Money, or a Bridge to " afford a convenient Leap."

B e l l.

Prithee leave Fooling.

R o v e.

I am in serious Earnest I assure you; I'll drink with you, game with you, go into any Scheme or Frolic with you, but war Matrimony.—Nay, if you'll come to the Tavern this Evening, I'll drink your Mistress's Health in a Bumper; but as to your conjugal Scheme, I'll have nothing to do with that Business positively.————

B e l l.

Well, well, I'll take you at your Word, and meet you at ten exactly at the same Place we were at last Night; then and there I'll let you know what further Measures I've concerted.

R o v e.

Till then, farewel, *a-propos*,—do you know that I've seen none of my Relations yet?

B e l l.

Time enough To-morrow.

R o v e.

Ay, ay, To-morrow will do,—well, your Servant.
[*Exit* Rovewell.

BELL.

Rovewell, yours,—see the Gentleman down Stairs,—
and d'ye hear, come to me in my Study that I may give
you a Letter to *Harriet*, and hark ye, Sir,——Be fure
you fee *Harriet* yourfelf; and let me have no Meffages
from that officious Go-between, her Mrs. *Slipflop* of a
Maid, with her unintelligible Jargon of hard Words, of
which fhe neither knows the Meaning nor Pronun-
ciation.—(*Exit* Brifk.) I'll write to her this Moment, acquaint her with the foft Tumult of my Defires, and, if poffible, make her mine this very Night.— [*Exit repeating.*
Love firft taught Letters for fome Wretch's Aid,
Some banifh'd Lover, or fome captive Maid.——

SCENE *The Upholfterer's Houfe.*

Enter HARRIET *and* TERMAGANT.

TERM.

WELL, but Ma'am, he has made Love to you fix
Weeks *fuccefsfully*; he has been as conftant in his
'*Moors* poor Gentleman, as if you had the *Subverfion* of
'*State* to fettle upon him—and if he flips thro' your Fin-
gers, now Ma'am, you have nobody to *depute* it to but
yourfelf.

HAR.

Lard *Termagant*, how you run on!—I tell you again
and again my pride was touched, becaufe he feemed to prefume on his Opulence, and my Father's Diftreffes.

TER.

La, Mifs *Harriet*, how can you be fo *paradropfical* in
your '*Pinions?*

HAR.

Well, but you know tho' my Father's Affairs are ruin'd
I am not in fo defperate a Way; confider my Uncle's Fortune is no Trifle, and I think that Profpect intitles me to
give myfelf a few Airs before I refign my Perfon.

TER.

I grant ye Ma'am, you have very good Pretenfions; but
then it's waiting for dead Men's Shoes: I'll venture to be
perjur'd Mr. *Bellmour* ne'er *difclaim'd* an *Idear* of your
Father's Diftrefs——

HAR.

H A R.

Suppofing that.

T E R M.

Suppofe Ma'am—I know it *difputably* to be fo.

H A R.

Indifputably I guefs you mean ;——but I'm tired of wrangling with you about Words.

T E R M.

By my troth you're in the right on't ;—there's ne'er a fhe in all old *England,* (as your Father calls it) is Miftrefs of fuch *phifology,* as I am. Incertain I am, as how you does not know nobody that puts their Words together with fuch a *Curacy* as myfelf. I once lived with a *Miftus,* Ma'am,—*Miftus !*—She was a Lady—a great Brewer's Wife !—and fhe wore as fine Cloaths as any Perfon of Quality, let her get up as early as fhe will—and fhe ufed to call me—*Tarmagant,* fays fhe,—What's the *Signification* of fuch a Word—and I always told her—I told her the *Importation* of all my Words, though I could not help laughing, Mifs *Harriet,* to fee fo fine a Lady, fuch a downright *Ignoranimus.*

H A R.

Well,—but pray now *Tarmagant,* would you have me directly upon being afked the Queftion, throw myfelf into the Arms of a Man ?

T E R M.

O' my Confcience you did throw yourfelf into his Arms with fcarce a Shift on, that's what you did.

H A R.

Yes, but that was a Leap in the Dark, when there was no Time to think of it.

T E R M.

Well, it does not fignify *Argifying,* I wifh we were both warm in Bed ; you with Mr. *Bellmour,* and I with his Coxcomb of a Man ; inftead of being *manured* here with an old crafy Fool—*axing* your pardon Ma'am, for calling your Father fo—but he is a Fool, and the worft of Fools with his *Policies*—when his Houfe is full of *Statues* of *Bangcreffy.*

HAR

HAR.

It's too true *Tarmagant*,—yet he's my Father ſtill, and I can't help loving him.

TERM.

Fiddle faddle—Love him!—he's an *Anecdote* againſt Love.

HAR.

Huſh! here he comes!—

TERM.

No, it's your Uncle *Feeble*, poor Gentleman, I pity's him, eaten up with *Infirmaries*, to be taking ſuch pains with a Madman.

Enter FEEBLE.

HAR.

Well Uncle, have you been able to conſole him?

FEEB.

He wants no Conſolation Child,—lackaday,—I'm ſo infirm I can hardly move.—I found him tracing in the Map, Prince *Charles* of *Lorraine'* Paſſage over the *Rhine*, and comparing it with *Julius Cæſar's*.

TERM.

An old Blockhead—I've no Patience with him with his Fellows coming after him every Hour in the Day with News. Well now I wiſhes there was no ſuch a Thing as a News-paper in the World, with ſuch a Pack of Lies, and ſuch a deal of *Jab-jab* every Day.

FEEB.

Ay, there were three or four ſhabby Fellows with him when I went into his Room—I can't get him to think of appearing before the Commiſſioners To-morrow, to diſcloſe his Effects; but I'll ſend my Neighbour Counſellor *Codicil* to him,—don't be dejected *Harriet*, my poor Siſter, your Mother was a good Woman; I love you for her ſake, Child, and all I am worth ſhall be yours—But I muſt be going,—I find myſelf but very ill; good Night, *Harriet*, good Night.

[*Exit* Feeble.

HAR.

You'll give me leave to ſee you to the Door, Sir.

[*Exit* Harriet.

TERM.

T E R M.

O' my Confcience this Mafter of mine within here, might have pick'd up his Crums as well as Mr. *Feeble*, if he had any *Idear* of his bufinefs, I'm fure if I had not hopes from Mr. *Feeble*, I fhould not tarry in this Houfe—— By my Troth, if all who have nothing to fay to the *'fairs* of the Nation, would mind their own Bufinefs, and thofe who fhould take care of our *'fairs*, would mind their Bufinefs too, I fancy poor old *England* (as they call it) would fare the better among 'em——This old crazy Pate within here—playing the Fool—when the Man is paft his grand *Clytemnefter.*   [*Exit* Termagant.

SCENE *difcovers* QUIDNUNC *at a Table, with News Papers, Pamphlets, &c. all around him.*

Q U I D.

Six and three is nine—feven and four is eleven, and carry one—let me fee, 126 Million—199 Thoufand, 328—and all this with about—where, where's the amount of the Specie? Here, here—with about 15 Million in Specie, all this great Circulation! good, good,— why then how are we ruined?—how are we ruined? What fays the Land-Tax at 4 Shillings in the Pound, two Million! now where's my new Affeffment?—here,— here, the 5th part of Twenty, 5 in 2 I can't but 5 in 20 (*paufes*) right, 4 times—why then upon my new Affeff- ment there's 4 Million—how are we ruined?—what fays, Malt, Cyder, and Mum,—eleven and carry one, nought and go 2—good, good, Malt, Hops, Cyder, and Mum; then there's the Wine Licence, and the Gin Act— The Gin Act is no bad Article—If the People will fhoot Fire down their Throats, why in a Chriftian Country they fhould pay as much as poffible for Suicide—Salt! good— Sugar, very good—Window lights—good again!—— Stamp Duty, that's not fo well—It will have a bad Effect upon the News-Papers, and we fhan't have enough of Politics—But there's the Lottery—where's my new Scheme for a Lottery?—Here it is—Now for the Amount of the

C   whole

whole—How are we ruin'd? 7 and carry nought—
nought and carry 1———

Enter TERMAGANT.
TERM.

Sir, Sir,—

QUID.

Hold your Tongue you Baggage, you'll put me out—
nought and carry 1.

TERM.

Counsellor *Codicil* will be with you presently—

QUID.

Prithee be quiet Woman—how are we ruined?

TERM.

Ay, I'm *confidous* as how you may thank yourself for
your own *Ruination.*

QUID.

Ruin the Nation!—hold your Tongue you Jade, I'm
raising the Supplies within the Year,—how many did I
carry?

TERM.

Yes, you've carried your Pigs to a fine Market—

QUID.

Get out of the Room, Hussey—you Trollop, get out
of the Room—   *(turning her out.]*

Enter RAZOR, *with Suds on his Hands,* &c.

QUID.

Friend *Razor,* I am glad to see thee—well hast got
any News?

RAZOR.

A Budget! I left a Gentleman half shaved in my Shop
over the way; it came into my Head of a sudden, so I
could not be at ease till I told you—

QUID.

That's kind, that's kind, Friend *Razor*—never mind
the Gentleman, he can wait.—

RAZOR.

Yes, so he can, he can wait.—

QUID.

QUID.

Come, now let's hear, what is't?

RAZOR.

I fhaved a great Man's Butler to Day.——

QUID.

Did ye?

RAZOR.

I did.

QUID.

Ay;

RAZOR.

Very true. (*both fhake their Heads.*)

QUID.

What did he fay?

RAZOR,

Nothing.

QUID,

Hum—how did he look?

RAZOR,

Full of Thought.

QUID.

Ay! full of Thought—what can that mean?

RAZOR.

It muft mean fomething. (*ftaring at each other.*)

QUID.

Mayhap fomebody may be going out of Place.

RAZOR.

Like enough,—there's fomething at the Bottom, when
a great Man's Butler looks grave, things can't hold out
in this Manner, Mafter *Quidnunc!*—Kingdoms rife and
fall!—Luxury will be the ruin of us all, it will indeed.
(*Stares at him.*)

QUID.

Pray now, Friend *Razor*, do you find Bufinefs as cur-
rent now as before the War?

RAZOR.

No, no, I have not made a Wig the Lord knows when,
I can't mind it for thinking of my poor Country.

QUID.

That's generous, Friend *Razor*——

C 2　　　　　　　　　　　RAZOR.

RAZOR.

Yes, I can't gi'my Mind to any for thinking of my Country, and when I was in *Bedlam*, it was the same, I cou'd think of nothing else in *Bedlam*, but poor old *England*, and so they said as how I was incurable for it.——

QUID.

S'bodikins! they might as well say the same of me.

RAZOR.

So they might—well, your Servant Mr. *Quidnunc*, I'll go now and shave the rest of the Gentleman's Face—Poor Old *England*.   (*sighs and shakes his Head*) *going.*

QUID.

But hark ye, Friend *Razor*, ask the Gentleman if he has got any News.——

RAZOR.

I will, I will.

QUID.

And d'ye hear, come and tell me if he has.——

RAZOR.

I will, I will—poor Old *England* (*going returns*) O, Mr. *Quidnunc*, I want to ask you—pray now—

Enter TERMAGANT.

TERM.

Gemini! Gemini!—How can a Man have so little *Difference* for his Customers—

QUID.

I tell you, Mrs. *Malapert*.——

TERM.

And I tell you the Gentleman keeps such a Bawling yonder, for shame, Mr. *Razor* — you'll be a *Bankrupper* like my Master, with such a House full of Children as you have, pretty little things—that's what you will—

RAZOR.

I'm a coming, I'm a coming, Mrs. *Termagant*—I say Mr. *Quidnunc*, I can't sleep in my Bed for thinking what will come of the Protestants, if the Papists should get the better in the present War——

QUID.

I'll tell you—The Geographer of our Coffee-house was saying the other Day, that there is an huge Tract of
Land

Land about the Pole, where the Proteftants may retire, and that the Papifts will never be able to beat 'em thence, if the northern Powers hold together, and the grand *Turk* make a Diverfion in their Favour.

RAZOR.

That makes me eafy—I'm glad the Proteftants will know where to go if the Papifts fhou'd get the better (*going returns*) Oh! Mr. *Quidnunc* — hark'ye— *India* Bonds are rifen.

QUID.

Are they ?—how much ?

RAZOR.

A *Jew* Pedlar faid in my Shop as how they are rifen three Sixteenths—

QUID.

Why then that makes fome Amends for the Price of Corn—

RAZOR.

So it does, fo it does, if they but hold up, and the Pro-teftants know where to go, I fhall then have a Night's Reft mayhap.—   [*Exit* Razor.

QUID.

I fhall never be rightly eafy till thofe careening Wharfs at *Gibraltar* are repaired—

TERM.

Fiddle for your *Dwarfs, impair* your ruin'd Fortune, do that.

QUID.

If only one Ship can heave down at a time, there will be no end of it—and then, why fhould Watering be fo tedious there ?

TERM.

Look where your Daughter comes, and yet you'll be *ruinating* about *Give-a-halter,* while that poor thing is breaking her Heart.

Enter HARRIET.

QUID.

It's one Comfort, however, they can always have frefh Provifions in the *Mediterranean*—

HAR.

HAR.

Dear Papa, what's the *Mediterranean* to People in our Situation ?—

QUID.

The *Mediterranean*, Child ? Why if we fhould lofe the *Mediterranean*, we're all undone.

HAR.

Dear Sir, that's our Misfortune—we are undone already.

QUID.

No, no,—here, here Child—I have raifed the Supplies within the Year.

TERM.

I tell you, you're a *lunadic* Man.

QUID.

Yes, yes, I'm a Lunatic to be fure—I tell you, *Harriet*, I have faved a great deal out of my Affairs for you—

HAR.

For Heav'n's fake, Sir, don't do that—you muft give up every thing, my Uncle *Feeble*'s Lawyer will be here to talk with you about it—

QUID.

Poh, poh, I tell you, I know what I am about ;—you fhall have my Books and Pamphlets, and all the Manifeftoes of the Powers at War.—

HAR.

And fo make me a Politician, Sir ?

QUID.

It would be the Pride of my Heart to find I had got a Politician in Petticoats—a Female *Machiavel!* —S'bodikins, you might then know as much as moft people that talk in Coffee-houfes, and who knows but in time you might be a Maid of Honour, or Sweeper of the Mall, or—

HAR.

Dear Sir, don't I fee what you have got by Politics ?

QUID.

Pfhaw! my Country's of more Confequence to me, and let me tell you, you can't think too much of your Country in thefe worft of Times ; for Mr. *Monitor* has told us, that Affairs in the North, and the Proteftant Intereft, begin to grow TICKLISH.

TERM.

T e r m.

And your Daughter's Affairs are very TICKLISH too,
I'm fure.———

H a r.

Prithee *Termagant*———

T e r m.

I muft fpeak to him—I know you are in a TICK-
LISH Situation, Ma'am.

Q u i d.

I tell you, you Trull———

T e r m.

But I am convicted it is fo—and the pofture of my Affairs is very TICKLISH too—and fo I imprecate that
Mr. *Bellmour* wou'd come, and———

Q u i d.

Mr. *Bellmour* come! I tell you Mrs. *Saucebox*, that
my Daughter fhall never be married to a Man that has
not better Notions of the Balance of Power.

T e r m.

But what *Purvifion* will you make for her now with
your Balances?

Q u i d.

There again now!—Why do you think I don't know
what I'm about? I'll look in the Papers for a Match for
you, Child; there's often good Matches advertifed in the
Papers—Evil betide it,—Evil betide it—! I once thought
to have ftruck a great Stroke, that would have aftonifhed
all *Europe*,— I thought to have married my Daughter to
Theodore King of *Corfica*———

H a r.

What, and have me perifh in a Jail, Sir!

Q u i d.

S'bodikins my Daughter would have had her Coronation-
Day;—I fhould have been allied to a crowned Head, and
been FIRST LORD OF THE TREASURY OF CORSICA?
—But come,—now I'll go and talk over the *London
Evening*, till the *Gazette* comes in—I fhan't fleep to night
unlefs I fee the *Gazette*.

Enter

Enter CODICIL.

CODIC.

Mr. *Quidnunc* your Servant—the Door was open, and
I entered upon the Premifses—I'm juft come from the Hall.

QUID.

S'bodikins! This Man is now come to keep me at Home.

CODIC.

Upon my Word Mifs *Harriet's* a very pretty young Lady,
as pretty a young Lady as one would defire to have and
to hold. Ma'am your moft obedient; I have drawn my
Friend *Feeble's* Will, in which you have all his Goods and
Chattles, Lands and Hereditaments.

HAR.

I thank you Sir, for the Information———

CODIC.

And I hope foon to draw your Marriage Settlement for
my friend Mr. *Bellmour.*

HAR.

O Lud! Sir, not a Word of that before my Father—
I wifh you'd try, Sir, to get him to think of his Affairs—

CODIC.

Why yes, I have Inftructions for that Purpofe; Mr.
Quidnunc, I am inftructed to expound the Law to you.

QUID.

What, the Law of Nations?

CODIC.

I am inftructed, Sir, that you're a Bankrupt——*Quafi
bancus ruptus—Banque route faire*—and my Inftructions
fay further, that you are fummoned to appear before the
Commifsioners To-morrow———.

QUID.

That may be, Sir, but I can't go To-morrow, and fo I
fhall fend 'em Word—I am to be To-morrow at *Slaughter's*
Coffee-houfe with a private Committee about Bufinefs of
great Confequence to the Affairs of *Europe*———

CODIC.

Then, Sir, if you don't go, I muft inftruct you, that
you'll be guilty of a Felony: it will be deem'd to be done

malo

malo Animo—it is held so in the Books—and what says the Statute ? By the 5th *George* 2d, *Cap*. 30. Not surrendering or imbezzeling is Felony without Benefit of Clergy.

QUID.

Ay,—you tell me News——

CODIC.

Give me leave, Sir,——I am instructed to expound the Law to you ; Felony is thus described in the Books *Felonia*, saith *Hotoman, de Verbis feudalibus, significat capitale facinus*, a capital Offence.

QUID.

You tell me News, you do indeed.

CODIC.

It was so apprehended by the *Goths* and the *Longobards*, and what saith Sir *Edward Coke* ? *Fieri debeat felleo animo.*

QUID.

You've told me News—I did not know it was Felony ; but if the Flanders Mail should come in while I am there—— I shall know nothing at all of it————

CODIC.

But why should you be uneasy ? *cui bono*, Mr. *Quidnunc, cui bono* ?

QUID.

Not uneasy ! If the Papists should beat the Protestants.

CODIC.

But I tell you, they can get no Advantage of us. The Laws against the further Growth of Popery will secure us —there are Provisoes in Favour of Protestant Purchasers under Papists—10th *Geo*. I. Cap. 4. and 6 *Geo*. II. Cap. 5.

QUID.

Ay !

CODIC.

And besides *Popish* Recusants can't carry Arms, so can have no Right of Conquest, *Vi & armis*.

QUID.

That's true—that's true—I'm easier in my Mind—

CODIC.

To be sure, what are you uneasy about ? The Papists can have no Claim to *Silesia*—

D   QUID.

QUID.

Can't they?

CODIC.

No, they can fet up no Claim—If the Queen on her
Marriage had put all her Lands into *Hotchpot* then indeed—
and it feemeth, faith *Littleton*, that this Word *Hotchpot* is
in *Englifh* a Pudding——

QUID.

You reafon very clearly, Mr. *Codicil*, upon the Rights
of the Powers at War, and fo now if you will, I am ready
to talk a little of my Affairs.

CODIC.

Nor does the Matter reft here ; for how can fhe fet up
a Claim, when fhe has made a Conveyance to the Houfe
of *Brandenburgh ?* the Law, Mr. *Quidnunc*, is very fevere
againft fraudulent Conveyances——

QUID.

S'bodikins, you have fatisfied me——

CODIC.

Why therefore then—if he will levy Fines and fuffer a
common Recovery, he can bequeathe it as he likes in *feodum
fimplex*, provided he takes care to put in *fes Heres*.

QUID.

I'm heartily glad of it,—fo that with regard to my
Effects——

CODIC.

Why then fuppofe fhe was to bring it to a Tryal at
Bar——

QUID.

I fay with regard to the full Difclofure of my Effects—

CODIC.

What wou'd fhe get by that ?—it would go off upon a
fpecial Pleading—and as to Equity—

QUID.

Pray muft I now furrender my Books and my Pamphlets ?

CODIC.

What wou'd Equity do for her ? Equity can't relieve
her, he might keep her at leaft twenty Years before a
Mafter to fettle the Account——

QUID.

QUID.

You have made me eafy about the Proteftants in this War, you have indeed—fo that with regard to my appearing before the commiffioners.

CODIC.

And as to the *Ban of the Empire,* he may demur to that, For all Tenures by *Knight's fervice* are abolifhed, and the Statute 12 *Char.* II. has declared all Lands to be held under a *Common Socage.*

QUID.

Pray now, Mr. *Codicil,* muft not my Creditors appear to prove their debts ?———

CODIC.

Why therefore then, if they're held in *Common Socage,* I fubmit it to the Court,—whether the Empire can have any Claim to *Knight's Service* ;—they can't call to him for a fingle Man for the Wars—*Unum Hominem ad Guerram* ;—for what is *Common Socage ?*—*Socagium idem eft quod Servitium focæ*—the Service of the Plough,

QUID.

I'm ready to attend 'em—But pray now, when my Certificate is figned,—it is of great Confequence to me to know this. I fay, Sir, when my Certificate is figned, Mayn't I then—Hey ! *(ftarting up)* Hey !—What do I hear ?

CODIC.

I apprehend,—I humbly conceive when your Certificate is figned———

QUID.

Hold your Tongue Man—did not I hear the *Gazette ?* *Newfman, (within)* Great News in the *London Gazette.*

QUID.

Yes, yes it is—it is the *Gazette*—*Termagant* run you Jade *(turns her out)* *Harriet* fly, it is the *Gazette*—
　　　　　　　　　　　　　　　(turns her out.

CODIC.

The Law in that Cafe, Mr. *Quidnunc, prima facie.*—

QUID.

I can't hear you,—I have not Time,—*Termagant,* run, make Hafte.—　　　　　　[*ftamps violently.*]

CODIC.

I fay, Sir, it is held in the Books———

　　　　　　　　　　QUID.

QUID.

I care for no Books—I want the Papers.—*(stamping.)*

CODIC.

Throughout all the Books,—Bo! the Man is *non compos,* and his Friends, inftead of a Commiffion of Bankruptcy, fhould take out a Commiffion of Lunacy.   [*Exit* Cod.

Enter TERMAGANT.

TERM.

What do you keep fuch a Bauling for? the Newfman fays as how the Emperor of *Mocco* is dead.

QUID.

The Emperor of *Morocco!*

TERM.

Yes, him.

QUID.

My poor dear Emperor of *Morocco!* *(burfts into Tears)*

TERM.

Ah! you old Don *Quikfett!*—Ma'am, Ma'am,—Mifs *Harriet,* go your ways into the next Room, there's Mr. *Bellmour's* Man there, Mr. *Bellmour* has fent you a Billydore.——

HAR.

Oh, *Termagant,* my Heart is in an Uproar,—I don't know what to fay,—where is he? let me run to him this Inftant.   (*Exit* Harriet.

QUID.

The Emperor of *Morocco* had a Regard for the Balance of *Europe,* *(fighs)* well, well, come, come, give me the Paper.

TERM.

The Newfman would not truft, becaufe you're a *Bank-rupper,* and fo I paid two Pence Halfpenny for it.—

QUID.

Let's fee,—let's fee—

TERM.

Give me my Money then—   (*running from him.*)

QUID.

Give it me this Inftant, you Jade—   (*after her.*)

TERM.

Give me my Money, I fay—   (*from him.*)

QUID.

I'll teach you, I will you Baggage.   (*after her.*)

TERM.

T e r m.

I won't part with it till I have my Money. *(from him.)*

Q u i d.

I'll give you no Money, Huffey.　　　*(after her.)*

T e r m.

Your Daughter fhall marry Mr. *Bellmour. (from him.)*

Q u i d.

I'll never accede to the Treaty,　　　*(after her.)*

T e r m.

Go you old Fool.　　　　　*(from him.)*

Q u i d.

You vile Minx, worfe than the Whore of *Babylon.*
　　　　　　　　　　　　(after her.)

T e r m.

There, you old crack'd brain'd Politic,—there's your
Paper for you.　　　　*(throws it down, and Exit.*

Q u i d.　*(fitting down.)*

Oh ! Heavens !—I'm quite out of Breath,—a Jade, to
keep my News from me—what does it fay ? what does
it fay ? what does it fay ? *(Reads very faft while opening
the Paper.)* " Whereas a Commiffion of Bankrupt is a-
" warded and iffued forth againft *Abraham Quidnunc,* of
" the Parifh of St. *Martin's* in the *Fields, Upholfterer,*
" *Dealer,* and *Chapman,* the faid Bankrupt is hereby re-
" quired to furrender himfelf." Po, what fignifies this
Stuff ? I don't mind myfelf, when the Balance of Power
is concerned.—However, I fhall be read of, in the fame
Paper, in the *London Gazette,* by the Powers abroad ;
together with the *Pope,* and the *French King,* and the
Mogul, and all of 'em—good, good, very good,—here's
a Pow'r of News,—let me fee, *(reads)* " Letters from
" the Vice Admiral, dated *Tyger* off *Calcutta."—(mutters
to himfelf very eagerly)* Oddfheart, thofe Baggages will interrupt me, I hear their Tongues a-going, clack, clack,
clack, I'll run into my clofet, and lock myfelf up.—A
Vixen !—a Trollop,—to want Money from me,—when
I may have occafion to buy *The State of the Sinking Fund,*
or *Faction Detected,* or *The Barrier Treaty,*—or,—and
befides, how could the Jade tell but To-morrow we may
have a *Gazette* Extraordinary ?　　　*[Exit.*

End of the Firft A C T.

ACT II.

SCENE, *the* UPHOLSTERER's *House.*

Enter QUIDNUNC.

QUID.

W HERE, where, where is he?—Where's
Mr. *Pamphlet?*—Mr. *Pamphlet!*—*Termagant,*
Mr. a—a—*Termagant, Harriet, Termagant.*
you vile Minx, you faucy—

Enter TERMAGANT.

Here's a Racket indeed !

QUID.

Where's Mr. *Pamphlet?* you Baggage if he's gone—

TERM.

Did not I *intimidate* that he's in the next Room—why
fure the Man's out of his Wits.

QUID.

Shew him in here then—I would not mifs feeing him
for the Difcovery of the North-Eaft Paffage.

TERM.

Go you old Gemini Gomini of a Politic. [*Exit* Term.

QUID.

Shew him in I fay,——I had rather fee him than the
whole State of the Peace at *Utrecht,* or 'the *Paris A-la-
main,*' or the Votes, or the Minutes, or—Here he comes
—the beft political Writer of the Age.

Enter

Enter PAMPHLET.

*(With a Surtout Coat, a Muff, a long Campaign Wig out
of Curl, and a Pair of black Garters, buckled under the
Knees.)*

Q u i d.

Mr. *Pamphlet,* I am heartily glad to fee you,—as glad
as if you were an Exprefs from the *Groyn,* or from *Ber-
lin,* or from *Zell,* or from *Calcutta* over Land, or from——

PAMPH.

Mr. *Quidnunc,* your Servant,—I'm come from a Place
of great Importance.——

Q u i d.

Look ye there now!—well, where, where?

PAMPH.

Are we alone?

Q u i d.

Stay, ftay, till I fhut the Door,—now, now, where
do you come from?

PAMPH.

From the Court of Requefts.

(laying afide his Surtout Coat.)

Q u i d.

The Court of Requefts, *(whifpers)* are they up?

PAMPH.

Hot work.——

Q u i d.

Debates arifing may be.

PAMPH.

Yes, and like to fit late.

Q u i d.

What are they upon?

PAMPH.

Can't fay,——

Q u i d.

What carried you thither?

PAMPH.

I went in hopes of being taken up.——

Q u i d.

Lookye there now. *(fhaking his head)*

PAMPH.

PAMPH.

I've been aiming at it thefe three Years.——

QUID.

Indeed! *(ftaring at him.)*

PAMPH.

Indeed,——Sedition is the only thing an Author can live by now.——Time has been I could turn a Penny by an Earthquake; or live upon a Jail-Diftemper; or dine upon a bloody Murder;——but now that's all over,——nothing will do now but roafting a Minifter——or telling the People, that they are ruined——the People of *England* are never fo happy as when you tell 'em they are ruined.

QUID.

Yes, but they an't ruined——I have a Scheme for paying off the national Debt.

PAMPH.

Let's fee, let's fee *(puts on his Spectacles)* well enough! well imagined,——a new Thought this——I muft make this my own *(afide)* filly, futile, abfurd,——abominable, this will never do——I'll put it in my Pocket and read it over in the morning for you——now look you here——I'll fhew you a Scheme *(rummaging his Pockets)* no that's not it——that's my conduct of the Miniftry, by a Country gentleman——I prov'd the Nation undone here, this fold hugely,——and here now, here's my Anfwer to it, by a noble Lord;——this did not move among the Trade.——

QUID.

What, do you write on both Sides?

PAMPH.

Yes, both Sides,——I've two hands Mr. *Quidnunc,*——alway impartial, *Ambo dexter.*——Now here, here's my Dedication to a great Man——touch'd Twenty for this——and here,——here's my Libel upon him——

QUID.

What, after being obliged to him?

PAMPH.

Yes, for that Reafon,——it excites Curiofity——Whitewafh and Blacking-ball Mr. *Quidnunc!* *in utrumque paratus*——no thriving without it.

QUID.

QUID.

What have you here in this Pocket?

(prying eagerly.)

PAMPH.

That's my Account with *Jacob Zorobabel,* the *Broker,*
for writing Paragraphs to raiſe or tumble the Stocks or the
Price of Lottery Tickets, according to his Purpoſes.

QUID.

Ay, how do you do that?

PAMPH.

As thus,—To-day the Proteſtant Intereſt declines, *Ma-
draſs* is taken, and *England's* undone; then all the long
Faces in the Alley look as diſmal as a Blank, and ſo *Jacob* buys away and thrives upon our Ruin.—Then To-
morrow, we're all alive and merry again, *Pondicherry's*
taken; a certain Northern Potentate will ſhortly ſtrike a
Blow, to aſtoniſh all *Europe,* and then every true born
Engliſhman is willing to buy a Lottery Ticket for twenty
or thirty Shillings more than its worth; ſo *Jacob* ſells
away, and reaps the Fruits of our Succeſs.

QUID.

What, and will the People believe that now?

PAMPH.

Believe it!—believe any thing,—no Swallow like a
true-born *Engliſhman's*—a Man in a Quart Bottle, or a
Victory, it's all one to them,—they give a Gulp—and
down it goes,—glib, glib.——

QUID.

Yes, but they an't at the Bottom of Things?

PAMPH.

No, not they, they dabble a little, but can't dive——

QUID.

Pray now Mr. *Pamphlet,* what do you think of our Situation?

PAMPH.

Bad, Sir, bad,—and how can it be better?—the people
in Power never ſend to me,—never conſult me,—it
muſt be bad—Now here, here, [*goes to his looſe Coat*]
here's a Manuſcript!—this will do the Buſineſs, a Maſter-
piece,—I ſhall be taken up for this.——

E   QUID.

QUID.

Shall ye?

PAMPH.

As fure as a Gun I fhall,—I know the Bookfeller's a Rogue, and will give me up.

QUID.

But pray now what fhall you get by being taken up?

PAMPH.

I'll tell you—(*whifpers*) in order to make me hold my Tongue.

QUID.

Ay, but you won't hold your Tongue for all that.

PAMPH.

Po, po, not a Jot of that,—abufe 'em the next Day.

QUID.

Well, well, I wifh you Succefs,—but do you hear no News? have you feen the *Gazette?*

PAMPH.

Yes, I've feen that,—great News, Mr. *Quidnunc,*—but harkye!—(*whifpers*) and kifs Hands next week.

QUID.

Ay!

PAMPH.

Certain.

QUID.

Nothing permanent in this World.——

PAMPH.

All his Vanity.——

QUID.

Ups and Downs.——

PAMPH.

Ins and Outs.——

QUID.

Wheels within Wheels ——

PAMPH.

No fmoak without Fire.

QUID.

All's well that Ends well.

Each in deep Thought without looking at the other.

PAMPH,

PAMPH.

It will laſt our Time.

QUID.

Whoever lives to ſee it, will know more of the Matter.

PAMPH.

Time will tell all.

QUID.

Ay, we muſt leave all to the Determination of Time. Mr. *Pamphlet,* I'm heartily oblig'd to you for this Viſit,—I love you better than any Man in *England.*

PAMPH.

And for my part Mr. *Quidnunc,*—I love you better than I do *England* itſelf.

QUID.

That's kind, that's kind,—there's nothing I would not do Mr. *Pamphlet,* to ſerve you.

PAMPH.

Mr. *Quidnunc,* I know you're a Man of Integrity and Honour,—I know you are,—and now ſince we have open'd our Hearts, there is a Thing Mr. *Quidnunc,* in which you can ſerve me,— you know, Sir,—this is in the Fullneſs of our Hearts,—you know you have my Note for a Trifle,—hard dealing with Aſſignees, now, could not you to ſerve a Friend, could not you throw that Note into the Fire?

QUID.

Hey ! but would that be honeſt?

PAMPH.

Leave that to me, a refin'd Stroke of Policy,—Papers have been deſtroyed in all Governments.

QUID.

So they have,—it ſhall be done, it will be political, it will indeed—Pray now Mr. *Pamphlet,* what do you take to be the true political Balance of Power?

PAMPH.

What do I take to be the Balance of Power?

QUID.

Ay, the Balance of Power.

E 2

PAMPH.

PAMPH.

The Balance of Power,—what do I take to be the Balance of Power, the Balance of Power (*shuts his Eyes*) what do I take to be the Balance of Power?

QUID.

The Balance of Power, I take to be, when the Court of Aldermen sits.

PAMPH.

No, no,—

QUID.

Yes, yes.—

PAMPH.

No, no, the Balance of Power is when the Foundations of Government and the Superstructures are natural.

QUID.

How d'ye mean natural?

PAMPH.

Prithee be quiet Man,—this is the Language.—The Balance of Power is—when Superstructures are reduc'd to proper Balances, or when the Balances are not reduc'd to unnatural Superstructures.

QUID.

Po, po, I tell you it is when the Fortifications of *Dunquerque* are demolish'd.——

PAMPH.

But I tell you Mr. *Quidnunc.*

QUID.

I say Mr. *Pamphlet.*——

PAMPH.

Hear me Mr. *Quidnunc.*

QUID.

Give me leave Mr. *Pamphlet.*——

PAMPH.

I must observe, Sir,——

QUID.

I am convinc'd Sir.——

PAMPH.

That the Balance of Power——

QUID.

That the Fortifications at *Dunquerque.*

Both in a Passion.

PAMPH.

PAMPH.

Depends upon the Balances and Superstructures.——

QUID.

Constitute the true Political Equilibrium.——

PAMPH.

Nor will I converse with a Man——

QUID.

And Sir, I never desire to see your Face,——

PAMPH.

Of such anti-constitutional Principles.——

QUID.

Nor the Face of any Man who is such a *Frenchman* in his Heart, and has such Notions of the Balance of Power.   [*Exeunt.*

QUIDNUNC (*Re-enters.*)

Ay, I've found him out,——such abominable Principles, I never desire to converse with any Man of his Notions,—— no, never while I live.——

Re-enter PAMPHLET.

PAMPH.

Mr. *Quidnunc,* one Word with you if you please:

QUID.

Sir, I never desire to see your Face.——

PAMPH.

My Property, Mr. *Quidnunc,*——I shan't leave my Pro- perty in the House of a Bankrupt, (*twisting his Handker- chief round his Arm*) a silly, empty, incomprehensible Blockhead.

QUID.

Blockhead! Mr. *Pamphlet.*——

PAMPH.

A Blockhead to use me thus, when I have you so much in my Power.——

QUID.

In your Power!

PAMPH.

In my Power, Sir,—it's in my Power to hang you.

QUID.

To hang me!

PAMPH.

PAMPH.

Yes, Sir; to hang you——(*drawing on his Coat*) Did not you propose, but this Moment, did not you desire me to combine and confederate to burn a Note, and defraud your Creditors—

QUID.

I desire it!

PAMPH.

Yes, Mr. *Quidnunc*, but I shall detect you to the World. I'll give your Character.——You shall have a Six-penny touch next Week.

Flebit et insignis totâ cantabitur urbe. [*Exit* Pamphlet.

QUID.

Mercy on me, there's the Effect of his anti-constitutional Principles.—The Spirit of his whole Party, I never desire to exchange another Word with him.

Enter TERMAGANT.

TERM.

Here's a Pother indeed !—did you call me ?

QUID.

No, you Trollop, no.——

TERM.

Will you go to Bed ?

QUID.

No, no, no, no,—I tell you, no.

TERM.

Better to go to Rest, Sir; I heard a Doctor of Physic say as how, when a Man is past his grand CRIME,—what the *Deuce* makes forget my Word ?—his Grand CRIME-HYSTERIC, nothing is so good against *Indiscompositions* as Rest taken in its *prudish natalibus.*——

QUID.

Hold your prating,——I'll not go to Bed, I'll step to my Brother *Feeble*, I want to have some Talk with him, and I'll go to him directly.   [*Exit* Quidnunc.

TERM.

Go thy ways for an old *Hocus-pocus* of a News-monger——You'll have good Luck if you find your Daughter here when you come back, Mr. *Bellmour* will be here in the Intrim, and if he does not carry her off

why

why then I fhall think him a mere *fhilly fhally Feller* ; and
by my Troth I fhall think him as bad a *Politifhing* as
yourfelf.—Well, as I live and breathe, I wonders what
the *Dickens* the Man fees in thefe News-Papers to be for
ever *toxicated* with them—Let me fee one of them, to try
if I can *veftigate* any thing——*(takes the News-Paper and
reads.)*

 " Yefterday at Noon arrived at his Lodgings in *Pall-*
" *Mall, John Stukly,* Efq; for the Remainder of the
" Winter-Seafon."

 Where the *Dewil* has the Man been?—who knows
him, or cares a minikin Pin about him?—He may go to
Jericho for what I cares.——

 " The fame Day, Mr. *William Tabby,* an eminent
" Man-Milliner was married to Mifs *Jenkins,* Daughter
" of Mr. *Jenkins,* a confiderable *Haberdafher* in Bear-
" binder Lane."——

 What the *Dickens* is this to me?—can't Mifs *Jenkins*
and her Man-Milliner go to Bed, and hold their
Tongues?—why muft they kifs and tell?

 " By Advices from *Violenna*—this is *Policies* now—
(reads to herfelf)—" and promifes a general Peace."—
Why can't that make the old Curmudgeon happy?—

 " By Letters from *Paris*"—this is more Policies—
(reads to herfelf) " and all feems tending to a general Rup-
" ture."—What the *Dewil* does the *Feller* mean?—Did
not he tell me this Moment there was to be Peace, and
now its bloody News again—To go to tell me fuch an
impudent Lie to my Face!

 " At the Academy in *Effex-Street,* Grown People are—
" taught to *dance.*"

 Grown People are taught to dance—I likes that well
enough—I fhould like to be *betterer* in my dancing—I likes
the *Figerre* of a *Minute* as well as a *Figerre* in Speech—*(dances
and fings)* But fuch *Trumpry* as the News is, with Kings,
and Cheefemongers, and Bifhops, and *Highwayrman,* and
Ladies Prayer-Books, and Lap-Dogs, and the *Domodary*
and *Camomile,* and Ambaffadors, and Hair-Cutters, all
higgledy piggledy together——As I hope for *Marcy* I'll
never read another Paper—and I wifhes old *Quidnunc*
would do the fame—if the Man would do as I do, there
would be fome Senfe in it,—if inftead of his Policies, he
would *manure* his Mind like me, and read good *Altars,* and
improve

improve himſelf in fine *Langidge,* and *Bombaſt,* and polite *Accolliſſments*———   [*Exit ſinging.*

Scene *the Street.*

Enter Bellmour, Rovewell *and* Brisk, *in Liquor.*

BELL.

Women ever were, and ever will be fantaſtic Beings,
vain, capricious, and fond of Miſchief———

BRISK.

Well argued, Maſter.

ROVEWELL. *(ſings.)*

Deceit is in every Woman,
But none in a Bumper can be my brave Boys,
But none in a Bumper can be.

BELL.

To be inſulted thus, with ſuch a contemptuous Anſwer
to a Meſſage of ſuch tender Import, ſhe might methinks
at leaſt have treated me with good Manners, if not with a
more grateful Return.———

ROVE.

Split her Manners, let's go and drink t'other Bumper
to drown Sorrow.

BELL.

I'll ſhake off her Fetters,—I will *Briſk,* this very Night
I will—

BRISK.

That's right, Maſter, and let her know we have found
her out, and as the Poet ſays,

‘ *She that will not when ſhe may,*
‘ *When ſhe will, ſhe ſhall have nay,* Maſter.

BELL.

Very true, *Briſk,* very true, the Ingratitude of it touches
to the quick,—my dear *Rovewell,* only come and ſee me
take a final Leave.—

ROVE.

No truly, not I, none of your virtuous Minxes for me,
I'll ſet you down there, if you've a mind to play the Fool—
I know ſhe'll melt you with a Tear, and make a Puppy of
you with a Smile, and ſo I'll not be Witneſs to it.

BELL.

You're quite miſtaken, I aſſure you,—you'll ſee me moſt
manfully upbraid her with her Ingratitude, and with more
Joy than a fugitive Galley Slave, eſcape from the Oar,
to which I have been chain'd.

BRISK.

B R I S K.

Mafter, Mafter, now's our Time, for look by the Glimmering of yonder Lamp, who comes along by the Wall there.—

B E L L.

Her Father, by all that's Lucky,—my dear *Rovewell,* let's drive off.

R O V E.

I'll fpeak to him for you, Man—

B E L L.

Not for the World—prithee come along—   [*Exeunt.*
Enter QUIDNUNC, *with a dark Lanthorn.*

Q U I D.

If the Grand *Turk* fhould actually commence open Hof- tility, and the *Houfe-bug Tartars* make a Diverfion upon the Frontiers, why then it's my Opinion—Time will dif- cover to us a great deal more of the Matter.

W A T C H (*within.*)

Paft Eleven o'Clock, a Cloudy Night.

Q U I D.

Hey! paft Eleven o'Clock,—'Sbodikins, my Brother *Feeble* will be gone to bed,—but he fhan't fleep till I have fome Chat with him. Hark'ye Watchman, Watchman.

Enter WATCHMAN.

W A T C H.

Call, Mafter.

Q U I D.

Ay, ftep hither, ftep hither, have you heard any News?

W A T C H.

News, Mafter!

Q U I D.

Ay, about the *Pruffians* or the *Ruffians?*

W A T C H.

Ruffians, Mafter.

Q U I D.

Yes, or the Movements in *Pomerania?*

W A T C H.

La, Mafter, I knows nothing———poor Gentleman (*pointing to his Head*) Good Night to you Mafter,—paft Eleven o'Clock.   [*Exit* Watchman.

Q U I D.

That Man now has a Place under the Government, and
F   he

he won't speak. But I'm losing Time (*knocks at the Door*)
Hazy Weather(*looking up.*)The Wind's fix'd in that Quarter, and we shan't have any Mails this Week to come,—
come about good Wind, do, come about.

Enter a Servant Maid.

MAID.

La, Sir, is it you?

QUID.

Is your Master at home, Child?

MAID.

Gone to Bed, Sir.

QUID.

Well, well, I'll step up to him.

MAID.

Must not disturb him for the World, Sir.———

QUID.

Business of the utmost Importance.———

MAID.

Pray consider, Sir, my Master an't well.———

QUID.

Prithee be quiet Woman; I must see him. [*Exeunt.*

SCENE, *a Room in* FEEBLE'S *House.*

Enter FEEBLE, *in his Night Gown.*

FEEB.

I was just stepping into Bed;—bless my Heart what
can this Man want?—I know his Voice,—I hope no
new Misfortune brings him at this Hour.

QUID.

Hold your Tongue you foolish Hussey,—he'll be glad
to see me.—Brother *Feeble,*—Brother *Feeble,* (*within.*)

FEEB.

What can be the Matter?

Enter QUIDNUNC.

QUID.

Brother *Feeble,* I give you Joy,—the *Nabob*'s demolish'd,
(*sings*) Britons *strike home, revenge,* &c.

FEEB.

Lackaday, Mr. *Quidnunc,* how can you serve me thus?

QUID.

Suraja Dowla is no more.

FEEB.

Poor Man! he's stark staring mad.———

QUID.

Q u i d.

Our Men diverted themfelves with killing their Bul-
locks and their Camels, till they diflodg'd the Enemy from
the Octagon, and the Counterfcarp, and the Bunglo.—

F e e b.

I'll hear the reft to-morrow Morning,—oh! I'm ready to die.

Q u i d.

Odfheart Man be of good Chear,—the new Nabob,
Jaffier Ally Cawn, has acceded to a Treaty; and the *Englifh* Company have got all their Rights in the *Phirmaud*
and the *Hufhbulhoorums*

F e e b.

But dear heart Mr. *Quidnunc,* why am I to be difturb'd
for this?

Q u i d.

We had but two Seapoys killed, three Chokeys, four
Gaul-walls, and two Zemidars. (*fings*) *Britons never fhall
be Slaves.*

F e e b.

Would not to-morrow Morning do as well for this?

Q u i d.

Light up your Windows, Man, light up your Windows. *Chandernagore* is taken.

F e e b.

Well, well, I'm glad of it—good Night. (*going*)

Q u i d.

Here, here's the *Gazette.*————

F e e b.

Oh, I fhall certainly faint. (*fits down*)

Q u i d.

Ay, ay, fit down, and I'll read it to you. (*Reads.*) nay,
don't run away—I've more News to tell you, there's an
Account from *Williamfburgh* in *America*—the Superinten-
dant of *Indian* Affairs—

F e e b.

Dear Sir, dear Sir,—(*avoiding him*)

Q u i d.

Has fettled Matters with the *Cherokees*—(*following him*)

F e e b.

Enough, enough,—(*from him*)

F 2   Q u i d.

QUID.

In the same Manner he did before with the *Catabaws.*
(*after him.*)

FEEB.

Well, well, your Servant.——(*from him*)

QUID.

So that the back Inhabitants——(*after him*)

FEEB.

I wish you would let me be a quiet Inhabitant in my
own House.——

QUID.

So that the back Inhabitants will now be secur'd by the
Cherokees and *Catabaws.*——

FEEB.

You'd better go home, and think of appearing before
the Commissioners.——

QUID.

Go home! no, no, I'll go and talk the Matter over at
our Coffee-house.——

FEEB.

Do so, do so.——

QUID.

(*Returning*) Mr. *Feeble,*——I had a Dispute about the
Balance of Power,——pray now can you tell——

FEEB.

I know nothing of the Matter——

QUID.

Well, another Time will do for that—I have a great
deal to say about that (*going, returns*) right, I had like to
have forgot, there's an Erratum in the last *Gazette.*——

FEEB.

With all my Heart——

QUID.

Page 3d, Line 1, Col. 1st, and 3d, for *Bombs* read *Booms.*

FEEB.

Read what you will——

QUID.

Nay, but that alters the Sense, you know,—well, now
your Servant. If I hear any more News I'll come and
tell you.——

FEEB.

For Heaven's Sake no more——

QUID.

QUID.

I'll be with you before you're out of your firſt Sleep—
FEEB.

Good-night, Good-night———   [*Runs off.*
QUID.

I forgot to tell you—the Emperor of *Morocco* is dead—
(*bawling after him*) ſo—now I've made him happy—
I'll go and knock up my Friend *Razor,* and make him
happy too ;—and then I'll go and ſee if any Body is up at
the Coffee-houſes,—and make them all happy there too.
—[*Exit.* Quidnunc,

SCENE a STREET. *A ſhabby Houſe with a Barber's
Pole up,—and Candles burning on the outſide.*

Enter QUIDNUNC, *with a dark Lanthorn.*

QUID.

Ah Friend *Razor !*—he has a great Reſpect for a re-
joicing Night.—Who knows but he has heard ſome more
Particulars.———   [*knocks.*
RAZOR *looking out of the Window.*
RAZOR.

Anan !

QUID.

Friend *Razor.*

RAZOR.

My Maſter *Quidnunc !* I'm rejoicing for the News.—
will you partake of a pipe ?—I'll open the Door.

QUID.

Not now, Friend *Razor.*

RAZOR.

I've ſomething to tell you—I'll come down.

QUID.

This may be worth ſtaying for—What can he have
heard !

Enter RAZOR, *in a Cap, a Pipe in his Mouth, and a
Tankard in his hand.*

RAZOR.

Say, here's to you, Maſter *Quidnunc:*

QUID.

What have you heard ? What have you heard ?—
RAZOR.

RAZOR.

The Confumers of Oats are to meet next Week.

QUID.

Thofe Confumers of Oats have been meeting any time thefe ten Years to my Knowledge, and I never cou'd find what they are about.

RAZOR.

Things an't right, I fear—its enough to put down a Body's Spirits.————   [*Drinks.*

QUID.

No, nothing to fear—I can tell you fome good News —a certain great Potentate has not heard High-Mafs, the Lord knows when.

RAZOR.

That puts a Body in Spirits again. (*drinks*) Here, drink no wooden Shoes.

QUID.

With all my Heart—(*drinks*) Good Liquor this, Mafter *Razor,* of a cold Night.

RAZOR.

Yes,—I put a Quatern of Britifh Brandy in my Beer— whu !—Do you know what a Rebel my Wife is.

QUID.

A Rebel !

RAZOR.

Ay, a Rebel—I earned Nineteen-pence half-penny to Day, and fhe wanted to lay out all that great Sum upon the Children—whu—but I bought thofe Candles for the good of my Country, to rejoice with as a Body may fay—a little Virginy for my Pipe and this Sup of Hot.— whu————

QUID.

Ay, you're an Honeft Man, and if every body did like you and me, what a Nation we fhou'd be.—

RAZOR.

Ay, very true,—(*fhakes his Head*)

QUID.

I can give you the Gazette to read.

RAZOR.

Can you ! a thoufand Thanks,—I'll take it Home to you when I have done.—(*drinks and ftaggers.*)

QUID.

QUID.

Friend Razor, you begin to be a little in for't.

RAZ.

Yes, I have a whirligigg of a Head. —— but a body
shou'd get drunk sometimes for the good of one's Country.

QUID.

Well, I shall be at home in half an Hour!—Hark'ye.

RAZ.

—Anan!

QUID.

I have made a rare discovery,—Florida will be able to
supply Jamaica with Peet for their Winters firings.   I
had it from a deep Politician.

RAZ.

Ay! I am glad the Poor People of Jamaica will have
Florida Peet to burn.——   *Exeunt.*

SCENE *The Upholsterer's House.*

Enter BELLMOUR, *and* HARRIET.

HAR.

MR. Bellmour, pray Sir— I desire, Sir, you'll not
follow me from Room to Room.

BELL.

Indulge me but a moment.

HAR.

No, Mr. Bellmour, I've seen too much of your Temper,—I'm touch'd beyond all Enduring at your unmanly
Treatment.

BELL.

Unmanly, Madam.

HAR.

Unmanly, Sir, to presume upon the Misfortunes of
my Family, and insult me with the formidable menaces
that, " Truly you have done, you'll be no more a Slave
to me." — Oh fye, Mr. Bellmour, I did not think a
Gentleman capable of it.

BELL.

But you won't consider.

HAR.

Sir, I wou'd have Mr. Bellmour understand, that tho'

my

my Father's Circumstances are Embarass'd, I have still an Uncle, who can, and will place me in a State of Affluence, and then, Sir, your Declarations.—

BELL.

My dearest Harriet, they were but hasty Words, let me now entreat you suffer me to convey you hence, far from your Father's Roof, where we may at length enjoy that Happiness, of which we have long cherish'd the loved Idea.—What say you, Harriet.

HAR.

I don't know what to say—my Heart's at my Lips. — Why don't you take me then.

Enter TERMAGANT.

TER.

Undone, Undone! I'm all over in a flustration—old Jimini Gomini's coming.

HAR.

O Lud, what is to be done now?

TER.

The Devil! what can be done? I have it—don't flustrate yourself—I'll find some Nonsense News for him — away with you both into that Room. Quick, quick.

[They Exit.

Let me see—have I nothing in my Pocket for the Old Hocus Pocus to read? Pawsh! that's Mr. Bellmour's Letter to Miss Harriet — I envelop'd that Secret for all Pains to purvent me. — Old Politic must not have an Ideer of that Business—Stay, stay, is there ne'er an old Trumpery News-paper?— this will do. — *[Puts it in her Pocket.]* Now let the Gazette of a Fellow come as soon as he will.

Enter QUIDNUNC.

QUID.

Fy upon it —fy upon it! — all the Coffee Houses shut up—Where is my Salmon's Gazetteer, and my map of the World? — In that Room I fancy — I won't sleep till I know the Geography of all these Places.   *Going.]*

TERM.

Sir, Sir, Sir!

QUID.

Q u i d.

What's the Matter?

T e r m.

Here has been Mr.———He with the odd Name.

Q u i d.

Mr. D———that writes the pretty Verses upon all Public Occasions———

T e r m.

Ay, Mr. *Reptile*—the same. He says as how there are some Assays of his in this Paper—*(searches her Pockets)* And he desires you will give him your Ideer of them.

Q u i d.

That I will—let me see!—

T e r m.

The Deuce fetch it—here is something disintangles in my Pocket—there, there it is.—*(gives the Paper and drops the letter)* Pray amuse it before you go to Bed—or had not you better go, and read it in Bed—

Q u i d.

No, I'll read it here.—

T e r m.

Do so,—he'll call in the morning,—I'll get him to Bed I warrant me, and then Miss *Harriet* may Elope as fast as she will.——   [*Exit.*

Q u i d.

Hey!—this is an old News-Paper, I see.—What's this? *takes up the Letter)* here may be some News.—" To Miss *Harriet Quidnunc.*"—Let me see—[*reads.*

   " My dearest *Harriet,*

" Why will you keep me in a state of suspence? I
" have given you every proof of the sincerest Constancy
" and Love. Surely then, now that you see your Fa-
" ther's Obstinacy, you may determine to consult your
" own Happiness; if you will permit me to wait on you
" this Evening, I will convey you to a Family, who
" will take the tenderest Care of your Person, till you
" resign it to the Arms of
        " Your Eternal Admirer
                " *Bellmour.*"

G   So

So, fo, here's Policy detected—why *Harriet*, Daughter!—*Harriet!*—She has not made her Escape I hope—So Madam,———

Enter HARRIET *and* BELLMOUR.

Hey, the Enemy in our camp.

HAR.

Mr. *Bellmour* is no Enemy, Sir.—

QUID.

No! What does he lurk in my House for?

BELL.

Sir, my Defigns are honourable, you fee Sir, I am above concealing myfelf.

QUID.

Ay, thanks to *Termagant*, or I fhou'd have been undermined here by you.———

TERM. *(looking in)*

What the Devil is here to do now?—I am all over in a Quandery.

QUID.

Now, Madam, an't you a falfe Girl—an undutiful Child?—But I can get intelligence you fee—*Termagant* is my Friend, and if it had not been for her———

Enter TERMAGANT.

TERM.

Oh my Stars and Garters! here's fuch a piece of work—What fhall I do?—My poor dear Miss *Harriet* —*(cries bitterly.)*

QUID.

What is there any more News? What has happen'd now?

TERM.

Oh Madam, Madam, forgive me my dear Ma'am— I did not do it purpofe—I did not, as I hope for Mercy I did not———

QUID.

Is the Woman crazy?———

TERM.

I did not intend to give it him;—I would have feen him gibbeted firft, I found the Letter in your Bed-
Cham-

Chamber— I knew it was the fame I delivered to you—
and my Curiofity did make me peep into it, fays my
Curiofity, " Now *Termagant*, you may gratify yourfelf
" by finding out the Contents of that Letter, which you
" have fo violent an itching for."— My Curiofity did
fay fo— and then I own my refpect for you did fay to me,
" Huffey, how dare you meddle with what does not
" belong to you? Keep your Diftance, and let your
" Miftrefs's Secrets alone." And then upon that, in
comes my Curiofity again, " Read it, I tell you, *Ter-*
" *magant*, a Woman of Spirit fhou'd know every thing."
" Let it alone, you Jade," fays my Refpect, " it's as
" much as your Place is worth," " What fignification's
" a Place with an old Bankrupper," fays my Curiofity,
" there's more Places than one, and fo read it, I tell
" you, *Termagant*."— I did read it, what could I do,—
Heav'n help me — I did read it, I don't go to deny it,
I don't,—I don't—I don't—   [*crying very bitterly.*]

Q U I D.

And I have read it too, don't keep fuch an Uproar,
Woman—

T E R M.

And after I had read it, thinks me, I'll give this to
my Miftrefs again, and her Germanocus of a Father
fhall never fee it—and fo as my ill Stars would have it,
as I was giving him a News Paper, I run my Hand into
the Lion's Mouth.—   [*crying.*

B E L L.

What an unlucky jade fhe has been.   [*afide.*

H A R.

Well, there's no Harm done, *Termagant* ; for I don't
want to deceive my Father.

Q U I D.

Yes, but there is harm done. (*knocking.*) Hey, what's
all this knocking—Step and fee, *Termagant*.

T E R M.

Yes, Sir.———   [*Exit.*

Q U I D.

A Waiter from the Coffee-houfe mayhap with fome
News — You fhall go to the Round Houfe, Friend —
I'll carry you there myfelf, and who knows but I may

meet

meet a Parliament Man in the Round House to tell him some Politicks.

Enter ROVEWELL.

ROVE.

But I say I will come in, my Friend shan't be murder'd amongst you——

BELL.

'Sdeath, *Rovewell!* what brings you here?

ROVE.

I have been waiting in a Hackney Coach for you these two Hours, and split me, but I was afraid they had smother'd you between two Feather Beds.

Enter TERMAGANT.

TERM.

More Misfortunes—here comes the Watch.

QUID.

The best News I ever heard.

Enter WATCHMAN.

QUID.

Here, Thieves, Robbery, Murder, I charge 'em both, take 'em directly.

WATCH.

Stand and deliver in the King's Name, seize 'em, knock 'em down——

BELL.

Don't frighten the Lady — here's my Sword — I surrender.

ROVE.

You Scoundrels—Stand off Rascals—

WATCH.

Down with him—down with him—   [*fight.*

Enter RAZOR *in his first Cloaths — with the Gazette in his Hand.*——

RAZOR.

What, a fray at my Master *Quidnunc's* — knock him down,— knock him down — [*folds up the Gazette, and strips to fight.*

QUID.

Quid.

That's right, that's right—hold him faft.—*Watch-*
men feize Rove. *and* Razor *puts on his Cloaths.*

Rove.

You have overpowered me, you Rafcals—

Term.

I believe as fure as any thing, as how he's a High-
warman, and as how it was he that robb'd the Mail.

Quid.

What rob the Mail and ftop all the News,—fearch
him—fearch him—he may have the Letters belonging
to the Mail in his Pockets now—Ay, here's one Letter—
" To Mr. *Abraham Quidnunc,*"—Let's fee what it is—
" Your dutiful Son, *John Quidnunc.*"

Rove.

That's my Name, and *Rovewell* was but affumed.

Quid.

What and am I your Father?

Razor.

(looks at him) Oh my dear Sir, *(embraces him and*
powders him all over) 'tis he fure enough—I remember
the Mole on his Cheek—I fhav'd his firft Beard.

Quid.

Juft return'd from the Weft-Indies, I fuppofe.

Rove.

Yes, Sir; the owner of a rich Plantation.

Quid.

What by ftudying Politicks?

Rove.

By a rich Planter's Widow; and I have now For-
une enough to make you happy in your old Age.

Razor.

And I hope I fhall fhave him again.

Rove.

So thou fhalt, honeft *Razor,*—in the mean time let
me entreat you beftow my Sifter upon my Friend *Bell-*
mour here.

Quid.

He may take her as foon as he pleafes,—'twill make
an excellent Paragraph in the News Papers.

Term.

TERM.

There, Madam, calcine your Perſon to him.

QUID.

What are the Spaniards doing in the Bay of Honduras?

ROVE.

Truce with Politicks for the Preſent, if you pleaſe Sir.—We'll think of our own Affairs firſt—before we concern ourſelves about the Balance of Power.

RAZOR.

With all my Heart, I'm rare happy.

Come Maſter Quidnunc *now with News ha' done,*
Bleſs'd in your Wealth, your Daughter and your Son ;
May Diſcord ceaſe, Faction no more be ſeen,
Be High and Low for Country King and Queen.

F I N I S.

THE
CITIZEN.
A
FARCE.

As it is performed at the

THEATRE ROYAL
IN
COVENT-GARDEN.

THE THIRD EDITION.

By ARTHUR MURPHY, Esq.

Æque neglectum pueris senibusque nocebit. Hor.

LONDON:

Printed for P. Vaillant, T. Caslon,
W. Griffin, T. Lowndes, W. Nicoll,
T. Becket, and S. Bladon. 1770.

[Price One Shilling.]

THE Author's compliments to Mifs EL-
LIOT, and he defires to infcribe to her the
following fcenes. She need not be alarmed at
a dedication, the propriety of which will ftrike
every reader, who remembers that Mifs ELLLIOT
and the CITIZEN made their firft appearance
on the ftage together, and that her uncommon
talents gave the piece the beft and moft effec-
tual protection. Elegance of figure ; a voice
of pleafing variety, a ftrong expreffion of humour, not impaired, but rendered exquifite, by
delicacy ; thefe were circumftances that fecured
the farce at firft, and have fince brought it into
favour. No author ever met with a better pa-
tronage ; and though the CITIZEN, like other
things of this kind, has many faults, yet it has
this peculiar merit, that it produced, in the
character of MARIA, a genuine comic genius.
The CITIZEN claims another praife. When
all the little arts of theatrical malice were con-
fpiring againft her, it recommended Mifs EL-
LIOT to the notice of Mr. BEARD, and obtained
for her that generous treatment, which *that
manager* feems determined to extend to real
merit. The Author, therefore, defires Mifs
ELLIOT's acceptance of this Farce, for the defects of which he makes no apology, becaufe,
fhould the moft fevere judge in this kind re-
folve to arm himfelf with criticifms, let him
but look at the acting of MARIA, *and he will
forget them all.*

Dramatis

Dramatis Personæ.

DRURY-LANE.

MEN.

Old Philpot,	Mr. Baddeley.
Young Philpot,	Mr. King.
Sir Jasper Wilding,	Mr. Burton.
Young Wilding,	Mr. Lee.
Beaufort,	Mr. Packer.
Dapper,	Mr. Vaughan.
Quilldrive,	Mr. Ackman.

WOMEN.

Maria,	Miss Elliot.
Corinna,	Mrs. Hippisley.

COVENT-GARDEN.

MEN.

Old Philpot,	Mr. Shuter.
Young Philpot,	Mr. Woodward.
Sir Jasper Wilding,	Mr. Dunstall.
Young Wilding,	Mr. Dyer.
Beaufort,	Mr. Baker.
Dapper,	Mr. Costollo.
Quilldrive,	Mr. Perry.

WOMEN.

Maria,	Mrs. Mattocks.
Corinna,	Miss Cockayne.

Servants, &c.

THE
CITIZEN.

ACT I. SCENE I.

YOUNG WILDING, BEAUFORT, *and* WILL
following.

Wilding.

HA, ha, my dear Beaufort! A fiery young fellow like you, melted down into a fighing, love-fick dangler after a high heel, a well-turn'd ancle, and a fhort petticoat!

Beau. Pr'ythee, Wilding, don't laugh at me—Maria's charms——

Wild. Maria's charms! And fo now you would fain grow wanton in her praife, and have me liften to your raptures about my own fifter! Ha, ha, poor Beaufort! ——Is my fifter at home, Will?

Will. She is, Sir.

Wild. How long has my father been gone out?

Will. This hour, Sir.

Wild. Very Well. Pray give Mr. Beaufort's compliments to my fifter, and he is come to wait upon her ——(*Exit* Will.) You will be glad to fee her I fuppofe, Charles.

Beau. I live but in her prefence.

Wild. Live but in her prefence! How the devil could the young baggage raife this riot in your heart? 'Tis more than her brother could ever do with any of her fex.

B

Beau.

Beau. Nay, you have no reason to complain; you are come up to town, post-haste, to marry a wealthy citizen's daughter, who only saw you last season at Tunbridge, and has been languishing for you ever since.

Wild. That's more than I do for her; and, to tell you the truth, more than I believe she does for me— This is a match of prudence, man! bargain and sale! —My reverend dad and the old put of a citizen finish-ed the business at Lloyd's Coffee-house by inch of candle—a mere transferring of property!—" Give " your son to my daughter, and I will give my " daughter to your son." That's the whole affair, and so I am just arrived to consummate the nuptials.

Beau. Thou art the happiest fellow——

Wild. Happy! so I am—what should I be otherwise for? If Miss Sally—upon my soul I forget her name—

Beau. Well! that is so like you——Miss Sally Philpot.

Wild. Ay! very true——Miss Sally Philpot—— she will bring fortune sufficient to pay off an old in-cumbrance upon the family-estate, and my father is to settle handsomely upon me——and so I have reason to be contented, have not I?

Beau. And you are willing to marry her without having one spark of love for her?

Wild. Love!——why I make myself ridiculous enough by marrying, don't I, without being in love into the bargain? What! am I to pine for a girl that is willing to go to bed to me? Love of all things!— My dear Beaufort, one sees so many people breathing raptures about each other before marriage, and din-ning their insipidity into the ears of all their ac-quaintance; " My dear Ma'am, don't you think " him a sweet man? a charminger creature never " was." Then he, on his side—" My life, my angel, " oh! she's a paradise of ever blooming sweets." And then in a month's time, " He's a perfidious wretch! " I wish I had never seen his face——the devil was " in me when I had any thing to say to him"—— " Oh! damn her for an inanimate piece——I wish " she'd poison'd herself with all my heart." That is

ever the way; and fo you fee love is all nonfenfe;
well enough to furnifh romances for boys and girls
at circulating libraries; that is all, take my word for it.

Beau. Pho! this is all idle talk; and, in the mean
time, I am ruin'd.

Wild. How fo?

Beau. Why, you know the old couple have bargain'd your fifter away.

Wild. Bargain'd her away! and will you pretend you
are in love?——Can you look tamely on and fee her
barter'd away at Garraway's, like logwood, cochineal,
or indigo? Marry her privately, man, and keep it a
fecret till my affair is over.

Beau. My dear Wilding, will you propofe it to her?

Wild. With all my heart—She is very long a coming——I'll tell you what, if fhe has a fancy for you,
carry her off at once—But, perhaps, fhe has a mind to
this cub of a citizen, Mifs Sally's brother.

Beau. Oh, no! he's her averfion.

Wild. I have never feen any of the family, but my
wife that is to be—my father-in-law and my brother-
in-law, I know nothing of them. What fort of a
fellow is the fon?

Beau. Oh! a diamond of the firft water! a buck,
Sir! a blood! every night at this end of the town;
at twelve next day he fneaks about the Change, in a
little bit of a frock and a bob-wig, and looks like a
fedate book-keeper in the eyes of all who behold him.

Wild. Upon my word, a gentleman of fpirit.

Beau. Spirit!——he drives a phaeton two ftory
high, keeps his girl at this end of the town, and is
the gay George Philpot all round Covent-Garden.

Wild. Oh, brave!——and the father——

Beau. The father, Sir——But here comes Maria;
take his picture from her. [*She fings within.*]

Wild. Hey! fhe is mufical this morning; fhe holds
her ufual fpirits, I find.

Beau. Yes, yes, the fpirit of eighteen, with the idea
of a lover in her head.

Wild. Ay! and fuch a lover as you too! tho' ftill
in her teens, fhe can play upon all your foibles, and

B 2 treat

treat you as she does her monkey, tickle you, torment you, enrage you, sooth you, exalt you, depress you, pity you, laugh at you——*Ecce signum!*

Enter MARIA *singing.*

Wild. The same giddy girl!——Sister; come, my dear——

Maria. Have done, brother; let me have my own way—I will go through my song.

Wild. I have not seen you this age; ask me how I do?

Maria. I won't ask you how you do—I won't take any notice of you, I don't know you.

Wild. Do you know this gentleman then? Will you speak to him?

Maria. No, I won't speak to him; I'll sing to him; it's my humour to sing. [*Sings.*]

Beau. Be serious but for a moment, Maria; my all depends upon it.

Maria. Oh! sweet Sir, you are dying, are you? then positively I will sing the song; for it is a description of yourself—mind it, Mr. Beaufort—mind it—Brother, how do you do? [*kisses him*] Say nothing, don't interrupt me——[*Sings.*]

Wild. Have you seen your city lover yet?

Maria. No; but I long to see him; I fancy he is a curiosity.

Beau. Long to see him, Maria!

Maria. Yes, long to see him—[Beaufort *fiddles with his lip, and looks thoughtful.*] Brother, brother! [*goes to him softly, beckons him to look at* Beaufort] do you see that? [*mimicks him*] mind him; ha, ha.

Beau. Make me ridiculous if you will, Maria; so you don't make me unhappy, by marrying this citizen.

Maria. And would not you have me marry, Sir? What, I must lead a single life to please you, must I? upon my word you are a pretty gentleman to make laws for me. [*Sings.*]

Can it be, or by law, or by equity said,
That a comely young girl ought to die an old maid?

Wild. Come, come, Miss Pert, compose yourself a little—this will never do.

Maria. My crofs, ill-natur'd brother! but it will do
—Lord! what do you both call me hither to plague
me? I won't ftay among ye—*à l'honeur, à l'honeur—*
[*running away.*] *à l'honeur.*

Wild. Hey, hey, Mifs Notable! come back, pray
Madam, come back——[*Forces her back.*]

Maria. Lord of Heaven! what do you want!

Wild. Come, come, truce with your frolicks, Mifs
Hoyden, and behave like a fenfible girl; we have
ferious bufinefs with you.

Maria. Have you? Well, come, I will be fenfible—
there, I blow all my folly away—'Tis gone, 'tis gone,
and now I'll talk fenfe; come——Is that a fenfible
face?

Wild. Po, po, be quiet, and hear what we have to
fay to you.

Maria. I will, I am quiet. It is charming weather;
it will be good for the country, this will.

Wild. Po, ridiculous! how can you be fo filly?

Maria. Blefs me! I never faw any thing like you—
there is no fuch thing as fatisfying you—I am fure it
was very good fenfe, what I faid—Papa talks in that
manner—Well, well! I'll be filent then—I won't
fpeak at all; will that fatisfy you? [*Looks fullen*]

Wild. Come, come, no more of this folly, but mind
what is faid to you—You have not feen your city
lover, you fay?

[*Maria fhrugs her fhoulders, and fhakes her head.*]

Wild. Why don't you anfwer?

Beau. My dear Maria, put me out of pain.

[*Maria fhrugs her fhoulders again.*]

Wild. Po! don't be fo childifh, but give a rational
anfwer.

Maria. Why, no, then; no——no, no, no, no,
no——I tell you no, no, no.

Wild. Come, come, my little giddy fifter, you muft
not be fo flighty; behave fedately, and don't be a girl
always.

Maria. Why don't I tell you I have not feen him—
but I am to fee him this very day.

Beau.

Beau. To see him this day, Maria?

Maria. Ha, ha!—look there, brother; he is beginning again—But don't fright yourself, and I'll tell you all about it—My papa comes to me this morning—by the by, he makes a fright of himself with this strange dress—Why does he not dress as other gentlemen do, brother?

Wild. He dresses like his brother fox-hunters in Wiltshire.

Maria. But when he comes to town, I wish he would do as other gentlemen do here——I am almost asham'd of him——But he comes to me this morning——" Hoic! hoic! our Moll——Where is the sly " puss——Tally ho !"——Did you want me papa? ——" Come hither, Moll, I'll *gee* you a husband, " my girl; one that has mettle enow——he'll take " cover, I warrant un——Blood to the bone."

Beau. There now, Wilding, did not I tell you this?

Wild. Where are you to see the young citizen?

Maria. Why, papa will be at home in a hour, and then he intends to drag me into the city with him, and there the sweet creature is to be introduced to me— The old gentleman, his father, is delighted with me: but I hate him, an old ugly thing.

Wild. Give us a description of him; I want to know him.

Maria. Why, he looks like the picture of Avarice, sitting with pleasure upon a bag of money, and trembling for fear any body should come and take it away— He has got square-toed shoes, and little tiny buckles, a brown coat, with small round brass buttons, that looks as if it was new in my great-grandmother's time, and his face all shrivell'd and pinch'd with care, and he shakes his head like a mandarine upon a chimney-piece——" Ay, ay, Sir Jasper, you are " right—and then he grins at me—I profess she is a " very pretty bale of goods. Ay, ay, and my son Bob " is a very sensible lad—ay, ay! and I will under- " write their happiness for one and a half *per cent.*"

Wild. Thank you, my dear girl; thank you for this account of my relations.

Beau.

Beau. Deftruction to my hopes! Surely, my dear little angel, if you have any regard for me——

Maria. There, there, there he is frighten'd again.
[*Sings*, Deareft creature, &c.]

Wild. Pfhaw! give over thefe airs——liften to me, and I'll inftruct you how to manage them all.

Maria. Oh! my dear brother, you are very good—but don't miftake yourfelf; though juft come from a boarding-fchool, give me leave to manage for myfelf——There is in this cafe a man I like, and a man I don't like——It is not you I like (*to* Beaufort)—no—no—I hate you——But let this little head alone; I know what to do——I fhall know how to prefer one, and get rid of the other.

Beau. What will you do, Maria?

Maria. Ha, ha, I can't help laughing at you. [*Sings.*
        Do not grieve me,
        Oh! relieve me, &c.

Wild. Come, come, be ferious Mifs Pert, and I'll inftruct you what to do—The old cit, you fay, admires you for your underftanding; and his fon would not marry you, unlefs he found you a girl of fenfe and fpirit?

Maria. Even fo—this is the character of your giddy fifter.

Wild. Why then I'll tell you—You fhall make him hate you for a fool, and fo let the refufal come from himfelf.

Maria. But how—how, my dear brother? Tell me how?

Wild. Why you have feen a play with me, where a man pretends to be a downright country oaf, in order to rule a wife and have a wife.

Maria. Very well—what then? what then?—Oh!—I have it—I underftand you—fay no more—'tis charming; I like it of all things; I'll do it, I will; and I will fo plague him, that he fhan't know what to make of me—He fhall be a very toad-eater to me; the four, the fweet, the bitter, he fhall fwallow all, and all fhall work upon him alike for my diverfion. Say nothing of it—it's all among ourfelves; but I won't be cruel. I hate ill-nature, and then who knows but I may like him? *Beau.*

Beau. My dear, Maria, don't talk of liking him.

Maria. Oh! now you are beginning again.

[*Sings*, Voi Amanti, &c. *and exit.*]

Beau. 'Sdeath, Wilding, I shall never be your brother-in-law at this rate.

Wild. Pshaw, follow me; don't be apprehensive——I'll give her farther instructions, and she will execute them I warrant you; the old fellow's daughter shall be mine, and the son may go shift for himself elsewhere.

SCENE II. *Old* Philpot's *House.*

Enter OLD PHILPOT, DAPPER, *and* QUILLDRIVE.

Old Phil. Quilldrive, have those dollars been sent to the Bank, as I order'd?

Quill. They have, Sir.

Old Phil. Very well!—Mr. Dapper, I am not fond of writing any thing of late; but at your request——

Dap. You know I would not offer you a bad policy.

Old Phil. I believe it—Well, step with me to my closet, and I will look at your policy——How much do you want upon it?

Dap. Three thousand; you had better take the whole; there are very good names upon it.

Old Phil. Well, well, step with me, and I'll talk to you—Quilldrive, step with those bills for acceptance —This way, Mr. Dapper, this way.   [*Exeunt.*

QUILLDRIVE *solus.*

Quill. A miserly old rascal! digging, digging money out of the very hearts of mankind; constantly, constantly scraping together, and yet trembling with anxiety for fear of coming to want. A canting old hypocrite! and yet under his veil of sanctity, he has a liquorish tooth left—running to the other end of the town slily every evening, and there he has his solitary pleasures in holes and corners.

GEORGE PHILPOT, *peeping in.*

G. Phil. Hist, hist!——Quilldrive!

Quill. Ha, Master George!

I

G. Phil.

G. Phil. Is Square-toes at home?

Quill. He is.

G. Phil. Has he afk'd for me?

Quill. He has.

G. Phil. [*Walks in on tip-toe.*] Does he know I did not lay at home?

Quil. No; I funk that upon him.

G. Phil. Well done; I'll give you a choice gelding to carry you to Dulwich of a Sunday—Damnation!—up all night—ftripped of nine hundred pounds--pretty well for one night!—Picqued, repicqued, flamm'd, and capotted every deal!—Old Dry-beard fhall pay all—is forty feven good? no—fifty good? no! no, no, no—to the end of the chapter—Cruel luck!—Damn me, 'tis life tho'—this is life—'sdeath! I hear him coming [*runs off and peeps*]—no, all's fafe—I muft not be caught in thefe cloaths, Quilldrive—

Quill. How come you did not leave them at Madam Corinna's, as you generally do?

G. Phil. I was afraid of being too late for old Square-toes, and fo I whipt into a hackney-coach, and drove with the windows up, as if I was afraid of a bumbailey.—Pretty cloaths, an't they?

Quill. Ah! Sir—

G. Phil. Reach me one of my mechanic city frocks—no—ftay—it's in the next room, an't it?

Quill. Yes, Sir.

G. Phil. I'll run and flip it on in a twinkle. [*Exit.*

QUILLDRIVE *folus.*

Quill. Mercy on us! what a life does he lead? Old Cojer within here will fcrape together for him, and the moment young Mafter comes to poffeffion, " Ill got, ill gone," I warrant me; a hard card I have to play between 'em both—drudging for the old man, and pimping for the young one—The father is a refervoir of riches, and the fon is a fountain to play it all away in vanity and folly!

Re-enter GEORGE PHILPOT.

G. Phil. Now I'm equipp'd for the city—Damn the city—I wifh the Papifhes would fet fire to it again

C   —I hate

—I hate to be beating the hoof here among them—
Here comes father—no;—it's Dapper—Quilldrive,
I'll give you the gelding.

Quill. Thank you, Sir.   [*Exit.*

Enter DAPPER.

Dap. Why you look like a devil, George.

G. Phil. Yes, I have been up all night; loft all
my money, and I am afraid I muft fmafh for it.

Dap. Smafh for it—what have I let you into the
fecret for? Have not I advifed you to trade upon your
own account—and you feel the fweets of it—How
much do you owe in the city?

G. Phil. At leaft twenty thoufand.

Dap. Poh, that's nothing! Bring it up to fifty or
fixty thoufand, and then give 'em a good crafh at
once—I have enfured the fhip for you.

G. Phil. Have you?

Dap. The policy's full; I have juft touch'd your
father for the laft three thoufand.

G. Phil. Excellent! are the goods re-landed?

Dap. Every bale—I have had them up to town,
and fold them all to a packer for you.

G. Phil. Bravo!—and the fhip is loaded with rubbifh, I fuppofe?

Dap. Yes; and is now proceeding on the voyage.

G. Phil. Very well—and to-morrow, or next day,
we fhall hear of her being loft upon the Goodwin,
or funk betwen the Needles.

Dap. Certainly.

G. Phil. Admirable! and then we fhall come upon the underwriters.

Dap. Directly.

G. Phil. My dear Dapper!   [*Embraces him.*

Dap. Yes; I do a dozen every year. How do
you think I can live as I do, otherwife?

G. Phil. Very true; fhall you be at the club after
Change?

Dap. Without fail.

G. Phil. That's right; it will be a full meeting:
we fhall have Nat Pigtail, the dry-falter, there; and
Bob Reptile, the Change-broker; and Soberfides, the
                                              banker

banker—we shall all be there. We shall have deep doings.

Dap. Yes, yes; well, a good morning; I must go now and fill up a policy for a ship that has been lost these three days.

G. Phil. My dear Dapper, thou art the best of friends.

Dap. Ay, I'll stand by you—It will be time enough for you to break, when you see your father near his end; then give 'em a smash; put yourself at the head of his fortune, and begin the world again—Good morning.   [*Exit.*

G. PHILPOT, *solus.*

G. Phil. Dapper, adieu—Who now in my situation would envy any of your great folks at the court-end! A Lord has nothing to depend upon but his estate—He can't spend you a hundred thousand pounds of other people's money—no—no—I had rather be a little bob-wig citizen, in good credit, than a commissioner of the customs—Commissioner!—The King has not so good a thing in his gift, as a commission of bankruptcy—Don't we see them all with their country seats at Hogsdon, and at Kentish-town, and at New-ington-butts, and at Islington; with their little flying Mercuries tipt on the top of the house, their Apollos, their Venus's and their leaden Hercules's in the garden; and themselves sitting before the door, with pipes in their mouths, waiting for a good digestion—Zoons! here comes old Dad; now for a few dry maxims of left-handed wisdom, to prove myself a scoundrel in sentiment, and pass in his eyes for a hopeful young man likely to do well in the world.

Enter OLD PHILPOT.

Old Phil. Twelve times twelve is 144.

G. Phil. I'll attack him in his own way—Commission at two and a half *per cent.*

Old. Phil. There he is, intent upon business! What, plodding, George?

G. Phil. Thinking a little of the main chance, Sir.

Old Phil. That's right; it is a wide world, George.

G. Phil. Yes, Sir, but you instructed me early in the rudiments of trade.

Old

Old Phil. Ay, ay! I inſtill'd good principles into thee.

G. Phil. So you did, Sir—principal and intereſt is all I ever heard from him. [*aſide*] I ſhall never forget the ſtory you recommended to my earlieſt notice, Sir.

Old Phil. What was that, George? It is quite out of my head.

G. Phil. It intimated, Sir, how Mr. Thomas Inkle, of London, merchant, was caſt away, and was afterwards protected by a young lady, who grew in love with him, and how he afterwards bargained with a planter to ſell her for a ſlave.

Old Phil. Ay, ay, [*laughs*] I recollect it now.

G. Phil. And when ſhe pleaded being with child by him, he was no otherwiſe mov'd than to raiſe his price, and make her turn better to account.

Old Phil. [*Burſts into a laugh.*] I remember it—ha, ha!—there was the very ſpirit of trade! ay—ay—ha, ha!

G. Phil. That was calculation for you——

Old Phil. Ay, ay.

G. Phil. The Rule of Three—If one gives me ſo much; what will two give me?

Old Phil. Ay, ay.   [*Laughs.*]

G. Phil. That was a hit, Sir.

Old Phil. Ay, ay.

G. Phil. That was having his wits about him.

Old Phil. Ay, ay! It is a leſſon for all young men. It was a hit indeed, ha! ha! [*Both laugh.*]

G. Phil. What an old negro it is.   [*Aſide.*]

Old Phil. Thou art a ſon after my own heart, George.

G. Phil. Trade muſt be minded—A penny ſav'd, is a penny got——

Old Phil. Ay, ay! [*Shakes his head, and looks cunning.*]

G. Phil. He that hath money in his purſe, won't want a head on his ſhoulders.

Old Phil. Ay, ay.

G. Phil. Rome was not built in a day—Fortunes are made by degrees—Pains to get, care to keep, and fear to looſe——

Old Phil. Ay, ay.

G. Phil. He that lies in bed, his eſtate feels it.

Old Phil. Ay, ay, the good boy.

G. Phil. The old Curmudgeon [*aside.*] thinks nothing mean that brings in an honeſt penny.

Old Phil. The good boy! George, I have great hopes of thee.

G. Phil. Thanks to your example; you have taught me to be cautious in this wide world——Love your neighbour, but don't pull down your hedge.

Old Phil. I profeſs it is a wiſe ſaying—I never heard it before; it is a wiſe ſaying; and ſhews how cautious we ſhould be of too much confidence in friendſhip.

G. Phil. Very true.

Old Phil. Friendſhip has nothing to do with trade.

G. Phil. It only draws a man in to lend money.

Old Phil. Ay, ay——

G. Phil. There was your neighbour's ſon, Dick Worthy, who was always cramming his head with Greek and Latin at ſchool; he wanted to borrow of me the other day, but I was too cunning.

Old Phil. Ay, ay—Let him draw bills of exchange in Greek and Latin, and ſee where he will get a pound ſterling for them.

G. Phil. So I told him—I went to him to his garret, in the Minories; and there I found him in all his miſery! and a fine ſcene it was—There was his wife in a corner of the room, at a waſhing tub, up to the elbows in ſuds; a ſolitary pork-ſtake was dangling by a bit of pack-thread, before a melancholy fire; himſelf ſeated at a three-legg'd table, writing a pamphlet againſt the German war; a child upon his left-knee, his right-leg employ'd in rocking a cradle with a brattling in it— And ſo there was buſineſs enough for them all—His wife rubbing away [*mimicks a waſher-woman*] and he writing on, "The king of Pruſſia ſhall have no more "ſubſidies; Saxony ſhall be indemnify'd—He ſhan't "have a foot in Sileſia." There is a ſweet little baby! [*to the child on his knee*] then he rock'd the cradle, huſh ho! huſh ho!—then twiſted the griſkin, [*ſnaps his fingers*] huſh ho! "The Ruſſians ſhall have Pruſſia," [*writes*] The wife [*waſhes and ſings*] he—"There's a dear." Round goes the griſkin again, [*ſnaps his Finger*] " and Canada muſt be reſtor'd" [*writes*]—and ſo you have a picture of the whole family. *Old*

Old. Phil. Ha, ha! What becomes of his Greek and Latin now? Fine words butter no parfnips—He had no money from you, I fuppofe, George?

G. Phil. Oh! no; charity begins at home, fays I.

Old Phil. And it was wifely faid—I have an excellent faying when any man wants to borrow of me—I am ready with my joke—"a fool and his money are foon parted"—ha, ha, ha!

G. Phil. Ha, ha——An old fkin-flint. [*Afide.*]

Old Phil. Ay, ay——a fool and his money are foon parted——ha, ha, ha!

G. Phil. Now if I can wring a handfome fum out of him, it will prove the truth of what he fays. [*Afide.*] And yet trade has its inconveniencies—Great houfes ftopping payment!

Old Phil. Hey—what! you look chagrin'd!—Nothing of that fort has happen'd to thee, I hope?——

G. Phil. A great houfe at Cadiz—— Don John de Alvarada—The Spanifh Galleons not making quick returns——and fo my bills are come back.

Old Phil. Ay!——[*Shakes his head.*]

G. Phil. I have indeed a remittance from Meffina. That voyage yields me thirty *per cent.* profit—But this blow coming upon me——

Old Phil. Why this is unlucky——how much money?

G. Phil. Three and twenty hundred.

Old Phil. George, too many eggs in one bafket; I'll tell thee, George, I expect Sir Jafper Wilding here prefently to conclude the treaty of marriage I have on foot for thee: then hufh this up, fay nothing of it, and in a day or two you pay thefe bills with his daughter's portion.

G. Phil. The old rogue [*afide.*] That will never do, I fhall be blown upon Change—Alvarada will pay in time—He has open'd his affairs—He appears a good man.

Old Phil. Does he?

G. Phil. A great fortune left; will pay in time, but I muft crack before that.

Old Phil. It is unlucky! A good man you fay he is?

G. Phil. No body better. *Old*

Old Phil. Let me see——Suppose I lend this money?

G. Phil. Ah, Sir.

Old Phil. How much is your remittance from Meffina?

G. Phil. Seven hundred and fifty.

Old Phil. Then you want fifteen hundred and fifty.

G. Phil. Exactly.

Old Phil. Don Alvarada is a good man you fay?

G. Phil. Yes, Sr.

Old Phil. I will venture to lend the money—You muft allow me commiffion upon thofe bills for taking them up for honour of the drawer.

G. Phil. Agreed.

Old Phil. Lawful intereft, while I am out of my money.

G. Phil. I fubfcribe.

Old Phil A power of attorney to receive the monies from Alvarada, when he makes a payment.

G. Phil. You fhall have it.

Old Phil. Your own bond.

G. Phil. To be fure.

Old Phil. Go and get me a check—You fhall have a draught on the bank.

G. Phil. Yes, Sir, (*going.*)

Old Phil. But ftay—I had forgot—I muft fell out for this—Stocks are under *par*——You muft pay the difference.

G. Phil. Was ever fuch a leech, (*afide*). By all means, Sir.

Old Phil. Step and get me a check.

G. Phil. A fool and his money are foon parted. [*afide.*
[*Exit* G. Philpot.

OLD PHILPOT, *Solus.*

What with commiffion, lawful intereft, and his paying the difference of the ftocks, which are higher now than when I bought in, this will be no bad morning's work; and then in the evening, I fhall be in the rareft fpirits for this new adventure I am recommended to—Let me fee—what is the lady's name, [*Takes a letter out.*] Corinna! ay, ay, by the defcrip-

tion

tion she is a bale of goods—I shall be in rare spirits—
Ay, this is the way, to indulge one's passions and yet
conceal them, and to mind one's business in the city
here, as if one had no passions at all—I long for the
evening methinks—Body o'me—I am a young man
still.

Enter QUILDRIVE.

Quill. Sir Jasper Wilding, Sir, and his daughter.

Old Phil. I am at home.

Enter Sir JASPER *and* MARIA.

[*Sir Jasper dressed as a Fox-hunter, and singing.*

Old Phil. Sir Jasper, your very humble servant.

Sir Jasp. Master Philpot, I be glad to zee ye, I
am indeed.

Old Phil. The like compliment to you, Sir Jasper.
Miss Maria, I kiss your fair hand.

Maria. Sir, your most obedient.

Sir Jasper. Ay, ay, I ha brought un to zee you—
There's my girl—I ben't asham'd of my girl.

Maria. That's more than I can say of my father—
luckily these people are as much strangers to decorum
as my old gentleman, otherwise this visit from a lady
to meet her lover would have an odd appearance——
Tho' but late a boarding-school girl, I know enough
of the world for that.   [*Aside.*

Old Phil. Truly she is a blooming young lady, Sir
Jasper, and I verily shall like to take an interest in her.

Sir Jasp. I ha brought her to zee ye, and zo your zon
may ha' her as soon as he will.

Old Phil. Why she looks three and a half *per cent.*
better than when I saw her last.

Maria. Then there is hopes that in a little time, I
shall be above *par*—he rates me like a lottery-ticket.
                                               [*Aside.*

Old Phil. Ay, ay, I doubt not, Sir Jasper: Miss has
the appearance of a very sensible, discreet young lady;
and to deal freely, without that she would not do for
my son—George is a shrewd lad, and I have often
heard him declare, no consideration should ever prevail
on him to marry a fool.

Maria,

Maria. Ay, you have told me so before, old gentleman, and I have my cue from my brother; and
if I don't soon give master George a surfeit of me, why
then I am not a notable girl. [*Aside.*]

Enter GEORGE PHILPOT.

G. Phil. A good clever old cuff this—after my own
heart—I think I'll have his daughter, if it's only for
the pleasure of hunting with him.

Sir Jasp. Zon-in-law, gee us your hand—What
zay you? Are you ready for my girl?

G. Phil. Say grace as soon as you will, Sir, I'll fall
too.

Sir Jasp. Well zaid—I like you—I like un master
Philpot—I like un—I'll tell you what, let un talk to
her now.

Old Phil. And so he shall—George, she is a bale of
goods; speak her fair now, and then you'll be in cash.

G. Phil. I think I had rather not speak to her now—
I hate speaking to those modest women—Sir,—Sir, a
word in your ear; had not I better break my mind,
by advertising for her in a new's-paper?

Old Phil. Talk sense to her, George; she is a notable girl———and I'll give the draft upon the bank
presently.

Sir Jasp. Come along, master Philpot———come
along; I ben't afraid of my girl——come along.
[*Exeunt* Sir Jasp. *and* Old Phil.]

Maria. A pretty sort of a lover they have found
for me. [*Aside.*]

G. Phil. How shall I speak my mind to her? She
is almost a stranger to me. [*Aside.*]

Maria. Now I'll make the hideous thing hate me if
I can. [*Aside.*]

G. Phil. Ay, she is as sharp as a needle, I warrant
her. [*Aside.*]

Maria. When will he begin?—Ah, you fright! You
rival Mr. Beaufort! I'll give him an aversion to me,
that's what I will; and so let him have the trouble of
breaking off the match: not a word yet—he is in a fine
confusion [*Looks foolish*] I think I may as well sit down,
Sir.   D   *G. Phil.*

G. Phil. Ma'am—I—I—I—[*frighted.*]—I'll hand you a chair, Ma'am——there, Ma'am.

[*Bows awkwardly.*

Maria. Sir, I thank you.

G. Phil. I'll fit down too.   [*In confusion.*]

Maria. Heigho!

G. Phil. Ma'am!

Maria. Sir!

G. Phil. I thought——I——I——did not you say something, Ma'am?

Maria. No, Sir; nothing.

G. Phil. I beg your pardon, Ma'am.

Maria. Oh! you are a fweet creature. [*Afide.*]

G. Phil. The ice is broke now; I have begun, and fo I'll go on.[*Sits filent, looks foolifh, and fteals a look at her.*

Maria. An agreeable interview this!

G. Phil. Pray, Ma'am, do you ever go to concerts?

Maria. Concerts! what's that, Sir?

G. Phil. A mufick meeting.

Maria. I have been at a Quaker's meeting; but never at a mufick meeting.

G. Phil. Lord, Ma'am, all the gay world goes to concerts——She notable! I'll take courage, fhe is nobody——will you give me leave to prefent you a ticket for the Crown and Anchor, Ma'am.

Maria. [*Looking fimple and awkward.*]—A ticket— what's a ticket?

G. Phil. There, Ma'am, at your fervice.

Maria. [*Curtfys awkwardly.*] I long to fee what a ticket is.

G. Phil. What a curtfy there is for the St. James's end of the town! I hate her; fhe feems to be an ideot.

[*Afide.*

Maria. Here's a charming ticket he has given me. [*Afide.*] And is this a ticket, Sir?

G. Phil. Yes, Ma'am——And is this a ticket.

[*Mimicks her afide.*

Maria. [*Reads.*] For fale by the candle, the following goods—thirty chefs ftraw hats—fifty tubs chip hats—pepper, fago, borax——ha—ha! Such a ticket!

. *Phil.*

G. Phil. I—I—I have made a miftake Ma'am——here, here is the right one.

Maria. You need not mind it, Sir,—I never go to fuch places.

G. Phil. No, Ma'am—I don't know what to make of her—Was you ever at the White-Conduit-houfe?

Maria. There's a queftion. [*Afide.*] Is that a nobleman's feat?

G. Phil. [*Laughs.*] Simpleton!—No Mifs—is it not a nobleman's feat—Lord! it's at Iflington.

Maria. Lord Iflington!——I don't know my Lord Iflington.

G. Phil. The town of Iflington.

Maria. I have not the honour of knowing his Lordfhip.

G. Phil. Iflington is a town, Ma'am.

Maria. Oh! it's a town.

G. Phil. Yes, Ma'am.

Maria. I am glad of it.

G. Phil. What is fhe glad of?

Maria. A pretty hufband my papa has chofe for me.
[*Afide.*

G. Phil. What fhall I fay to her next? Have you been at the burletta, Ma'am?

Maria. Where?

G. Phil. The burletta.

Maria. Sir, I would have you to know that I am no fuch perfon——I go to burlettas! I am not what you take me for.

G. Phil. Ma'am——

Maria. I'm come of good people, Sir; and have been properly educated as a young girl ought to be.

G. Phil. What a damn'd fool fhe is. [*Afide.*]—The burletta is an opera, Ma'am.

Maria. Opera, Sir! I don't know what you mean by this ufage——to affront me in this manner!

G. Phil. Affront! I mean quite the reverfe, Ma'am; I took you for a connoiffeur.

Maria. Who me a connoiffeur, Sir! I defire you won't call me fuch names; I am fure I never fo much as thought of such a thing. Sir, I won't be call'd a connoisseur——I won't——I won't——I won't.

[Bursts out a crying.

G. Phil. Ma'am, I meant no offence—A connoisseur is a virtuoso.

Maria. Don't virtuoso me! I am no virtuoso, Sir, I would have you to know it—I am as virtuous a girl as any in England, and I will never be a virtuoso.

[Cries bitterly.

G. Phil. But, Ma'am, you mistake me quite.

Maria. [*In a passion, choaking her tears and sobbing.*] Sir, I am come of as virtuous people as any in England—My family was always remarkable for virtue—My mamma [*bursts out*] was as a good a woman as ever was born, and my aunt Bridget [*sobbing*] was a virtuous woman too——And there's my sister Sophy makes as good and as virtuous a wife as any at all—And so, Sir, don't call me a virtuoso——I won't be brought here to be treated in this manner, I won't—I won't—I won't. *[Cries bitterly.*

G. Phil. The girl's a natural—So much the better. I'll marry her, and lock her up—Ma'am, upon my word you misunderstand me.

Maria Sir [*drying her tears*] I won't be call'd connoisseur by you nor any body—And I am no virtuoso—I'd have you to know that.

G. Phil. Ma'am, connoisseur and virtuoso are words for a person of taste.

Maria. Taste! [*Sobbing.*]

G. Phil. Yes, Ma'am.

Maria. And did you mean to say as how I am a person of taste?

G. Phil. Undoubtedly.

Maria. Sir, your most obedient humble servant; Oh! that's another thing—I have a taste to be sure.

G. Phil. I know you have, Ma'am——O you're a cursed ninny. *[Aside.*

Maria. Yes, I know I have——I can read tolerably; and I begin to write a little.

G. Phil. Upon my word, you have made a great progress!——What could old Square-Toes mean by

passing

paſſing her upon me for a ſenſible girl? And what a
fool I was to be afraid to ſpeak to her——I'll talk to
her openly at once——Come ſit down, Miſs——Pray
Ma'am, are you inclin'd to matrimony?

Maria. Yes, Sir.

G. Phil. Are you in love?

Maria. Yes, Sir.

G. Phil. Thoſe naturals are always amorous [*aſide.*]
How ſhould you like me?

Maria. Of all things——

G. Phil. A girl without ceremony, [*aſide*] Do you
love me?

Maria. Yes, Sir.

G. Phil. But you don't love any body elſe?

Maria. Yes, Sir.

G. Phil. Frank and free, (*aſide*). But not ſo well
as me?

Maria. Yes, Sir.

G. Phil. Better may be?

Maria. Yes, Sir.

G. Phil. The devil you do! [*aſide.*] And, perhaps,
if I ſhould marry you I ſhould have a chance to be
made a——

Maria. Yes, Sir.

G. Phil. The caſe is clear; Miſs Maria, your very
humble ſervant; you are not for my money, I promiſe you.

Maria. Sir.

G. Phil. I have done, Ma'am, that's all, and I take
my leave.

Maria. But you'll marry me?

G. Phil. No, Ma'am, no;—No ſuch thing—You
may provide yourſelf a huſband elſewhere, I am your
humble ſervant.

Maria. Not marry me, Mr. Philpot?——But you
muſt——my papa ſaid you muſt——And I will have
you.

G. Phil. There's another proof of her nonſenſe,
[*aſide.*] Make yourſelf eaſy, for I ſhall have nothing
to do with you.

Maria.

Maria. Not marry me Mr. Philpot? (*bursts out in tears*) but I say you shall, and I will have a husband, or I'll know the reason why—You shall—You shall—

G. Phil. A pretty sort of a wife they intend for me here——

Maria. I wonder you an't asham'd of yourself to affront a young girl in this manner. I'll go and tell my papa—I will—I will—I will.   [*crying bitterly.*

G. Phil. And so you may—I have no more to say to you—and so your servant, Miss—your servant.

Maria. Ay! and by goles! my brother Bob shall fight you.

G. Phil. What care I for your brother Bob? [*going.*

Maria. How can you be so cruel, Mr. Philpot? how can you—oh--[*cries and strugles with him. Exit* G. Phil. Ha! ha! I have carried my brother's scheme into execution charmingly; ha! ha! He will break off the match now of his own accord——Ha! ha! This is charming; this is fine; this is like a girl of spirit.

END of the FIRST ACT.

⸭⸺⸭⸺⸭⸺⸭⸺⸭⸺⸭⸺⸭⸺⸭⸺⸭⸺⸭⸺⸭⸺

ACT II.   SCENE I.

Enter CORINNA, TOM *following her.*

Cor. AN elderly gentleman did you say?

Tom. Yes; that says he has got a letter for you, Ma'am.

Cor. Desire the gentleman to walk up stairs. [*Exit.* Tom.] These old fellows will be coming after a body —but they pay well, and so——Servant, Sir.

Enter OLD PHILPOT.

Old Phil. Fair Lady, your very humble servant— Truly a blooming young girl! Madam, I have a letter here for you from Bob Poacher, whom, I presume, you know.

Cor. Yes, Sir, I know Bob Poacher—He is a very good friend of mine; (*reads to herself*) he speaks so handsomely of you, Sir, and says you are so much of
the

the gentleman, that, to be sure, Sir, I shall endeavour
to be agreeable, Sir.

Old Phil. Really you are very agreeable—You see
I am punctual to my hour.

[*Looks at his watch.*

Cor. That is a mighty pretty watch, Sir.

Old Phil. Yes, Madam, it is a repeater; it has been
in our family for a long time—This is a mighty pretty
lodging—I have twenty guineas here in a purse, here
they are; (*turns them out upon the table*) as pretty
golden rogues as ever fair fingers play'd with.

Cor. I am always agreeable to any thing from a
gentleman.

Old Phil. There are [*aside.*] some light guineas
among them——I always put off my light guineas in
this way——You are exceedingly welcome, Madam.
Your fair hand looks so tempting, I must kiss it——
Oh! I could eat it up—Fair lady, your lips look so
cherry——They actually invite the touch; (*kisses*)
really it makes the difference of *cent. per cent.* in one's
constitution—You have really a mighty pretty foot
—Oh, you little rogue—I could smother you with
kisses—Oh you little delicate, charming—[*kisses her.*

GEORGE PHILPOT, *within.*

G. Phil. Gee-houp!—Awhi!—Awhi! Gallows!
Awhi!

Old Phil. Hey——What is all that?—Somebody
coming!

Cor. Some young rake, I fancy, coming in whether
my servants will or no.

Old Phil. What shall I do?—I would not be seen
for the world——Can't you hide me in that room?

Cor. Dear heart! no, Sir——These wild young
fellows take such liberties——He may take it into his
head to go in there, and then you will be detected—
Get under the table—He shan't remain long whoever
he is—Here—Here, Sir, get under here.

Old Phil. Ay, ay; that will do——Don't let him
stay long--Give me another buss--Wounds! I could—

Cor. Hush!——Make haste.

Old Phil. Ay; ay; I will fair lady—[*Creeps under the table and peeps out.*] Don't let him ſtay long.

Cor. Huſh! Silence! you will ruin all elſe.

Enter G. PHILPOT, *dreſs'd out.*

G. Phil. Sharper do your work—Awhi! Awhi! So my girl——how doſt do?

Cor. Very well, thank you—I did not expect to ſee you ſo ſoon—I thought you was to be at the club—— The ſervants told me you came back from the city at two o'clock to dreſs, and ſo I concluded you would have ſtaid all night as uſual.

G. Phil. No; the run was againſt me again, and I did not care to purſue ill-fortune. But I am ſtrong in caſh, my girl.

Cor. Are you?

G. Phil. Yes, yes——Suſkins in plenty.

Old Phil. [*peeping*] Ah the ungracious! Theſe are your haunts, are they?

G. Phil. Yes, yes; I am ſtrong in caſh——I have taken in old curmudgeon ſince I ſaw you.

Cor. As how, pray?

Old Phil. [*peeping out*] Ay, as how; let us hear, pray.

G. Phil. Why, I'll tell you.

Old Phil. [*peeping*] Ay! let us hear.

G. Phil. I talk'd a world of wiſdom to him.

Old Phil. Ay!

G. Phil. Tipt him a few raſcally ſentiments of a ſcoundrelly kind of prudence.

Old Phil. Ay!

G. Phil. The old curmudgeon chuckled at it.

Old Phil. Ay, ay; the old curmudgeon! ay, ay.

G. Phil. He is a ſad old fellow!

Old Phil. Ay! Go on.

G. Phil. And ſo I appear'd to him as deſerving of the gallows as he is himſelf.

Old Phil. Well ſaid boy, well ſaid—Go on.

G. Phil. And then he took a liking to me—Ay, ay, ſays he, ay, friendſhip has nothing to do with trade— George, thou art a ſon after my own heart; and then as I dealt out little maxims of penury, he grinn'd like a Jew broker, when he has cheated his principal of an eighth *per cent.*——And cried ay, ay, that is the very spirit of trade——A fool and his money are soon parted——(*mimicking him*) and so, on he went, like Harlequin in a French comedy, tickling himself into a good humour, till, at last, I tickled him out of fifteen hundred and odd pounds.

Old Phil. I have a mind to rise and break his bones—But then I discover myself—Lie still, Isaac, lie still.

G. Phil. Oh! I understand trap——I talked of a great house stopping payment——The thing was true enough, but I had no dealing with them.

Old. Phil. Ay, ay.

G. Phil. And so, for fear of breaking off a match with an ideot he wants me to marry, he lent me the money, and cheated me tho'.

Old Phil. Ay, you have found it out—Have ye?

G. Phil. No old usurer in England, grown hard-hearted in his trade, could have dealt worse with me—I must have commission upon these bills for taking them up for honour of the drawer—Your bond—Lawful interest, while I am out of my money; and the difference for selling out of the stocks——an old miserly good for nothing skin-flint.

Old Phil. My blood boils to be at him—Go on, can you tell us a little more?

G. Phil. Po! he is an old curmudgeon—And so I will talk no more about him—Come give me a kiss.

[*They kiss.*

Old Phil. The young dog, how he fastens his lips to her!

G. Phil. You shall go with me to Epsom next Sunday.

Cor. Shall I? That's charming.

G. Phil. You shall, in my chariot—I drive.

Cor. But I don't like to see you drive.

G. Phil. But I like it, I am as good a coachman as any in England—There was my lord—What d'ye call him—He kept a stage-coach for his own driving, but, Lord! he was nothing to me.

E   *Cor.*

Cor. No!

G. Phil. Oh! no—I know my road-work, my girl, —When I have my coachman's hat on—is my hat come home?

Cor It hangs up yonder! but I don't like it.

G. Phil. Let me fee it———Ay! the very thing——— Mind me when I go to work———Throw my eyes about a few———Handle the braces———Take the off-leader by the jaw———Here you———how have you curbed this horfe up?———Let him out a link, do you blood of a—Whoo Eh!—Jewel—Button!—Whoo Eh! Come here, you Sir, how have you coupled Gallows? you know he'll take the bar of Sharper—Take him in two holes, do——There's four pretty little knots as any in England———Whoo Eh!

Cor. But can't you let your coachman drive?

G. Phil. No, no——See me mount the box, handle the reins, my wrift turned down, fquare my elbows, ftamp with my foot———Gee up!——Off we go——— Button, do you want to have us over!——Do your work do—Awhi! awhi!———There we bowl away; fee how fharp they are———Gallows!—Softly up hi' [*whiftles*]there's a public-houfe—Give 'em a mouthful of water, do—And fetch me a dram—Drink it off— Gee up! Awhi! Awhi!———There we go fcrambling altogether———Reach Epfom in an hour and forty-three minutes, all Lombard-ftreet to an egg-fhell, we do—There's your work my girl!—Eh! damn me.

Old. Phil. Mercy on me! What a profligate de-dauched young dog it is.

Enter YOUNG WILDING.

Wild. Ha! my little Corinna———Sir, your fervant.

G. Phil. Your fervant, Sir.

Wild. Sir, your Servant.

G. Phil. Any commands for me, Sir?

Wild. For you, Sir?

G. Phil. Yes, for me, Sir?

Wild. No, Sir, I have no commands for you.

G. Phil. What's your bufinefs?

Wild. Bufinefs!

G. Phil. Ay, bufinefs.

Wild.

Wild. Why, very good business I think—My little
Corinna—My life—My little——

G Phil. Is that your business?—Pray, Sir,——Not
so free, Sir.

Wild. Not so free!

G. Phil. No, Sir! that lady belongs to me.

Wild. To you, Sir!

G. Phil. Yes, to me.

Wild. To you! Who are you?

G. Phil. As good a man as you.

Wild. Upon my word!——Who is this fellow,
Corinna? Some journeyman-taylor, I suppose, who
chuses to try on the gentleman's cloaths before he
carries them home.

G. Phil. Taylor!—What do you mean by that?
You lie! I am no taylor.

Wild. You shall give me satisfaction for that!

G. Phil. For what?

Wild. For giving me the lie.

G. Phil. I did not.

Wild. You did, Sir.

G. Phil. You lie; I'll bet you five pounds I did not
—But if you have a mind for a frolick—Let me put
by my sword—Now, Sir, come on [*In a boxing attitude.*

Wild. Why, you scoundrel, do you think I want
to box? Draw, Sir, this moment.

G. Phil. Not I——come on.

Wild. Draw, or I'll cut you to pieces.

G. Phil. I'll give you satisfaction this way [*pushes
at him.*]

Wild. Draw, Sir, Draw; You won't draw!——
There, take that, Sirrah—and that—and that, you
scoundrel.

Old Phil. Ay, ay; well done; lay it on—[*peeps out.*

Wild. And there you rascal; and there.

Old Phil. Thank you; thank you—Could not you
find in your heart to lay him on another for me?

Cor. Pray, don't be in such a passion, Sir.

Wild. My dear, Corinna, don't be frighten'd; I
shall not murder him.

Old Phil. I am fafe here—lie ftill Ifaac, lie ftill—
I am fafe——

Wild. The fellow has put me out of breath. [*Sits down.*] [Old Philpot's *watch ftrikes ten under the table*] Whofe watch is that? [*ftairs round*] Hey! what is all this? [*looks under the table*] your humble fervant, Sir! Turn out pray, turn out—You won't—Then I'll unfhell you. [*Takes away the table.*] Your very humble fervant, Sir.

G. Phil. Zounds! my father there all this time!
[*Afide.*]

Wild. I fuppofe you will give me the lie too?

Old Phil. [*Still on the ground.*] No Sir; not I truly, But the gentleman there may divert himfelf again if he has a mind.

Wild. No, Sir, not I; I pafs.

Old Phil. George, you are there I fee.

G. Phil. Yes, Sir, and you are there I fee.

Wild. Come rife—Who is this old fellow?

Cor. Upon my word I don't know—As I live and breathe I don't—he came after my maid, I fuppofe; I'll go and afk her—let me run out of the way, and hide myfelf from this fcene of confufion.
[*Exit* Corinna.

G. Phil. What an Imp of hell fhe is. [*Afide.*

Wild. Come, get up Sir; you are too old to be beat.

Old Phil. [*Rifing.*] In troth, fo I am—But there you may exercife yourfelf again if you pleafe.

G. Phil. No more for me, Sir—I thank you.

Old Phil. I have made but a bad voyage of it—The fhip is funk, and ftock and block loft. [*Afide.*

Wild. Ha, ha! upon my foul, I can't help laug at his old fquare toes—As for you, Sir, you have had what you deferv'd—Ha, ha! you are a kind cull, I fuppofe—ha, ha! And you, reverend dad, you muft come here tottering after a punk, ha, ha!

Old Phil. Oh! George! George!

G. Phil. Oh! father! father!

Wild. Ha, ha! what father and fon! And fo you have found one another out, ha, ha!——Well, you

3   may

may have bufinefs, and fo, gentlemen, I'll leave you
to yourfelves.   [*Exit.*

G. Phil. This is too much to bear——What an in-
famous jade fhe is! All her contrivance!——don't be
angry with me, Sir—I'll go my ways this moment, tie
myfelf up in this matrimonial noofe—and never have
any thing to do with thefe courfes again.   [*Going.*

Old Phil. And hark you, George; tie me up in a
real noofe, and turn me off as foon as you will. [*Exeunt.*

Enter BEAUFORT, *dreffed as a lawyer, and* SIR JAS-
PER WILDING, *with a bottle and glafs in his hand.*

Beau. No more, Sir Jafper, I can't drink any more.

Sir Jafp. Why you be but a weezen-fac'd drinker,
mafter Quagmire—come, man, finifh this bottle.

Beau. I beg to be excufed—you had better let me
read over the deeds to you.

Sir Jafp. Zounds! it's all about out-houfes, and
meffuages, and barns, and ftables, and orchards, and
meadows, and lands and tenements, and woods and
underwoods, and commons, and backfides. I am o'the
commiffion for Wilts, and I know the ley, and fo truce
with your jargon, mafter Quagmire.

Beau. But, Sir, you don't confider, marriage is an
affair of importance——it is contracted between per-
fons, firft confenting; fecondly, free from canonical
impediments; thirdly, free from civil impediments,
and can only be diffolved for canonical caufes or levi-
tical caufes——See *Leviticus* xviii. and xxviii Harry
VIII. chapter vii.

Sir Jafp. You fhall drink t'other Bumper, an you
talk of ley.

Enter a Servant.

Ser. Old Mr. Philpot, Sir, and his fon.

Sir Jafp. Wounds! that's right, they'll take me
out of the hand of this lawyer here.   [*Exit.*

BEAUFORT, *folus.*

Beau. Well done, Beaufort! thus far you have
play'd your part, as if you had been of the pumple-
nofe family of Furnival's-Inn.

Sir

Sir Jasp. Master Philpot, I be glad you are come; this man here has so plagued me with his ley, but now we'll have no more about it, but sign the papers at once.

Old Phil. Sir Jasper, twenty thousand Pounds you know is a great deal of money——I should not give you so much, if it was not for the sake of your daughter's marrying my son; so that if you will allow me discount for prompt payment, I will pay the money down.

G. Phil. Sir, I must beg to see the young lady once more, before I embark; for to be plain, Sir, she appears to me a mere natural.

Sir Jasp. I'll tell you what, youngster, I find my girl a notable wench—and here, here's zon Bob.

Enter YOUNG WILDING.

Sir Jasp. Bob, gee us your hand——I ha' finish'd the business—and zo now—here, here, here's your vather-in-law.

Old Phil. Of all the birds in the air, is that he ![*Aside.*

G. Phil. He has behav'd like a relation to me already. [*Aside.*

Sir Jasp. Go to un man—that's your vather——

Wild. This is the strangest accident——Sir—— Sir——[*stifling a laugh*] I——!—Sir—upon my soul, I can't stand this. [*Bursts out a laughing.*]

Old Phil. I deserve it! I deserve to be laught at.
[*Aside.*

G. Phil. He has shewn his regard to his sister's family already. [*Aside.*

Sir Jasp. What's the matter, Bob? I tell you this is your vather-in-law--[*Pulls* Old Philpot *to him.*]Master Philpot, that's Bob—Speak to un Bob—speak to un—

Wild. Sir—I—I am [*stifles a laugh*] I say, Sir—— I am, Sir—extremely proud—of—of——

G. Phil. Of having beat me, I suppose. [*Aside.*

Wild. Of the honour, Sir—of—of— [*Laughs.*

G. Phil. Ay! that's what he means. [*Aside.*

Wild. And, Sir—I—I— this opportunity—I cannot look him in the face——[*bursts out into a laugh*] ha, ha! I cannot stay in the room——[*Going.*

Sir

Sir Jasp. Why the volks are all mad, I believe! you shall stay, Bob; you shall stay. [*Holds him.*

Wild. Sir I——I cannot possibly——

[*Whispers his father.*

Old Phil. George, George! what a woeful figure do we make!

G. Phil. Bad enough of all conscience, Sir.

Sir Jasp. An odd adventure, Bob. [*Laughs heartily.*

Old Phil. Ay! there now he is hearing the whole affair, and is laughing at me.

Sir Jasp. Ha, ha! Po, never mind it——a did not hurt un.

Old Phil. It's all discover'd.

Sir Jasp. Ha, ha!——I told ye zon Bob could find a hare squat upon her form with any he in Christendom —ha, ha! never mind it man, Bob meant no harm— here, here, Bob—here's your vather, and there's your brother——I should like to ha'zeen un under the table.

Wild. Gentlemen, your most obedient.

[*Stifling a laugh.*

Old Phil. Sir, your servant—He has lick'd George well——and I forgive him.

Sir Jasp. Well, young gentleman, which way is your mind now.

G. Phil. Why, Sir, to be plain, I find your daughter an ideot.

Sir Jasp. Zee her again then——zee her again ——here, you, sirrah, send our Moll hither.

Ser. Yes, Sir.

Sir Jasp. Very well then, we'll go into t'other room, crack a bottle, and settle matters there; and leave un together——Hoic! hoic——Our Moll—— Tally over

Enter MARIA.

Maria. Did you call me, papa?

Sir Jasp. I did, my girl—There, the gentleman wants to speak with you—Behave like a clever wench as you are——come along my boys——Master Quagmire, come and finish the business.

[*Exit singing, with* Old Philpot *and* Beaufort, *manent* George *and* Maria.]

G. Phil.

G. Phil. I know she is a fool, and so I will speak to her without ceremony—Well, Miss, you told me you could read and write?

Maria. Read, Sir, Heavens !——[*Looking at him.* ha, ha, ha !

G. Phil. What does she laugh at ?

Maria. Ha, ha, ha, ha !

G. Phil. What diverts you so, pray ?

Maria. Ha, ha, ha ! What a fine taudry figure you have made of yourself ? ha, ha !

G. Phil. Figure, Madam !

Maria. I shall die, I shall die ! ha, ha, ha !

G. Phil. Do you make a laughing-stock of me ?

Maria. No, Sir, by no means——ha, ha, ha !

G. Phil. Let me tell you, Miss, I don't understand being treated thus.

Maria. Sir, I can't possibly help it—I—I—ha, ha !

G. Phil. I shall quit the room, and tell your papa, if you go on thus.

Maria. Sir, I beg your pardon a thousand times---I am but a giddy girl--I cannot help it--I--I--ha, ha !

G. Phil. Ma'am, this is down right insult.

Maria. Sir, you look somehow or other——I don't know how, so comically——ha, ha ha !

G. Phil. Did you never see a gentleman dress'd before ?

Maria. Never like you---I beg your pardon, Sir---ha, ha, ha !

G. Phil. Now here is an ideot in spirits---I tell you this is your ignorance——I am dress'd in high taste.

Maria. Yes, so you are——ha, ha, ha !

G. Phil. Will you have done laughing ?

Maria. Yes, Sir, I will——I will——there—— there——there——I have done.

G. Phil. Do so then, and behave yourself a little sedate.

Maria. I will, Sir;——I won't look at him, and then I shan't laugh——

G. Phil. Let me tell you, Miss, that nobody understands dress better than I do.

Maria. Ha, ha, ha !

G. Phil. She's mad sure.

Maria.

Maria. No, Sir, I am not mad—I have done, Sir—
I have done—I assure you, Sir, that no body is more
averse from ill manners, and would take greater pains
not to affront a gentleman——ha, ha, ha!

G. Phil. Again! Zounds! What do you mean!
you'll put me in a passion, I can tell you, presently.

Maria. I can't help it—Indeed I can't—Beat me if
you will, but let me laugh--I can't help it—ha, ha, ha!

G. Phil. I never met with such usage in my life.

Maria. I shall die—Do, Sir, let me laugh—It will
do me good---ha, ha, ha !

[*Falls down in a fit of laughing.*]

G. Phil. If this is your way, I won't stay a moment
longer in the room——I'll go this moment and tell
your father.

Maria. Sir, Sir, Mr. Philpot, don't be so hasty, Sir
—I have done, Sir ; it's over now---I have had my
laugh out—I am a giddy girl—but I'll be grave——
I'll compose myself and act a different scene with
him from what I did in the morning. I have all the
materials of an impertinent wit, and I will now
twirl him about the room, like a boy setting up his
top with his finger and thumb. [*Aside.*]

G. Phil. Miss, I think you told me you can read
and write.

Maria. Read, Sir ! Reading is the delight of my
life——Do you love reading, Sir ?

G. Phil. Prodigiously—How pert she is grown—I
have read very little, and I'm resolv'd for the future
to read less. [*Aside.*] What have you read, Miss?

Maria. Every thing.

G. Phil. You have ?

Maria. Yes, Sir, I have.

G. Phil. Oh ! brave—and do you remember what
you read, Miss?

Maria. Not so well as I could wish—Wits have
short memories.

G. Phil. Oh ! you are a wit too ?

Maria. I am—and do you know that I feel myself
provok'd to a simile now ?

G. Phil. Provok'd to a simile !——Let us hear it !

F *Maria.*

Maria. What do you think we are both like?

G. Phil. Well——

Maria. Like Cymon and Iphigenia in Dryden's fable.

G. Phil. Jenny in Dryden's fable!

Maria. *The fanning breeze upon her bosom blows;*
         To meet the fanning breeze her bosom rose.

That's me——now you.

He trudg'd along, unknowing what he sought,
And whistled as he went [mimicks] *for want of thought.*

G. Phil. This is not the same girl. [*Disconcerted.*

Maria. Mark again, mark again:

The fool of nature stood with stupid eyes,
And gaping mouth that testified surprize.

                    [*He looks foolish, she laughs at him.*

G. Phil I must take care how I speak to her; she is not the fool I took her for.   [*Aside.*

Maria. You seem surpriz'd, Sir——but this is my way—I read, Sir, and then I apply—I have read every thing; Suckling, Waller, Milton, Dryden, Landsdown, Gay, Prior, Swift, Addison, Pope, Young, Thompson.

G. Phil. Hey! the devil—what a clack is here!

                    [*He walks a-cross the stage.*

Maria. [*Following him eagerly.*] Shakespear, Fletcher, Otway, Southern, Rowe, Congreve, Wicherly, Farquhar, Cibber, Vanbrugh, Steel, in short every body; and I find them all wit, fire, vivacity, spirit, genius, taste, imagination, raillery, humour, character, and sentiment—Well done, Miss Notable! you have play'd your part like a young actress in high favour with the town.   [*Aside.*

G. Phil. Her tongue goes like a water-mill.

Maria. What do you say to me now, Sir?

G. Phil. Say!—I don't know what the devil to say.
                    [*Aside.*

Maria. What's the matter, Sir? Why you look as if the stocks were fallen—or like London-bridge at low water—or like a waterman when the Thames is frozen—or like a politician without news—or like a prude without scandal—or like a great lawyer without a brief—or like some lawyers with one—or——

G. Phil.

G. Phil. Or like a poor devil of a husband henpeck'd by a wit, and so say no more of that—What a capricious piece here is! [*Aside.*

Maria. Oh, fy! you have spoil'd all—I had not half done.

G. Phil. There is enough of all conscience—You may content yourself.

Maria. But I can't be so easily contented——I like a simile half a mile long.

G. Phil. I see you do.

Maria. Oh! And I make verses too—verses like an angel—off hand—extempore——Can you give me an extempore?

G. Phil. What does she mean!—no, Miss—I have never a one about me.

Maria. You can't give me an extempore—Oh! for shame, Mr. Philpot—I love an extempore of all things; and I love the poets dearly, their sense so fine, their invention rich as Pactolus.

G. Phil. A poet rich as Pactolus! I have heard of Pactolus in the city.

Maria. Very like.

G. Phil. But you never heard of a poet as rich as he.

Maria. As who?

G. Phil. Pactolus—He was a great Jew merchant—liv'd in the ward of Farringdon without.

Maria. Pactolus, a Jew merchant! Pactolus is a river.

G. Phil. A river!

Maria. Yes—don't you understand geography?

G. Phil. The girl's crazy!

Maria. Oh! Sir—if you don't understand geography, you are nobody—I understand geography, and I understand orthography; you know I told you I can write—and I can dance too—will you dance a minuet? [*Sings and dances.*

G. Phil. You shan't lead me a dance, I promise you.

Maria. Oh! very well, Sir——you refuse me—— remember you'll hear immediately of my being married to another, and then you'll be ready to hang yourself.

G. Phil. Not I, I promise you.

Maria. Oh! very well—very well—remember——
mark my words—I'll do it---you shall see---ha, ha!
[*Runs off in a fit of laughing.*]

GEORGE *solus.*

G. Phil. Marry you! I would as soon carry my wife
to live in Bow-street, and write over the door "Phil-
"pot's punch-house."

Enter OLD PHILPOT *and* Sir JASPER.

Sir Jasp. [*Singing*] "So rarely so bravely we'll hunt
"him over the downs, and we'll hoop and we'll hollow."
Gee us your hand, young gentleman; well——what
zay ye to un now?——Ben't she a clever girl?

G. Phil. A very extraordinary girl indeed.

Sir Jasp Did not I tell un zo——then you have
nothing to do but to consummate as soon as you will.

G. Phil. No, you may keep her, Sir——I thank
you——I'll have nothing to do with her.

Old Phil. What's the matter now, George?

G. Phil. Po! she is a wit.

Sir Jasp. Ay! I told un zo.

G. Phil. And that's worse than t'other——I am off,
Sir.

Sir Jasp. Odds heart! I am afraid you are no great
wit.

Enter MARIA.

Maria. Well, papa, the gentleman won't have
me.

Old Phil. The numskull won't do as his father bids
him; and so, Sir Jasper, with your consent I'll make a
proposal to the young lady myself.

Maria. How! what does he say?

Old Phil. I am in the prime of my days, and I can
be a brisk lover still—Fair Lady, a glance of your eye
is like the returning sun in the spring——It melts
away the frost of age, and gives a new warmth and
vigour to all nature.   [*Falls a coughing.*

Maria. Dear heart! I should like to have a scene
with him.

Sir

Sir Jaſp. Hey! What's in the wind now!——This won't take——My girl ſhall have fair play——No old fellow ſhall totter to her bed——What ſay you, my girl, will you rock his cradle?

Maria. Sir, I have one ſmall doubt——Pray can I have two huſbands at a time?

G. Phil. There's a queſtion now! She is grown fooliſh again.

Old Phil. Fair lady, the law of the land——

Sir Jaſp. Hold ye, hold ye; let me talk of law; I know the law better nor any on ye——Two huſbands at once——No; no——Men are ſcarce, and that's down-right poaching.

Maria. I am ſorry for it, Sir——For then I can't marry him, I ſee.

Sir Jaſp. Why not?

Maria. I am contracted to another.

Sir Jaſp. Contracted! To whom?

Maria. To Mr. Beaufort——That gentleman, Sir.

Old Phil. That gentleman!

Beau. Yes, Sir, [*Throws open his gown*] My name is Beaufort——And, I hope, Sir Jaſper, when you conſider my fortune, and my real affection for your daughter, you will generouſly forgive the ſtratagem I have made uſe of.

Sir Jaſp. Maſter Quagmire! What are you young Beaufort all this time?

Old Phil. That won't take, Sir——That won't take.

Beau. But it muſt take, Sir——You have ſign'd the deeds for your daughter's marriage; and, Sir Jaſper, by this inſtrument has made me his ſon-in-law.

Old Phil. How is this? How is this? Then, Sir Jaſper, you will agree to cancel the deeds, I ſuppoſe, for you know——

Sir Jaſp. Catch me at that, an ye can! I fulfill'd my promiſe, and your ſon refuſed, and ſo the wench has looked out ſlily for herſelf elſewhere. Did I not tell you ſhe was a clever girl? I ben't aſham'd o' my girl!——Our Moll, you have done no harm, and Mr.

Beaufort

Beaufort is welcome to you with all my heart. I'll
ftand to what I have figned, though you have taken
me by furprize.

Wild. Bravo! my fcheme has fucceeded rarely.

Old bil. And fo here I am bubbled and choufed
out of my money——George! George! what a day's
work have we made of it!——Well, if it muft be fo,
be it fo——I defire, young gentleman, you will come
and take my daughter away to-morrow morning——
And, I'll tell you what, here, here—Take my family
watch into the bargain; and I wifh it may play you
juft fuch another trick as it has me; that's all——I'll
never go intriguing with a family watch again.

Maria. Well, Sir! [*To* G. Phil.] what do you
think of me now? An't I a connoiffeur, Sir! and a
virtuofo——ha! ha!

G. Phil. Yes; and much good may do your hufband
——I have been connoiffeur'd among ye to fome purpofe——Bubbled at play——dup'd by my wench——
cudgel'd by a rake——laugh'd at by a girl——detected
by my father——and there is the fum total of all I
have got at this end of the town.

Old Phil. This end of the town! I defire never to
fee it again while I live——I'll pop into a hackney-
coach this moment, drive to Mincing-lane, and never
venture back to this fide of Temple-bar.   [*Going.*]

G. Phil. And, Sir, Sir!——fhall I drive you?

Old Phil. Ay, you or any-body.   [*Exit.*]

G. Phil. I'll overturn the old hocus at the firft corner.   [*Following him.*]

Sir Jafp. They fhan't go zo, neither——they fhall
ftay and crack a bottle.   [*Exit after them.*]

Maria. Well, brother, how have I play'd my part?

Wild.
Beau. } To a miracle.

Maria. Have I?——I don't know how that is——
Love urg'd me on to try all wily arts
To win your—[*To Beaufort.*] *No! not yours——*
    To win your hearts. [*To the Audience.*]
Your hearts to win is now my aim alone;
" There if I grow, the harveft is your own."

                              EPI-

EPILOGUE,

By OLD PHILPOT *and* GEORGE PHILPOT.

Fath. OH! George, George, George! 'tis such
      young rakes as you,
That bring vile jokes, and foul dishonour too,
Upon our city youth.
Geo. —————— ———'Tis very true.
Fath. St. James's end o'th' town———
Geo. —— ——— ——— No place for me.
Fath. No truly—no—their manners disagree
With ours intirely—yet you there must run,
To ape their follies———
Geo. —— ——— And so am undone.
Fath. There you all learn a vanity in vice,
You turn mere fops——you game
Geo. —— ——— ——— Oh damn the dice.
Fath. Bubbled at play———
Geo. —— ——— Yes, Sir———
Fath. —— ——— — By every common cheat.
Geo. Ay! here's two witnesses—[*Pulls out his pockets.*]
Fath. —— ——— You get well beat.
Geo. A witness too of that, [*shews his head*] and there's
      another.   [*To* Young Wilding.
Fath. You dare to give affronts———
Geo. —— —— ———Zounds such a pother!—
Fath. Affronts to gentlemen!
Geo. —— . ——— ——'Twas a rash action——
Fath. Damn'e, you lie! I'll give you satisfaction.
                    [*Mimicking.*]
Drawn in by strumpets, and detected too!
Geo. That's a sad thing, Sir! I'll be judg'd by you—
Fath. The dog he has me there——
Geo. —— ——— ——— Think you it right—
Under a table———
Fath. —— ——— Miserable plight!
Geo. For grave threescore to sculk with trembling
      knees,
And envy each young lover that he sees!
Think you it fitting thus abroad to roam?
Fath. Wou'd I had stay'd to cast accounts at home.

G e

Geo. Ay! there's another vice——

Fath. —— —— —— Sirrah give o'er,

Geo. You brood for ever o'er your much lov'd store,
And scraping *cent. per cent.* still pine for more.
At Jonathan's, where millions are undone,
Now cheat a nation, and now cheat your son.

Fath. Rascal, enough!

Geo. —— —— I could add, but am loth——

Fath. Enough!—this jury [*to the audience*] will con-
vict us both.

Geo. Then to the court we'd better make submission.
Ladies and gentlemen, with true contrition,
I here repent my faults—ye courtly train,
Farewel!—farewel, ye giddy and ye vain!
I now take up—forsake the gay and witty,
To live henceforth a credit to the city.

Fath. You see me here quite cover'd o'er with shame,
I hate long speeches——But I'll do the same.
Come, George——To mend is all the best
can boast.

Geo. Then let us in——

Fath. —— —— And this shall be our toast,
May Britain's thunder on her foes be hurl'd,

Geo. And London prove the market of the world!

F I N I S.

WHAT we must ALL come to:

A

COMEDY

In TWO ACTS,

As it was intended to be ACTED at the

THEATRE-ROYAL in COVENT-GARDEN.

——— Otium et oppidi
Laudat rura sui ———   HOR.
——— Nugæ seria ducent
In mala ———   HOR.

LONDON,

Printed for P. VAILLANT, facing Southampton-street,
in the Strand. MDCCLXIV.

(Price One Shilling.)

Advertisement.

THE idea of the Character of DRUGGET, *in the following piece, was taken from a paper written by Mr.* POPE, *and published in the* Guardian, *No.* 173. *The reader will perceive some strictures of true humour from thence inserted in this little Comedy. The violent differences between* Sir Charles *and* Lady Rackett *about a trifle, and the renewal of those differences by venturing, after they had subsided, to resume the object in thorough good humour, are, it is conceived, founded in Nature, because similar incidents often occur in real life. To shew the passions thus frivolously agitated, and to point out the ridicule springing from their various turns and shiftings, was the main drift of the ensuing scenes. But some people were determined not to hear, and the Author could not be induced by any private motives to send the Performers a second time into so painful a service as that of the Stage always is, when a few are unwilling to be entertained.*

Lincoln's Inn,
January 10, 1764.

Dramatis Personæ.

MEN.

Sir CHARLES RACKETT,	Mr. DYER.
DRUGGET,	Mr. SHUTER.
LOVELACE,	Mr. CUSHING.
WOODLEY,	Mr. WHITE.

WOMEN.

Lady RACKETT,	Miss ELLIOT.
Mrs. DRUGGET,	Mrs. PITT.
NANCY,	Miss HALLAM.
DIMITY,	Mrs. GREEN.

A Servant, &c.

WHAT we must ALL come to.

ACT I.

Enter WOODLEY *and* DIMITY.

Dimity.

O! Po!—no such thing—I tell you, Mr. Woodley, you are a mere novice in these affairs.

Wood. Nay, but listen to reason, Mrs. Dimity—has not your master, Mr. Drugget, invited me down to his country-house, in order to give me his daughter Nancy in marriage; and with what pretence can he now break off?

Dim. What pretence!—you put a body out of all patience—but go on your own way, Sir; my advice is all lost upon you.

Wood. Come now, do me justice—have not I fix'd an interest in the young lady's heart?

Dim. An interest in a fiddlestick?—You ought to have made love to the father and

B   mother

mother — what, do you think the way to get a wife, is by speaking fine things to the lady you've a fancy for? —— That was the practice, indeed, but things are alter'd now — you must address the old people, Sir; and never trouble your head about your mistress — None of your letters, and verses, and soft looks, and fine speeches, — " Have compassion, thou angelic creature, on a poor, dying" — Pshaw! stuff! nonsense! all out of fashion. — Go your ways to the old Curmudgeon, humour his whims — " I shall esteem it an honour, Sir, to be allied to a gentleman of your rank and taste." " Upon my word, he's a pretty young gentleman." — Then wheel about to the mother: " Your daughter, Ma'am, is the very model of you, and I shall adore her for your sake." " Here, come hither, Nancy, take this gentleman for better for worse." " La, Mama, I can never consent."—" I should not have thought of your consent — the consent of your relations is enough: why how now, Hussey! — So away you go to church, the knot is tied, and you quarrel like contrary elements all the rest of your lives — that's the way of the world now.

Wood. But you know, my dear Dimity, the old couple have received every mark of attention from me.

                                    Dim.

Dim. Attention ! to be sure you did not fall asleep in their company ; but what then ? —You should have entered into their characters, play'd with their humours, and sacrificed to their absurdities.

Wood. But if my temper is too frank —

Dim. Frank, indeed ! I hate the word, except when I receive a letter. — Have not you to do with a rich old shopkeeper, retired from business with an hundred thousand pounds in his pocket, to enjoy the dust of the London road, which he calls living in the country — and yet you must find fault with his situation ! — What if he has made a ridiculous gimcrack of his house and gardens, you know his heart is set upon it ; and could not you have commended his taste ? But you must be too frank ! — " Those walks and alleys are too regular— those evergreens should not be cut into such fantastic shapes."— And thus you advise a poor old mechanic, who delights in every thing that's monstrous, to follow nature—Oh, you're likely to be a successful lover !

Wood. But why should not I save a father-in-law from being a laughing-stock ?

Dim. Make him your father-in-law first—

Wood. Why he can't open his windows for the dust—he stands all day looking thro' a pane of glass; and he calls that living in the fresh air, and enjoying his own thoughts.

Dim.

Dim. Po! Po!—you have ruin'd yourfelf by talking fenfe to him ; and all your
nonfenfe to the daughter won't make amends
for it.—And then the mother ; how have
you play'd your cards in that quarter ?—She
wants a tinfel man of fafhion for her fecond
daughter—" Don't you fee (fays fhe) how
happy my eldeft girl is made by marrying
Sir Charles Rackett — Nancy fhall have a
man of quality too."

Wood. And yet I know Sir Charles Rackett perfectly well.

Dim. Yes, fo do I ; and I know he'll
make his lady wretched at laft—But what
then ? You fhould have humour'd the old
folks, — you fhould have been a talking
empty fop, to the good old lady ; and to
the old gentleman, an admirer of his tafte
in gardening. But you have loft him—he
is grown fond of this beau Lovelace, that's
here in the houfe with him ; the coxcomb
ingratiates himfelf by flattery, and you're
undone by franknefs.

Wood. And yet, Dimity, I won't defpair.

Dim. And yet you have reafon, a million
of reafons — To-morrow is fix'd for the
wedding-day ; Sir Charles and his lady are
to be here this very night—they are engag'd,
indeed, at a great rout in town, but they
take a bed here, notwithftanding. — The
family is fitting up for them ; Mr. Drugget
will keep ye all up, in the next room there,
till

till they arrive—and to-morrow the bufinefs
is over—and yet you don't defpair!—Hufh!
— hold your tongue; here he comes, and
Lovelace with him. — Step this way with
me, and I'll devife fomething, I warrant
you.—'Tis enough to vex a body, to fee an
old father and mother marrying their daughter as they pleafe, in fpite of all I can do.

[*Exeunt.*

Enter DRUGGET *and* LOVELACE.

Drug. And fo you like my houfe and
gardens, Mr. Lovelace.

Love. Oh! perfectly, Sir; they gratify my
tafte of all things. One fees villas where
nature reigns in a wild kind of fimplicity;
but then they have no appearance of art, no
art at all.

Drug. Very true, rightly diftinguifh'd:
—now mine is all art; no wild nature here;
I did it all myfelf.

Love. What, had you none of the great
proficients in gardening to affift you?

Drug. Lackaday! no, — ha! ha! I did
it all myfelf—I love my garden. The front
of my houfe, Mr. Lovelace, is not that very
pretty?

Love. Elegant to a degree!

Drug. Don't you like the fun-dial,
plac'd juft by my dining-room windows?

Love. A perfect beauty!

Drug.

Drug. I knew you'd like it — and the motto is so well adapted — *Tempus edax, & index rerum.* And I know the meaning of it — Time eateth and discovereth all things — ha! ha!—pretty, Mr. Lovelace!—I have seen people so stare at it as they pass by — ha! ha!

Love. Why now I don't believe there's a nobleman in the kingdom has such a thing.

Drug. Oh no—they have got into a false taste. — I bought that bit of ground, the other side of the road — and it looks very pretty—I made a duck-pond there, for the sake of the prospect.

Love. Charmingly imagin'd !

Drug. My leaden images are well —

Love. They exceed ancient statuary.—

Drug. I love to be surpriz'd at the turning of a walk with an inanimate figure, that looks you full in the face, and can say nothing to you, while one is enjoying one's own thoughts— ha! ha! — Mr. Lovelace, I'll point out a beauty to you — Just by the haw-haw, at the end of my ground, there is a fine Dutch figure, with a scythe in his hand, and a pipe in his mouth — that's a jewel, Mr. Lovelace.—

Love. That escap'd me: a thousand thanks for pointing it out—I observe you have two very fine yew-trees before the house.

Drug. Lackaday, Sir ! they look uncouth—I have a design about them — I intend

tend—ha! ha! it will be very pretty, Mr.
Lovelace — I intend to have them cut into
the fhape of the two giants at Guild-hall
—ha! ha!

Love. Exquifite!—Why then they won't
look like trees. —

Drug. Oh, no, no—not at all—I won't
have any thing in my garden that looks like
what it is—ha! ha!

Love. Nobody underftands thefe things
like you, Mr. Drugget.

Drug. Lackaday! it's all my delight now
—this is what I have been working for. I
have a great improvement to make ftill—I
propofe to have my evergreens cut into fortifications ; and then I fhall have the Moro
caftle, and the Havanna ; and then near it
fhall be fhips of myrtle, failing upon feas of
box to attack the town: won't that make my
place look very rural, Mr. Lovelace ?

Love. Why you have the moft fertile invention, Mr. Drugget.

Drug. Ha! ha! this is what I have been
working for. I love my garden — but I
muft beg your pardon for a few moments—
I muft ftep and fpeak with a famous nurfery-
man, who is come to offer me fome choice
things — Do go and join the company,
Mr. Lovelace —— my daughter Rackett
and Sir Charles will be here prefently —
I fhan't go to bed till I fee 'em — ha! ha!

I did

—I did all this myself, Mr. Lovelace —
this is what I have been working for — I
fin'd for Sheriff to enjoy thefe things— ha!
ha!   [*Exit.*

Love. Poor Mr. Drugget! Mynheer Van
Thundertentrunck, in his little box at the
fide of a dyke, has as much tafte and elegance. — However, if I can but carry off
his daughter, if I can rob his garden of that
flower — why then I fhall fay, " This is
what I have been working for."

Enter DIMITY.

Dim. Do lend us your affiftance, Mr.
Lovelace — you're a fweet gentleman, and
love a good-natur'd action.

Love. Why how now! what's the matter?

Dim. My mafter is going to cut the two
yew-trees into the fhape of two devils, I
believe; and my poor miftrefs is breaking
her heart for it.—Do, run and advife him
againft it—fhe is your friend, you know fhe
is, Sir.

Love. Oh, if that's all — I'll make that
matter eafy directly.

Dim. My miftrefs will be for ever oblig'd
to you; and you'll marry her daughter in
the morning.

Love. Oh, my rhetoric fhall diffuade him.

Dim. And, Sir, put him againft dealing
with that nurfery-man; Mrs. Drugget hates
him.   *Love.*

Love. Does fhe?

Dim. Mortally.

Love. Say no more, the bufinefs is done.
[*Exit.*

Dim. If he fays one word, old Drugget will never forgive him. — My brain was at it's laft fhift; but if this plot takes — So, here comes our Nancy.

Enter NANCY.

Nan. Well, Dimity, what's to become of me?

Dim. My ftars! what makes you up, Mifs?—I thought you were gone to bed!

Nan. What fhould I go to bed for? only to tumble and tofs, and fret, and be uneafy — they are going to marry me, and I am frighted out of my wits.

Dim. Why then you're the only young lady within fifty miles round, that would be frighten'd at fuch a thing.

Nan. Ah! if they would let me chufe for myfelf.

Dim. Don't you like Mr. Lovelace?

Nan. My mama does, but I don't; I don't mind his being a man of fafhion, not I.

Dim. And, pray, can you do better than follow the fafhion?

Nan. Ah! I know there's a fafhion for dreffing the hair, and a fafhion for new

C   bonnets

bonnets—but I never heard of a fashion for the heart.

Dim. Why then, my dear, the heart mostly follows the fashion now.

Nan. Does it?—Pray who sets the fashion of the heart?

Dim. All the fine ladies in London, o'my conscience.

Nan. And what's the last new fashion, pray?

Dim. Why to marry any fop, that has a few deceitful agreeable appearances about him; something of a pert phrase, a good operator for the teeth, and a tolerable taylor.

Nan. And do they marry without loving?

Dim. Oh! marrying for love has been a great while out of fashion.

Nan. Why then I'll wait till that fashion comes up again.

Dim. And then, Mr. Lovelace, I reckon—

Nan. Pshaw! I don't like him: he talks to me as if he was the most miserable man in the world, and the confident thing looks so pleas'd with himself all the while. — I want to marry for love, and not for card-playing — I should not be able to bear the life my sister leads with Sir Charles Rackett —and I'll forfeit my new cap, if they don't quarrel soon.

Dim. I'll be sworn they will — but what say you then to Mr. Woodley?

Nan.

Nan. Ah !—I don't know what to fay—
but I can fing fomething that will explain
my mind.

S O N G.

1.

WHEN firft the dear youth paffing by,
    Difclos'd his fair form to my fight,
I gaz'd, but I could not tell why ;
    My heart it went throb with delight.

2.

As nearer he drew, thofe fweet eyes
    Were with their dear meaning fo bright,
I trembled, and, loft in furprize,
    My heart it went throb with delight.

3.

When his lips their dear accents did try
    The return of my love to excite,
I feign'd, yet began to guefs why
    My heart it went throb with delight.

4.

We chang'd the ftol'n glance, the fond fmile,
    Which lovers alone read aright ;
We look'd, and we figh'd, yet the while
    Our hearts they went throb with delight.

5.

Confent I foon blufh'd, with a figh
    My promife I ventur'd to plight ;
Come, Hymen, we then fhall know why
    Our hearts they go throb with delight.

Enter WOODLEY.

Wood. My fweeteſt angel! I have heard all, and my heart overflows with love and gratitude.

Nan. Ah! but I did not know you was liſtening. You ſhould not have betray'd me ſo, Dimity: I ſhall be angry with you.

Dim. Well, I'll take my chance for that, — Run both into my room, and ſay all your pretty things to one another there, for here comes the old gentleman—make haſte away.— [*Exeunt Woodley and Nancy.*

Enter DRUGGET.

Drug. A forward preſuming coxcomb! Dimity, do you ſtep to Mrs. Drugget, and ſend her hither.

Dim. Yes, Sir;—It works upon him I ſee.— [*Exit.*

Drug. The yew-trees ought not to be cut, becauſe they'll help to keep off the duſt, and I am too near the road already— a ſorry ignorant fop!—When I am in ſo fine a ſituation, and can ſee every carriage that goes by.—And then to abuſe the nurſery-man's rarities!—A finer ſucking pig in lavender, with ſage growing in his belly, was never ſeen!—And yet he wants me not to have it—But have it I will.—

There's

There's a fine tree of knowledge too, with Adam and Eve in juniper; Eve's nofe not quite grown, but it's thought in the fpring will be very forward—I'll have that too, with the ferpent in ground-ivy—two poets in wormwood—I'll have them both. Ay; and there's a Lord Mayor's feaft in honey-fuckle; and the whole court of Aldermen in hornbeam: and three modern beaux in jeffamine, fomewhat ftunted: they all fhall be in my garden, with the Dragon of Wantley in box—all—all—I'll have 'em all, let my wife and Mr. Lovelace fay what they will—

Enter Mrs. DRUGGET.

Mrs. D. Did you fend for me, lovey?

Drug. The yew-trees fhall be cut into the giants of Guild-hall, whether you will or not.

Mrs. D. Sure my own dear will do as he pleafes.

Drug. And the pond, tho' you praife the green banks, fhall be wall'd round, and I'll have a little fat boy in marble, fpouting up water in the middle.

Mrs. D. My fweet, who hinders you?

Drug. Yes, and I'll buy the nurfery-man's whole catalogue—Do you think after retiring to live all the way here, almoft

four

four miles from London, that I won't do as
I pleafe in my own garden?

Mrs. D. My dear, but why are you in
fuch a paffion?

Drug. I'll have the lavender pig, and the
Adam and Eve, and the Dragon of Wantley,
and all of 'em—and there fhan't be a more
romantic fpot on the London road than
mine.

Mrs. D. I'm fure it's as pretty as hands
can make it.

Drug. I did it all myfelf, and I'll do
more—And Mr. Lovelace fhan't have my
daughter.—

Mrs. D. No! what's the matter now,
Mr. Drugget?

Drug. He fhall learn better manners than
to abufe my houfe and gardens.—You put
him in the head of it, but I'll difappoint
ye both—And fo you may go and tell Mr.
Lovelace that the match is quite off.

Mrs. D. I can't comprehend all this not
I—but I'll tell him fo, if you pleafe, my
dear—I am willing to give myfelf pain, if
it will give you pleafure : muft I give myfelf pain?—don't afk me, pray don't.

Drug. I am refolv'd, and it fhall be fo.

Mrs. D. Let it be fo then. *(Cries)* Oh!
oh! cruel man! I fhall break my heart if
the match is broke off—if it is not concluded to-morrow, fend for an undertaker,
and bury me the next day.

Drug.

Drug. How! I don't want that neither—

Mrs. D. Oh! oh!—

Drug. I am your lord and mafter, my dear, but not your executioner—Before George, it muft never be faid that my wife died of too much compliance—Cheer up, my love—and this affair fhall be fettled as foon as Sir Charles and Lady Rackett arrive.

Mrs. D. You bring me to life again—you know, my fweet, what an happy couple Sir Charles and his Lady are—they have been married thefe fix weeks, and have never had the leaft difference—Why fhould not we make our Nancy as happy?

Enter DIMITY.

Dim. Sir Charles and his Lady, Ma'am.

Mrs. D. Oh! charming! I'm tranf-ported with joy!—Where are they? I long to fee 'em. [*Exit.*

Dim. Well, Sir; the happy couple are arriv'd.

Drug. Yes, they do live happy, in-deed.

Dim. But how long will it laft?

Drug. How long! don't forbode any ill, you jade—don't, I fay—It will laft during their lives, I hope.

Dim. Well, mark the end of it—Sir Charles, I know, is gay and good-humour'd

3 —but

—but he can't bear the leaſt contradiction, no, not in the mereſt trifle.

Drug. Hold your tongue — hold your tongue.

Dim. Yes, Sir; I have done ;—and yet there is in the compoſition of Sir Charles a certain humour, which, like the flying gout, gives no diſturbance to the family till it ſettles in the head — When once it fixes there, mercy on very body about him! but here he comes.   [*Exit.*

Enter Sir CHARLES.

Sir Cha. My dear Sir, I kiſs your hand —but why ſtand on ceremony? to find you up thus late, mortifies me beyond ex-preſſion.

Drug. 'Tis but once in a way, Sir Charles.

Sir Cha. My obligations to you are in-expreſſible; you have given me the moſt amiable of girls; our tempers accord like uniſons in muſic.

Drug. Ah! that's what makes me happy in my old days; my children and my gar-den are all my care.

Sir Cha. And my friend Lovelace—he is to have our ſiſter Nancy, I find.

Drug. Why my wife is ſo minded.

Sir Cha. Oh, by all means, let her be made happy—A very pretty fellow Love-lace

lace—And as to that Mr.—Woodley I think you call him—he is but a plain underbred, ill-fashion'd fort of a—Nobody knows him, he is not one of us—Oh, by all means marry her to one of us.

Drug. I believe it muft be fo — Would you take any refrefhment?

Sir Cha. Nothing in nature—it is time to retire.

Drug. Well, well! good night then, Sir Charles—ha! here comes my daughter —good night, Sir Charles.

Sir Cha. Bon repos!

Drug. (*Going out*) My Lady Rackett, I'm glad to hear how happy you are, (*without*) I won't detain you now—there's your good man waiting for you—good night, my girl.

Sir Cha. I muft humour this old putt, in order to be remember'd in his will.

Enter Lady RACKETT.

Lady R. O la! — I'm quite fatigu'd — I can hardly move—why don't you help me, you barbarous man?

Sir Cha. There; take my arm— " Was ever thing fo pretty made to walk."

Lady R. But I won't be laugh'd at—I don't love you.

Sir Cha. Don't you?

D   *Lady*

Lady R. No. Dear me! this glove!
Why don't you help me off with my glove?
pſhaw!—Yow aukward thing, let it alone;
you an't fit to be about me, I might as well
not be married for any uſe you are of—
reach me a chair—You have no compaſſion
for me—I am ſo glad to ſit down—Why do
you drag me to routs—You know I hate
'em?

Sir Cha. Oh! there's no exiſting, no
breathing, unleſs one does as other people
of faſhion do.

Lady R. But I'm out of humour, I loſt
all my money.

Sir Cha. How much?

Lady R. Three hundred.

Sir Cha. Never fret for that — I don't
value three hundred pounds to contribute to
your happineſs.

Lady R. Don't you?—not value three
hundred pounds to pleaſe me?

Sir Cha. You know I don't.

Lady R. Ah! you fond fool!—but I hate
gaming—It almoſt metamorphoſes a woman
into a fury—do you know that I was frighted
at myſelf ſeveral times to-night—I had an
huge oath at the very tip of my tongue.

Sir Cha. Had ye?

Lady R. I caught myſelf at it—and ſo I
bit my lips—and then I was cramm'd up in
a corner of the room with ſuch a ſtrange

party

party at a whift-table, looking at black and red fpots—did you mind 'em?

Sir Cha. You know I was bufy elfewhere.

Lady R. There was that ftrange unaccountable woman, Mrs. Nightfhade—She behav'd fo ftrangely to her hufband, a poor, inoffenfive, good-natur'd, good fort of a good for nothing kind of man,—but fhe fo teiz'd him —"How could you play that card? Ah, you've a head, and fo has a pin—You're a numfcull, you know you are —Ma'am, he has the poorcft head in the world, he does not know what he is about; you know you don't—Ah fye!—I'm afham'd of you!"

Sir Cha. She has ferv'd to divert you, I fee.

Lady R. And then to crown all—there was my Lady Clackit, who runs on with an eternal volubility of nothing, out of all feafon, time, and place—In the very midft of the game fhe begins, "Lard, Ma'am, I was apprehenfive I fhould not be able to wait on your La'fhip—my poor little dog, Pompey—the fweeteft thing in the world,— a fpade led!—there's the knave—I was fetching a walk, Me'm, the other morning in the Park—a fine frofty morning it was— I love frofty weather of all things—Let me look at the laft trick—and fo Me'm, little Pompey—And if your La'fhip was to fee the dear creature pinch'd with the froft, and

mincing

mincing his fteps along the Mall —with his pretty little innocent face—I vow I don't know what to play—And fo, Me'm, while I was talking to Captain Flimfey — Your La'fhip knows Captain Flimfey—Nothing but rubbifh in my hand—I can't help it—And fo, Me'm, five odious frights of dogs befet my poor little Pompey — the dear creature has the heart of a lion, but who can refift five at once —And fo Pompey barked for affiftance—the hurt he receiv'd was upon his cheft—the doctor would not advife him to venture out till the wound is heal'd, for fear of an inflammation —Pray what's trumps?

Sir Cha. My dear, you'd make a moft excellent actrefs.

Lady R. Well, now let's go to bed—but Sir Charles, how fhockingly you play'd that laft rubber, when I ftood looking over you !

Sir Cha. My love, I play'd the truth of the game.

Lady R. No, indeed, my dear, you play'd it wrong.

Sir Cha. Po! nonfenfe! you don't underftand it.

Lady R. I beg your pardon, I am allow'd to play better then you.

Sir Cha. All conceit, my dear, I was perfectly right.

Lady

Lady R. No fuch thing, Sir Charles, the diamond was the play.

Sir Cha. Po! po! ridiculous! the club was the card againft the world.

Lady R. Oh, no, no, no, I fay it was the diamond.

Sir Cha. Zounds! Madam, I fay it was the club.

Lady R. What do you fly into fuch a paffion for?

Sir Cha. 'Sdeath and fury, do you think I don't know what I'm about? I tell you once more the club was the judgment of it.

Lady R. May be fo—have it your own way *(walks about, and fings.)*

Sir. Cha. Vexation! you're the ftrangeft woman that ever liv'd, there's no converf-ing with you — Look'ye here, my Lady Rackett—it's the cleareft cafe in the world, I'll make it plain in a moment.

Lady R. Well, Sir! ha! ha! ha! *(with a fneering laugh)*

Sir Cha. I had four cards left—a trump was led—they were fix—no, no, no, they were feven, and we nine—then you know — the beauty of the play was to —

Lady R. Well, now it's amazing to me, that you can't fee it—give me leave, Sir Charles—your left hand adverfary had led his laft trump—and he had before finefs'd the club, and rough'd the diamond—now if you had put on your diamond—

Sir

Sir Cha. Zoons ! Madam, but we play'd for the odd trick.

Lady R. And fure the play for the odd trick——

Sir Cha. Death and fury ! can't you hear me ?

Lady R. Go on, Sir.

Sir Cha. Zoons, hear me I fay—will you hear me ?

Lady R. I never heard the like in my life. *(Hums a tune, and walks about fretfully.)*

Sir Cha. Why then you are enough to provoke the patience of a Stoic.——*(Looks at her, and fhe walks about, and laughs uneafily.)* Very well, Madam ;—You know no more of the game than a hobby-horfe—no more than my coachman.

Lady R. Ha ! ha !——*(takes out a glafs, aud fettles her hair.)*

Sir Cha. You're a vile woman, and I'll not fleep another night under one roof with you.

Lady R. As you pleafe, Sir.

Sir Cha. Madam, it fhall be as I pleafe —I'll order my chariot this moment— *(going)* I know how the cards fhould be play'd as well as any man in England, that let me tell you —*(going)*—And when your family were ftanding behind counters, meafuring out tape, and bartering for Whitechapel needles, my anceftors, my anceftors, Madam, were fquandering away

whole

whole eftates at cards; whole eftates, my Lady Rackett—(*She hums a tune and he looks at her*)—Why then, by all that's dear to me, I'll never exchange another word with you, good, bad, or indifferent— Look'ye, my Lady Rackett—thus it ftood—the trump being led, it was then my bufinefs—

Lady R. To fineffe the club.

Sir Cha. Damn it, I have done with you for ever, and fo you may tell your father.   [*Exit.*

Lady R. What a paffion the gentleman's in! ha! ha! (*laughs in a peevifh manner*) I promife him, I'll not give up my judgment.

Enter Sir CHARLES.

Sir Cha. My Lady Rackett, look'ye, Ma'am — once more out of pure good-nature —

Lady R. Sir, I am convinc'd of your good-nature.

Sir Cha. That, and that only prevails with me to tell you, the club was the play.

Lady R. Well, be it fo—I have no objection.

Sir Cha. It's the cleareft point in the world — we were nine, and —

Lady R. And for that very reafon :—you know the club was the beft in the houfe.

Sir Cha. There is no fuch thing as talking to you — You're a bafe woman—I'll part from you for ever; you may live here with
                                        your

your father, and admire his fantaſtical evergreens, till you grow as fantaſtical yourſelf
—I'll ſet out for London this inſtant—(*Stops
at the door*) The club was not the beſt in
the houſe.

Lady R. How calm you are ! Well ! —
I'll go to bed ;—will you come ?—you had
better—come then—you ſhall come to bed
—not come to bed when I aſk you ?—Poor
Sir Charles ! [*Looks and laughs, then Exit.*

Sir Cha. That eaſe is provoking. (*Croſſes
to the oppoſite door, where ſhe went out*)—I tell
you the diamond was the play, and I here
take my final leave of you—(*walks back, as
faſt as he can*) I am reſolv'd upon it, and I
know the club was not the beſt in the
houſe. [*Exit.*

ACT II.

Enter DIMITY.

Dimity.

HA! ha! ha! oh! heavens! I ſhall expire in a fit of laughing—This is the
modiſh couple that were ſo happy—ſuch a
quarrel as they have had—the whole houſe
is in an uproar—ha! ha! A rare proof of
the happineſs they enjoy in high life. I ſhall
never

never hear people of fashion mention'd
again, but I shall be ready to die in a fit of
laughter—ho! ho! ho!

Enter DRUGGET.

Drug. Hey! how! what's the matter, Dimity—What am I call'd down stairs for?

Dim. Why there's two people of fashion
—(*Stifles a laugh.*)

Drug. Why you saucy minx!—Explain
this moment.

Dim. The fond couple have been together by the ears this half hour—are you
satisfied now?—

Drug. Ay!—what have they quarrell'd
—what was it about?

Dim. Something above my comprehen-
sion and your's too, I believe—People in high
life understand their own forms best—And
here comes one that can unriddle the whole
affair.   [*Exit.*

Enter Sir CHARLES.

Sir Cha. (*To the people within*) I say, let
the horses be put-to this moment—So, Mr.
Drugget.

Drug. Sir Charles, here's a terrible bustle
—I did not expect this—what can be the
matter?

E   *Sir*

Sir. Cha. I have been us'd by your daughter, in so base, so contemptuous a manner, that I am determin'd not to stay in this house to-night.

Drug. This is a thunder-bolt to me! after seeing how elegantly and fashionably you liv'd together, to find now all sunshine vanish'd—Do, Sir Charles, let me heal this breach, if possible.

Sir Cha. Sir, 'tis impossible—I'll not live with her a day longer.

Drug. Nay, nay, don't be over hasty,—let me intreat you, go to bed and sleep upon it —in the morning when you're cool —

Sir Cha. Oh, Sir, I am very cool, I assure —ha! ha!—it is not in her power, Sir, to —to—a—a—to disturb the serenity of my temper—Don't imagine that I'm in a passion —I'm not so easily ruffled as you may imagine—But quietly and deliberately I can resent ill usage—I can repay the injuries done me by a false, ungrateful, deceitful wife, with the severity, and at the same time with the composure of an old judge, harden'd in his office—That man, am I, Sir.

Drug. The injuries done you by a treacherous wife !—my daughter I hope—

Sir Cha. Her character is now fully known to me—she's a vile woman ! that's all I have to say, Sir.

Drug.

Drug. Hey! how!—a vile woman—what has fhe done—I hope fhe is not capable—

Sir Cha. I fhall enter into no detail, Mr. Drugget, the time and circumftances won't allow it at prefent—But depend upon it I have done with her—a low, unpolifh'd, uneducated, falfe, impofing—See if the horfes are put-to.

Drug. Mercy on me! in my old days to hear this.

Enter Mrs. DRUGGET.

Mrs. D. Deliver me! I am all over in fuch a tremble—Sir Charles, I fhall break my heart if there's any thing amifs.

Sir Cha. Madam, I am very forry for your fake—but there is no poffibility of living with her.

Mrs. D. My poor dear girl! What can fhe have done?

Sir Cha. What all her fex can do, the very fpirit of them all.

Drug. Ay! ay! ay!—She's bringing foul difgrace upon us—This comes of her marrying a man of fafhion.

Sir Cha. Fafhion, Sir!—That fhould have inftructed her better—She might have been fenfible of her happinefs—Whatever you may think of the fortune you gave her, my rank in life, claims refpect — claims obe-

E 2   dience,

dience, attention, truth, and love, from one raifed in the world as fhe has been by an alliance with me.

Drug. And let me tell you, however you may eftimate your quality, my daughter is dear to me.

Sir Cha. And, Sir, my character is dear to me.

Drug. Yet you muft give me leave to tell you——

Sir Cha. I won't hear a word.

Drug. Not in behalf of my own daughter ?

Sir Cha. Nothing can excufe her——'tis to no purpofe——She has married above her ; and if that circumftance makes the Lady forget herfelf, fhe at leaft fhall fee that I can and will fupport my own dignity.

Drug. But, Sir, I have a right to afk——

Mrs. D. Patience, my dear, be a little calm.

Drug. Mrs. Drugget, do you have patience, I muft and will enquire.

Mrs. D. Don't be fo hafty, my love ; have fome refpect for Sir Charles's rank ; don't be violent with a man of his fafhion.

Drug. Hold your tongue, woman, I fay——you're not a perfon of fafhion at leaft —— My daughter was ever a good girl.

Sir Cha. I have found her out.

Drug. Oh ! then it's all over——and it does not fignify arguing about it.

Mrs. D. That ever I fhould live to fee this hour !

Sir Cha. I know her thoroughly—and there is no fuch thing as being connected with her a moment longer.

Mrs. D. How the unfortunate girl could take fuch wickednefs in her head, I can't imagine—I'll go and fpeak to the unhappy creature this moment.   [*Exit.*

Sir Cha. She ftands detected now—detected in her trueft colours.

Drug. Well, grievous as it may be, let me hear the circumftances of this unhappy bufinefs.

Sir Cha. Mr. Drugget, I have not leifure now—but her behaviour has been fo exafperating, that I fhall make the beft of my way to town—My mind is fixed—She fees me no more, and fo, your fervant, Sir.
    [*Exit.*

Drug. What a calamity has here befallen us! as good a girl, and as well difpos'd till the evil communication of high life, and fafhionable vices, turn'd her to folly.

Enter LOVELACE.

Love. Joy! joy! Mr. Drugget, I give you joy.

Drug. Don't infult me, Sir—I defire you won't.

Love.

Love. Infult you, Sir!—is there any thing infulting, my dear Sir, if I take the liberty to congratulate you on—

Drug. There! there!—the manners of high life for you — He thinks there's nothing in all this — the ill behaviour of a wife he thinks an ornament to her character —Mr. Lovelace, you ſhall have no daughter of mine.

Love. My dear Sir, never bear malice— I have reconfider'd the thing, and curſe catch me if I don't think your notion of the Gulid-hall giants, and the court of Aldermen in hornbeam—

Drug. Well! well! well! there may be people of the court end of the town in hornbeam too.

Love. Yes, faith, ſo there may—and I believe I could recommend you a tolerable collection—however, with your daughter I am ready to venture.

Drug. But I am not ready—I'll not venture my girl with you —no more daughters of mine ſhall have their minds deprav'd by polite vices.

Enter WOODLEY.

Mr. Woodley—you ſhall have Nancy to your wife, as I promis'd you—take her to-morrow morning.

Wood.

Wood. Sir, I have not words to exprefs——

Love. What the devil is the matter with the old haberdafher now ?

Drug. And hark ye, Mr. Woodley—I'll make you a prefent for your garden, of a coronation dinner in greens, with the champion riding on horfeback, and the fword will be full grown before April next.

Wood. I fhall receive it, Sir, as your favour.

Drug. Ay, ay ! I fee my error in wanting an alliance with great folks—I had rather have you, Mr. Woodley, for my fon-in-law, than any courtly fop of 'em all. Is this man gone !— Is Sir Charles Rackett gone ?

Wood. Not yet ;—he makes a bawling yonder for his horfes—I'll ftep and call him to you.   [*Exit.*

Drug. I am out of all patience—I am out of my fenfes,—I muft fee him once more—Mr. Lovelace, you nor no perfon of fafhion, fhall ruin another daughter of mine.
                                    [*Exit.*

Love. Droll this !—damn'd droll ! And every fyllable of it Arabic to me—the queer old putt is as whimfical in his notions of life as of gardening. If this be the cafe—. I'll brufh, and leave him to his exotics.
                                    [*Exit.*

Enter

Enter Lady RACKETT, Mrs. DRUGGET,
and DIMITY.

Lady R. A cruel barbarous man! to
quarrel in this unaccountable manner; to
alarm the whole house, and expose me and
himself too.

Mrs. D. Oh! child! I never thought it
would have come to this — your shame
won't end here; it will be all over St.
James's parish by to-morrow morning.

Lady R. Well, if it must be so, there's
one comfort, the story will tell more to his
disgrace than mine.

Dim. As I'm a sinner, and so it will,
Madam. He deserves what he has met
with, I think.

Mrs. D. Dimity, don't you encourage
her—No, no, no, my dear child, the disgrace will be all your own.

Lady R. Will it?—I am sure I shan't
blush for any thing that has past—I know
a little more of the world than that comes
to.

Mrs. D. You shock me to hear you
speak so—I did not think you had been so
harden'd.

Lady R. Harden'd do you call it?—I have
liv'd in the world to very little purpose, if
such trifles as these are to disturb my rest.

Mrs.

Mrs. D. You wicked girl !—Do you call it a trifle to be guilty of falfhood to your huf-band's bed ?

Lady R. How !— (*Turns fhort, and ftares at her.*)

Dim. That ! that's a mere trifle indeed—I have been in as good places as any body, and not a creature minds it now, I'm fure.

Mrs. D. My Lady Rackett, my Lady Rackett, I never could think to fee you come to this deplorable fhame.

Lady R. Surely the bafe man has not been capable of laying any thing of that fort to my charge—(*Afide.*) All this is unaccount-able to me—ha ! ha ! —'tis ridiculous be-yond meafure.

Dim. That's right, Madam :—Laugh at it—you ferv'd him right.

Mrs. D. Charlotte ! Charlotte ! 'm aftonifh'd at your wickednefs.

Lady R. Well, I proteft and vow I don't comprehend all this— has Sir Charles ac-cus'd me ?

Mrs. D. Oh! too true he has—he has found you out, and you have behav'd bafely he fays.

Lady R. Madam !

Mrs. D. You have fallen into frailty like many others of your fex, he fays, and he is refolv'd to come to a feparation directly.

Lady R. Why then if he is fo bafe a wretch as to difhonour me in that manner, his heart fhall ake before I live with him again.

F   *Dim.*

Dim. Hold to that, Ma'am, and let his head ake into the bargain.

Mrs. D. Oh! what shall I do? it is all too true I find.

Lady R. True!—'tis false as scandal, and the vilest calumny that ever was invented.

Dim. Po! never go to deny it—own it Ma'am.

Lady R. Stand away;—don't talk to me —Sir Charles! Sir Charles!—Pray, Madam, let Mr. Woodley have my sister — I am unfortunate ever to have seen so vile a slanderer — is it possible that he could have talked thus meanly of me?

Mrs. D. Your poor father heard it as well as me.

Lady R. Then let your doors be open'd for him this very moment—let him return to London—if he does not, I'll lock myself up, and the false one shan't approach me, tho' he beg on his knees at my very door— a base injurous man!   [*Exit.*

Mrs. D. Dimity, do let us follow, and hear what she has to say for herself. [*Exit.*

Dim. She has excuse enough I warrant her —What a noise is here indeed!—I have liv'd in polite families, where there was no such bustle made about nothing.   [*Exit.*

Enter Sir CHARLES, *and* DRUGGET.

Sir Cha. 'Tis in vain Sir, my resolution is taken—   *Drug.*

Drug. Well, but confider, I am her father,—indulge me only till we hear what the girl has to fay in her defence.

Sir Cha. She can have nothing to fay—no excufe can palliate fuch behaviour.

Drug. Don't be too pofitive—there may be fome miftake.

Sir Cha. No miftake—did not I fee her, hear her myfelf?

Drug. Lackaday! I am an unfortunate man!

Sir Cha. She will be unfortunate too—with all my heart—She may thank herfelf—She might have been happy had fhe been fo difpos'd.

Drug. Why truly, I think fhe might.

Enter Mrs. DRUGGET.

Mrs. D. I wifh you'd moderate your anger a little—and let us talk over this affair with temper—my daughter denies every tittle of your charge.

Sir Cha. Denies it! denies it!

Mrs. D. She does indeed.

Sir Cha. And that aggravates her fault.

Mrs. D. She vows you never found her out in any thing that was wrong.

Sir Cha. So! She does not allow it to be wrong then!—Madam, I tell you again, I know her thoroughly, I fay I have found her out, and I am now acquainted with her character.

Mrs D. Then you are in oppofite ftories—She fwears, my dear Mr. Drugget, the poor girl fwears fhe never was guilty of the fmalleft infidelity to her hufband's bed in her born days.

Sir Cha. And what then ?—What if fhe does fay fo!

Mrs. D. And if fhe fays truly, it is hard her character fhould be blown upon without juft caufe.

Sir Cha. And is fhe therefore to behave ill in other refpects ? I never charg'd her with infidelity to me, Madam — there I allow her innocent.

Drug. And did not you charge her then?

Sir Cha. No, Sir, I never dreamt of fuch a thing.

Drug. Why then, if fhe's innocent, let me tell you, you're a fcandalous perfon.

Mrs. D. Prithee, my dear—

Drug. Be quiet—tho' he is a man of quality, I will tell him of it—did not I fine for fheriff ? — yes, you are a fcandalous perfon to defame an honeft man's daughter.

Sir Cha. What have you taken into your head now ?

Drug. You charg'd her with falfhood to your bed.

Sir Cha. No—never—never.

Drug. But I fay you did—you call'd yourfelf a cuckold—did not he, wife?

Mrs. D. Yes, Lovey, I'm witnefs.

Sir Cha. Po! po! po! no such thing——

Drug. But I aver you did——

Mrs D. You did indeed, Sir——

Sir Cha. But I tell you no——positively, no.

Drug. and Mrs. D. And I say yes —— positively yes——

Sir Cha. 'Sdeath, this is all madness——

Drug. You said you had found her out in the very fact——

Sir Cha. Mr. Drugget —— give me leave, Sir——

Drug. That she follow'd the ways of most of her sex——

Sir Cha. I said so——and what then?

Drug. There he owns it——owns that he call'd himself a cuckold —— and without rhyme or reason into the bargain ——

Sir Cha. I never own'd any such thing——

Drug. You own'd it even now——now—— now——now——

Enter DIMITY, *in a fit of laughing.*

Dim. What do you think it was all about——ha! ha!——the whole secret is come out, ha! ha!——It was all about a game of cards——ha! ha!——

Drug. A game of cards! ——

Dim. (*Laughing*) It was all about a club and a diamond (*runs out laughing.*)

Drug. And was that all, Sir Charles?

Sir Cha. And enough too, Sir——

Drug.

Drug. And was that what you found her out in?

Sir Cha. I can't bear to be contradicted, when I'm clear that I'm in the right.

Mrs. D. Oh!—I underſtand the affair now—this was only one of thoſe polite diſputes, which people of quality, who have nothing elſe to differ about, muſt always be liable to.

Drug. I never heard of ſuch a heap of nonſenſe in all my life—Woodley ſhall marry Nancy.

Mrs. D. Don't be in a hurry, my love, this will be all made up.

Drug. Why does not he go and aſk her pardon then?

Sir Cha. I beg her pardon! I won't debaſe myſelf to any of you—I ſhan't forgive her, you may reſt aſſur'd—. [*Exit.*

Drug. Now there—there's a pretty fellow for you—

Mrs. D. I'll ſtep and prevail on my Lady Rackett to ſpeak to him—then all will be well. [*Exit.*

Drug. A ridiculous ſop! I'm glad it's no worſe however.

Enter NANCY.

So Nancy—you ſeem in confuſion, my girl!

Nan. How can one help it?—With all this noiſe in the houſe, and you're going to
marry

marry me as ill as my fifter—I hate Mr.
Lovelace.

Drug. Why fo child?

Nan. I know thefe people of quality defpife us all out of pride, and would be glad
to marry us out of avarice.

Drug. The girl's right.

Nan. They marry one woman, live with
another, and love only themfelves.

Drug. And then quarrel about a card.

Nan. I don't want to be a gay lady—I
want to be happy.

Drug. And fo you fhall — don't fright
yourfelf, child — ftep to your fifter, bid her
make herfelf eafy—go, and comfort her, go—

Nan. Yes, Sir. [*Exit.*

Drug. I'll ftep and fettle the matter with
Mr. Woodley this moment. [*Exit.*

Enter Sir CHARLES, *with a pack of cards
in his hand.*

Sir Cha. Never was any thing like her behaviour—I can pick out the very cards I
had in my hand, and then 'tis as plain as the
fun—there—now—there—no—damn it—
no—there it was—now let's fee—They had
four by honours—and we play'd for the odd
trick—damnation! honours were divided—
ay!—honours were divided—and then a
trump was led—and the other fide had the
—confufion!—this prepofterous woman has
put

put it all out of my head (*puts the cards into his pocket.*) Mighty well, Madam; I have
done with you.

Enter Mrs. DRUGGET.

Mrs. D. Come, Sir Charles, let me
prevail—come with me and speak to her.

Sir Cha. I don't desire to see her face.

Mrs. D. If you were to see her all bath'd
in tears, I am sure it would melt your very
heart.

Sir Cha. Madam, it shall be my fault if
ever I'm so treated again—I'll have nothing
to say to her (*going, stops*) does she give up
the point?

Mrs. D. She does, she agrees to any
thing.

Sir Cha. Does she allow that the club was
the play?

Mrs. D. Just as you please—She's all
submission.

Sir Cha. Then I'll step and speak to her
—I never was clearer in any thing in my
life.   [*Exit.*

Mrs. D. Lord love 'em, they'll make it up
now—and then they'll be as happy as ever.
[*Exit.*

Enter NANCY.

Nan. Well! they may talk what they
will of taste, and genteel life—I don't think
it's natural—give me Mr. Woodley—La!
there's that odious thing coming this way.

Enter

Enter LOVELACE.

Love. My charming little innocent, I have not feen you thefe three hours.

Nan. I have been very happy thefe three hours.

Love. My fweet angel, you feem difconcerted—And you neglect your pretty figure —no matter for the prefent; in a little time I fhall make you appear as graceful and genteel as your fifter.

Nan. That is not what employs my thoughts, Sir.

Love. Ay, but my pretty little dear, that fhou'd engage your attention—to fet off and adorn the charms that nature has given you, fhould be the bufinefs of your life.

Nan. Ah! but I have learnt a new fong that contradicts what you fay, and tho' I am not in a very good humour for finging, yet you fhall hear it.

Love. By all means;—dont check your fancy—I am all attention.

Nan. It exprefles my fentiments, and when you have heard them you won't teize me any more.

SONG.

I.

TO dance, and to drefs, and to flaunt it about,
To run to Park, play, to affembly and rout,

To

To wander for ever in whim's giddy maze,
And one poor hair torture a million of ways,
To put, at the glafs, ev'ry feature to fchool,
And practife their art on each fop and each
    fool,
Of one thing to think, and another to tell,
Thefe, thefe are the manners of each giddy
    belle.

2.

To fmile, and to fimper, white teeth to difplay;
The time in gay follies to trifle away;
Againft ev'ry virtue the bofom to fteel,
And only of drefs the anxieties feel;
To be at Eve's ear, the infidious decoy,
The pleafure ne'er tafte yet the mifchief enjoy,
To boaft of foft raptures they never can know,
Thefe, thefe are the manners of each giddy
    beau.   [*Exit.*

Love. I muft have her notwithftanding
this—for tho' I am not in love, yet I'm in
debt.

Enter DRUGGET.

Drug. So, Mr. Lovelace! any news from
above-ftairs? Is this abfurd quarrel at an
end—have they made it up?

Love. Oh! a mere bagatelle, Sir—thefe
little fracas among the better fort of people
never laft long—elegant trifles caufe elegant
difputes, and we come together elegantly
again—as you fee—for here they come, in
perfect good humour.   *Enter*

Enter Sir CHARLES *and* Lady RACKETT,
Mrs. DRUGGET.

Sir Cha. Mr. Drugget, I embrace you,
Sir; you fee me now in the moft perfect
harmony of fpirits.

Drug. What, all reconcil'd again?

Lady R. All made up, Sir—I knew how
to bring the gentleman to—this is the firft
difference, I think we ever had, Sir
Charles.—

Sir Cha. And I'll be fworn it fhall be the
laft.

Drug. I am at eafe again—Sir Charles, I
can fpare you an image to put on the top of
your houfe in London.

Sir Cha. Infinitely oblig'd to you.

Mrs. D. My dear, they are as happy
now as two intriguing ducks in our pond
yonder—You'll give Nancy, to Mr. Lovelace?

Sir Cha. Oh, to be fure, my friend Lovelace muft be the man.

Lady R. And then my fifter and I fhall
be near neighbours, and we fhall fo rival
each other in the beau monde.

Drug. Well! well! I believe it muft be
fo—we'll talk of thefe matters in the morning—It's time to retire now—I am glad to
fee you happy again—and now I'll wifh you
a good night, Sir Charles—Mr. Lovelace,

this

this is your way—fare ye well both—I am glad your quarrels are at an end—This way, Mr. Lovelace — come, come my dear— come, we'll go and take care of one another,

[Exeunt Lovelace, Drugget, and Mrs. Drugget.

Lady R. Ah! your a sad man, Sir Charles, to behave to me as you have done—

Sir Cha. My dear, I grant it—and such an absurd quarrel too—ha! ha!

Lady R. Yes—ha! ha!— about such a trifle—

Sir Cha. It's pleasant how we could both fall into such an error—ha! ha!—

Lady R. Ridiculous beyond expression, —ha! ha!

Sir Cha. And then the mistake your father and mother fell into—ha! ha!

Lady R. That too is a diverting part of the story—ha! ha! but Sir Charles, must I I stay and live with my father till I grow as fantastical as his own evergreens?

Sir Cha. No, no, prithee — don't remind me of my folly.

Lady R. Ah! my relations were all standing behind counters selling White-chapel needles, while your family were spending great estates.

Sir Cha. Nay, nay, spare my blushes.

Lady R. How could you say so low a thing?—I don't love you.

Sir Cha. It was indelicate I grant it.

Lady.

Lady R. Am I a vile woman?

Sir. Cha. How can you, my angel?

Lady R. I ſhan't forgive you!—I'll have you on your knees for this. *(Sings and plays with him.)*—("Go, naughty man")—Ah! Sir Charles—

Sir Cha. The reſt of my life ſhall aim at convincing you how ſincerely I love—

Lady R. (Sings) "Go, naughty man, I can't abide you"—Well! come let us go to reſt *(Going.)* Ah, Sir Charles!—now it's all over, the diamond was the play—

Sir Cha. Oh no, no, no,—my dear! ha! ha!—It was the club indeed—

Lady R. Indeed, my love, you're miſtaken—

Sir Cha. Oh, no, no, no—

Lady R. But I ſay, yes, yes, yes—*(Both laughing.)*

Sir Cha. Pſhaw, no ſuch thing—ha! ha!—

Lady R. 'Tis ſo, indeed—ha! ha!—

Sir Cha. No—no—no—you'll make me die with laughing—

Lady R. Ay, and you make me laugh too—ha! ha! *(Toying with him.)*

Enter FOOTMAN.

Footm. Your honour's cap and ſlippers—

Sir Cha. Ay, give me my night cap—and here, take theſe ſhoes off *(He takes 'em off, and leaves 'em at a diſtance)* Indeed my
Lady

Lady Rackett, you make me ready to expire with laughing—ha! ha!—

Lady R. You may laugh—but I'm right notwithstanding —

Sir Cha. How can you say so?

Lady R. How can you say otherwise?

Sir Cha. Well now mind me, my Lady Rackett—We can now talk of this matter in good humour—

Lady R. So we can — and it's for that reason I venture to speak to you—are these the ruffles I bought for you?

Sir Cha. They are, my dear.

Lady R. They are very pretty—but indeed you play'd the card wrong—

Sir Cha. Po, there is nothing so clear—if you will but hear me—only hear me—

Lady R. Ah!—but do you hear me—the thing was thus—your club being the best in the house—

Sir Cha. How can you talk so!—(*Somewhat peevish.*)

Lady R. See there now —

Sir Cha. Now see—this was the affair—

Lady R. Pshaw! fiddlestick! hear me first.

Sir Cha. Po — no — damn it — let me speak—

Lady R. Well, to be sure you're a strange man—

Sir Cha. Plague and torture!—there is no such thing as conversing with you—

Lady

Lady R. Very well, Sir—fly out again—

Sir Cha. Look here now —here's a pack of cards—now you ſhall be convinc'd—

Lady R. You may talk till to-morrow, I know I'm right (*walks about.*)

Sir Cha. Why then by all that's perverſe, you are the moſt headſtrong—Can't you look here now—here are the very cards—

Lady R. Go on; you'll find it out at laſt—

Sir Cha. Damn it ! will you let a man ſhew you ! Po! it's all nonſenſe—I'll talk no more about it—(*Puts up the cards.*) Come, we'll go to bed (*Going.*) Now only ſtay a moment — (*Takes out the cards*) — Now, mind me — ſee here—

Lady R. No, it does not ſignify—your head will be clearer in the morning—I'll go to bed—

Sir Cha. Stay a moment, can't ye —

Lady R. No—my head begins to ake— (*Affectedly.*)

Sir Cha. Why then damn the cards— there—there— (*Throwing the cards about.*) and there, and there — you may go to bed by yourſelf—and confuſion ſeize me, If I live a moment longer with you — (*Putting on his ſhoes again.*)

Enter DIMITY.

Dim. Did you call, Sir?
Sir Cha. No—never—never—Madam—

5

Dim.

Dim. (*In a fit of laughing*)—What, at it again !

Lady R. Take your own way, Sir——

Sir Cha. Now then I tell you once more you are a vile woman.

Dim. Law! Sir — This is charming ! — I'll run and tell the old couple.   [*Exit.*

Sir Cha. (*Still putting on his shoes*)—You are the moſt perverſe obſtinate, nonſenſical——

Lady R. Ha ! ha ! don't make me laugh again, Sir Charles——

Sir Cha. Hell and the devil —will you ſit down quietly and let me convince you——

Lady R. I don't chuſe to hear any more about it——

Sir Cha. Why then, I believe you are poſſeſs'd — it is in vain to talk ſenſe and reaſon to you——

Lady R. Thank you for your compliment, Sir—ſuch a man (*With a ſneering laugh*) I never knew the like—(*Sits down.*)

Sir Cha. I promiſe you, you ſhall repent of this uſage—before you have a moment of my company again — it ſhan't be in a hurry you may depend, Madam—Now ſee here—I can prove it to a demonſtration (*Sits down by her, ſhe gets up.*) Lookye there again now—you have the moſt perverſe and peeviſh temper — I wiſh I had never ſeen your face—I wiſh I was a thouſand miles off from you—ſit down but one moment——

Lady R. I'm diſpos'd to walk about, Sir——

Sir

Sir Cha. Why then may I perish if ever
—a blockhead—an ideot I was to marry
(*Walks about*) such a provoking—impertinent—(*She sits down.*)—Damnation!—
I am so clear in the thing—She is not worth
my notice—(*Sits down, turns his back, and
looks uneasy.*) I'll take no more pains about
it—(*Pauses for some time, then looks at her.*)
Is not it very strange, that you won't hear
me ?

Lady R. Sir I am very ready to hear you—

Sir Cha. Very well then — very well —
you remember how the game stood — I'll
write it down and send it to Arthur's ;
and if the best judges there—

Lady R. I wish you'd untie my necklace,
it hurts me—

Sir Cha. Why can't you listen ? —

Lady R. I tell you it hurts me terribly—

Sir Cha. Death and confusion !—there is
no bearing this—farewell— [*Exit.*

Enter Mr. *and* Mrs. DRUGGET, WOODLEY,
LOVELACE, *and* NANCY.

Drug. What's here to do now ?

Lady R. Never was such a man born—
I did not say a word to the gentleman—
and yet he has been raving about the room
like a madman.

Drug. And about a club again, I sup-
H   pose,

poſe ; come hither, Nancy ; Mr. Woodley, ſhe is yours for life——

Mrs. D. My dear, how can you be ſo——

Drug. It ſhall be ſo——take her for life, Mr. Woodley.

Wood. My whole life ſhall be devoted to her happineſs——

Love. The devil! and ſo I am to be left in the lurch in this manner, am I?

Lady R. Oh! my dear Sir, this is no-thing—I have a lure to bring the gentleman back again ——

Drug. Never tell me——it's too late now—— Mr. Woodley, I recommend my girl to your care——I ſhall have nothing now to think of, but my greens, and my images, and my ſhrubbery —— tho', mercy on all married folks, ſay I! —— for theſe wranglings are, I am afraid, *What we muſt All come to.*

Lady Rachett, coming forward.

WHAT *we muſt all come to?* What ?—— Come to what?
Muſt broils and quarrels be the marriage lot?
If that's the wiſe, deep meaning of our poet,
The man's a fool! a blockhead! and I'll ſhew it.
What could induce him in an age ſo nice——
So fam'd for virtue, ſo refin'd from vice,
To form a plan ſo trivial, falſe, and low?
As if a belle could quarrel with a beau:

As

As if there were—in thefe thrice happy days,
One who from nature, or from reafon ftrays!
There's no crofs hufband now; no wrang-
    ling wife,—
The man is downright ignorant of life.
  'Tis the millennium this—devoid of guile,
Fair gentle Truth, and white-rob'd Can-
    dour fmile.
From every breaft the fordid love of gold
Is banifh'd quite—no boroughs now are
    fold!
Pray tell me, Sirs—(for I don't know, I
    vow,)
Pray—is there fuch a thing as Gaming now?
Do peers make laws againft that giant Vice,
And then at Arthur's break them in a trice?
No—no—our lives are virtuous all, auftere
    and hard; —
Pray, ladies,—do you ever fee a card?
Thofe empty boxes fhew you don't love
    plays;
The managers, poor fouls! get nothing now
    a days.
If here you come—by chance—but once a
    week,
The pit can witnefs that you never fpeak:
Penfive Attention fits with decent mien;
No paint, no naked fhoulders to be feen!
  And yet this grave, this moral, pious age,
May learn one ufeful leffon from the ftage.
Shun ftrife, ye fair, and once a conteft o'er,
Wake to a blaze the dying flame no more—

  I   From

From fierce debate fly all the tender Loves,
And Venus cries, " Coachman,—Put-to my
                doves,"
The genial bed no blooming Grace prepares,
" And every day becomes a day of cares."

FINIS.

THE
DESERT ISLAND,

A

DRAMATIC POEM,

IN

THREE ACTS.

As It is Acted at the

Theatre-Royal in Drury-Lane.

Te, dulcis conjux, te folo in littore fecum
Te veniente die, te decedente canebat.   Virg.

LONDON,

Printed for Paul Vaillant, facing Southampton ſtreet,
in the Strand. MDCCLXII.

[Price One Shilling and Six Pence.]

ADVERTISEMENT.

THE following Piece is founded on the *Isola Disabitata* of the celebrated ABBE METASTASIO: In reading the Performance of that great Genius, the present Writer received so exquisite a Pleasure, that he contracted a Passion for the Subject, and could not refrain from exercising his Pen upon it. In the Prosecution of his Plan, he knew enough of the modern Theatre, to perceive that it was thin of what our Play-followers call Business; and he was aware that on the Stage it might prove (to use *Milton's* Words) *very different from what among us passes for Best*. The same Remark was made by a Friend of the Author's, who thought it hazardous to offer to a popular Assembly a Piece, in which there were none of those Strokes that generally succeed with the Multitude. " Can't you," said he, " throw " in something here and there to season it more to " the public Appetite? — Suppose you were to " change the Title, and fix the Scene among the " *Anthropophagi*, or among the *Men, whose Heads* " *do grow beneath their Shoulders* — a few of those " extraordinary Personages exhibited on the Stage, " will prove very acceptable : — What think you " of an *Irish* Servant in it? — That certainly will " insure Success, the more especially if you add " some aerial Beings, and conclude the Whole " with a drunken Song by the Tars of *Old Eng-* " *land*." — The Author was sensible of the Force of these Observations; but the GREAT MILTON (mentioned above) stared him in the Face, with his Reflections on " the Error of introducing tri- " vial and vulgar Persons, which, by all Judicious, " hath been counted absurd, and brought in with- " out Discretion, CORRUPTLY to gratify the Peo- " ple."*—He therefore determined to preserve the

_____

* *Vide*. Preface to *Samson Agonistes*.

Integrity

ADVERTISEMENT.

Integrity of his original Design, and to try what would be the Effect of a simple Fable, with but few Incidents, supported entirely by the Spirit of Poetry, Sentiment, and Passion. To combine these three Qualities is indeed an arduous Task; and the Author, therefore, does not flatter himself that he has entirely succeeded in so difficult an Attempt.

In Justice to METASTASIO, he thinks proper to inform the mere *English* Reader, that he hath not been a Translator on this Occasion, but has followed the Impulse of his own Imagination, excepting in a few Passages. The ITALIAN POET gave the Fable; the present Writer made his own Use of it; or in other Words, the Ground-work, or *Canevas*, (as the *French* call it) is METASTASIO'S; for the Colouring Mr. *Murphy* is answerable.

He could not but be surprized to find that, on the first Nights the Scene in the third Act, between *Sylvia* and *Henrico*, was deemed equivocal. There is always a sufficient Number ready to ascribe to an Author various Meanings, which he never had, "and see at Cannon's what was never there."— To these Gentlemen he returns his Thanks; but the Species of Wit, which they are willing to allow him, he begs leave publickly to disclaim. The Character of a Girl, who has never seen a Man, and who has been taught to think of such a Being with Horror, is merely imaginary; but the possible, or Poetical Existence of such a Girl being once established, it is to be wished that the Critics would agree what Questions it is natural for her to ask on her first Interview with a Man. METASTASIO makes her say,

> *Che vuoi da me?*
> *Un Uom Sei dunque!*
> *Andiamo Insieme.*
> *Ah! troppo non trattenerti,* &c.

And

ADVERTISEMENT.

And thefe little Touches, (fo differently do we judge in *England*) were thought abroad to be delicate Strokes of the moft elegant Simplicity.

He could wifh it had been univerfaly underftood that it was not a TRAGEDY he offered to the Public, but a DRAMATIC POEM; that is to fay, a Piece with fome interefting Situations to engage the Affections, but which affords more Room for a Picturefque Imagnation to difplay itfelf, than is generally allowed to the more important Concerns of real Tragedy, where the Diftrefs fhould be always encreafing, where the Paffions fhould be always rifing to fuller and ftronger Emotions, and where of Courfe the Poet ought not to find Leifure for Imagery and Defcription. Had this been felt and acknowledged, no Body would have looked for another Kind of Entertainment than was promifed, and the Smiles arifing from SYLVIA'S Dread of a Man (on the firft Difcovery of him,) and her gradual Attachment to him in Compliance with natural Inftinct, would never have been judged inconfiftent with the Colour of the Whole. But if the Author of the *Defert Ifland* has erred in this, he has the Confolation of having erred with the greateft Poet now in *Europe*.

As many of the malevolent Writers of the Age have heretofore honoured the Author with their Abufe, and as he was apprehenfive that they ftill remained under the Oppreffion of their Dullnefs and Obfcurity, it was deemed proper to call them forth into Daylight, by exhibiting one general Reprefentative of them all on the Stage. For this he returns his Thanks to the Author of the Prologue; and if any needy Bookfellers, or unhappy Authors, can find their Account in taking further Liberties with him, he hereby declares, he fhould be forry not to have Merit enough to provoke fome of them, and for their Encouragement,

he

ADVERTISEMENT.

he adds in the Words of the noble Author of the *Characteristics*, that " He will never reply, un-
" less he should hear of them or their Works in
" any good Company a Twelve-month after."

Lincoln's Inn,
Jan. 26, 1760.   The AUTHOR.

PROLOGUE,

Written and Spoken by Mr. GARRICK,

In the Character of a DRUNKEN POET.

ALL, all shall out—all that I know and feel;
I will by Heav'n—to higher Powers appeal!—
Behold a Bard!—no Author of to-night—
No, no,—they can't say that, with all their spite:
Ay, you may frown (looking behind the scenes) *I'm at you,*
great and small—
Your Poet, Players, Managers and all!—
These Fools within here, swear that I'm in liquar—
My passion warms me—makes my utt'rance thicker;—
I totter too—but that's the Gout and Pain,—
French Wines, and living high, have been my bane.—
From all temptations now, I wisely steer me;
Nor will I suffer one fine woman near me.
And this I sacrifice, to give you pleasure—
For you I've coin'd my brains,—and here's the treasure!
                                    [Pulls out a Manuscript.
A treasure this, of profit and delight!
And all thrown by for this damn'd stuff to-night:—
This is a play would water ev'ry eye!—
If I but look upon't, it makes me cry:
This Play would tears from blood-stain'd Soldiers draw,—
And melt the bowels of hard hearted Law!
Would fore and aft the storm-proof Sailor rake;—
Keep turtle eating Aldermen awake!
Would the cold blood of ancient Maidens thrill,
And make ev'n pretty younger tongues lie still.

This

PROLOGUE.

This Play not ev'n Managers would refuse,—
Had Heav'n but giv'n 'em any brains to chuse!—

[*Puts up his Manuscript.*

Your Bard to-night, bred in the ancient school,
Designs and measures all by critic rule;
'Mongst Friends—it goes no farther—He's a Fool. }
So very classic, and so very dull—
His Desert Island is his own dear Skull:
No Soul to make the Play-house ring, and rattle,
No Trumpets, Thunder, Ranting, Storms, or Battle! }
But all your fine poetic Prittle-prattle.
The Plot is this—A Lady's cast away—
" Long before the beginning of the Play;"
And they are taken by a Fisherman, }
The Lady and the Child—'tis Bays's plan—
So on he blunders—He's an Irishman.— }
'Tis all alike—his comic stuff I mean— }
I hate all humour—it gives me the Spleen; }
So damn'em both, with all my heart, unsight, unseen.
But should you ruin him, still I'm undone—
I've try'd all ways to bring my Phœnix on—

[*Shewing his Play again.*

Flatter I can with any of their Tribe—
Can cut and slash—indeed I cannot bribe; }
What must I do then?—beg you to subscribe.
Be kind ye Boxes, Galleries, and Pit—
'Tis but a Crown a piece, for all this Wit:
All Sterling Wit—to puff myself I hate—
You'll ne'er supply your wants at such a rate!
'Tis worth your money, I would scorn to wrong ye,—
You smile consent—I'll send my hat among ye.

[*Going, he returns.*

So much beyond all praise your bounties swell!
Not my own Tongue, my Gra-ti-tude can tell— }
" A little Flattery sometimes does well."

[*Staggers off.*

Dramatis

Dramatis Personæ.

M E N.

FERDINAND, Husband to Constantia, } Mr. HOLLAND.

HENRICO, Friend to Ferdinand, } Mr. FLEETWOOD.

W O M E N.

CONSTANTIA,   Mrs. PRITCHARD.

SYLVIA, her Daughter,   Miss PRITCHARD.

SCENE, A DESERT ISLAND.

THE
DESERT ISLAND.

ACT I.

*The scene represents a vale in the Desert Island,
surrounded by rocks, caverns, grottos, flowering
shrubs, exotic trees, and plants growing wild.
On one side is a cavern in a rock, over the entrance
of which appears, in large characters, an unfinish-
ed inscription.* CONSTANTIA *is discovered at
work at the inscription, in a romantic habit of
skins, leaves, and flowers; in her hand she holds a
broken sword, and stands in act to finish the
imperfect inscription.*

After a short pause, she begins.

REST, rest my arm — ye weary
    sinews, rest —
Awhile forget your office — On
    this rock
Here sit thee down, and think thy-
    self to stone.   [*Sits down.*
— Would heav'n I could ! — [*rises.*] Ye shrubs,
    ye nameless plants,

        That

That wildy-gadding 'midft the rifted rocks
Wreathe your fantaftic fhoots;—ye darkfome trees,
That weave yon verdant arch above my head,
Shad'wing this folemn fcene;—ye mofs-grown
   caves,
Romantic grottos,—all ye objects drear,——
Tell me, in pity tell me, have ye feen,
Thro' the long feries of involving time,
In which you have inclos'd this lonely manfion,
Say, have ye feen another wretch like me?—
No, never!—You, in tend'reft fympathy,
Have join'd my plaits—you, at the midnight
   hour,
When with uprooted hair I've ftrew'd the earth,
And call'd my hufband gone;—have call'd in vain
Perfidious Ferdinand!—you, at that hour,
Have waken'd echo in each vocal cell,
Till ev'ry grove, and ev'ry mountain hoar,
Mourn'd to my grefs refponfive—Well you know
The ftory of my woes—Ev'n yonder marble
Relenting feels the touch; receives each trace
That forms the melancholy tale.—Tho' rude,
And inexpert my hand;—tho' all uncouth
The inftrument, yet there behold my work
Well nigh complete—let me about it ftreight.
     [_She advances toward the rock._

Ye deep engraven letters, there remain;
And if in future time refiftlefs fate
Should throw fome Briton on this difmal fhore;
Then fpeak aloud;—to his aftonifh'd fenfe
Relate my fad, my memorable cafe—
Alarm his foul, call out——   STOP

STOP TRAVELLER.

HERE

CONSTANTIA,

WITH HER LITTLE INFANT,

SYLVIA,

WAS DESERTED BY HER HUSBAND,

THE PERFIDIOUS

FERDINAND;

WHO PRETENDING TO LAND HER

FOR REFRESHMENT

FROM THE DANGERS OF A STORMY SEA,

BARBAROUSLY LEFT HER

ON THIS UNHOSPITABLE ISLAND,

WHERE SHE ENDED HER DEPLORABLE LIFE.

FRIEND!

WHOE'ER THOU ART,

PITY MY WRONGS,

BUT AGAINST MY HUSBAND,

(FOR LOVE LIKE MINE CANNOT FORGET

WHERE ONCE WITH DELIGHT IT FIXED)

I CHARGE YOU NEVER MEDITATE R - - - -

Revenge! — the word Revenge is wanting still.
Ye holy pow'rs! if with one pitying look
You'll deign to view me, grant my earnest pray'r!
Let me but finish this my sad inscription,
Then let this busy, this afflicted heart
Be still at once, and beat my breast no more.

[She goes on with her work.

Enter SYLVIA.

SYLVIA.

My dearest mother — oh! quite out of breath.

B 2 . CONSTAN-

CONSTANTIA.

What is the matter, child?

SYLVIA.

Why, ma'am, my heart,
Beats wild with joy — oh! such an incident! —

CONSTANTIA.

What incident, my sweet?

SYLVIA.

My little fawn,
My dear, my loveliest fawn, — for many days
Whose loss I've mourn'd; for whose dear sake
     I've left
No corner of the Isle unsearch'd;—this monument
O'er the dew-spangled lawn, with printless feet,
Came bounding to me; playful frisk'd about
With inexpressive airs of glad surprize,
With eager signs of transport — Big round tears
Stood trembling in his eye, and seem'd to speak
His fond regret still mingling with his joy.

CONSTANTIA.

And is it that, my love, delights thee so? —

SYLVIA.

And can you wonder, ma'am? — yes, that de-
     lights me,
Transports me, charms me; — he's my darling
     care,
My dear companion, my sweet little friend,
That loves me, gambols round me, watches still
With anxious tenderness my ev'ry motion,

                                        Pants

Pants on my bofom, leaps into my arms,
And wanders o'er me with a thoufand kiffes.
Before this time, he never once ftray'd from me;
—I thought I loft him;—but he's found again!
And can you wonder I'm tranfported thus!

CONSTANTIA.

Oh! happy ftate of innocence!—how fweet
Thy joys, fimplicity, e'er yet the mind
With artificial paffions learns to glow;
Ere taft has ta'en our fenfes to our fchool,
Has given each well-bred appetite her laws,
Taught us to feel imaginary blifs,
Or elfe expire in elegance of pain.

SYLVIA.

Nay, now, again, you're growing grave—'tis you
Give laws to appetite;—forbid each fenfe.
To minifter delight; your eyes are dimm'd
With conftant tears;—the rofes on your cheek
Fade like yon violets, when exceffive dews
Have bent their drooping melancholy heads;
Soon they repair their graces; foon recal
Their aromatic lives, and fmiling yield
To fighing Zephyr all their balmy fweets.
To grief you're ftill a prey; ftill wan defpair
Sits with'ring at your heart, and ev'ry feature
Has your directions to be fix'd in woe.
Nay, pr'ythee now clear up—you make me fad—
—Will you, Mama, forget your cares?——

CONSTANTIA.

Forget!——
Oh! fweet oblivion, thy all healing balm

To

To wretches you refuse! — can I forget
Perfidious Ferdinand? — His tyrant form
Is ever prefent — The deluding looks,
Endearing accents, and the foft regards
With which he led me to yon mofs-clad cave,
There to repofe awhile — oh! cruel man!
And you, ye confcious wilds, I call you falfe!
Accomblices in guilt! — The Zephyrs bland
That pant upon each leaf; — the melody
That warbles thro' your groves; the falling foun-
      tains
That at each deep'ning cadence lull the mind,
Were all fuborn'd againft me; all confpir'd
To wrap me in the filken folds of fleep.
Sudden I wake — where, where is Ferdinand?
I rave, I fhriek, — no Ferdinand replies; ——
Frantic I rove thro' all your winding glades,—
I feek the fhore, — no Ferdinand appears —
I climb yon craggy fteeps; I fee the fhip
Unfurling all her fails — I call aloud,
I ftamp, cry out; — deaf as the roaring fea
He catches ev'ry gale that blows from heav'n,
And cleaves his liquid way. ——

SYLVIA.

Why will you thus
Recal your paft afflictions? ——

CONSTANTIA.

Ah! what then,
Thou wretched Conftance, what were then thy
      feelings?

                           I rend

I rend my treſſes, — beat my breaſt in vain,
In vain ſtretch out theſe ineffectual arms,
Pierce with my frantic cries the wounded air,
Daſh my bare boſom on the flinty rock,
Then riſe again, and ſtrain my aching ſight,
To ſee the ſhip ſtill leſſ'ning to my view,
And take the laſt, laſt glimpſe, as far, far off
In the horizon's verge ſhe dwindles ſtill,
Grows a dim ſpeck, and mixes with the clouds
Juſt vaniſhing, — juſt loſt, — ah! ſeen no more.

SYLVIA.

I pr'ythee don't talk ſo — my heart dies in me —
Why won't you ſtrive a little to forget
This melancholy theme? — the twilight grey
Of morn but faintly ſtreaks the eaſt; the ſtars
ſtill glimmer thro' the whit'ning air; the groves
Are mute; yon all-devouring deep lies huſh'd;
The tuneful birds, and the whole brute creation
Still ſink in ſoft oblivious ſlumber wrapp'd,
Forgetful of their cares; — all, — all but you
Know ſome repoſe; — you paſs the dreary night
In tears and ceaſeleſs grief; then riſing wild
Anticipate the dawn, and here reſume
Your doleful taſk, or elſe aſcend the height
Of yonder promontory; their forlorn
You ſit, and hear the brawling waves beneath
Laſh the reſounding ſhore; your brimful eye
Still fix'd on that ſad quarter of the heav'ns
Where my hard father diſappear'd.

CONSTAN-

CONSTANTIA.

Yes, there
My melancholy loves to dwell; there loves
To sit, and pine over its hoard of grief;
To roll these eyes o'er all the sullen main,
In hopes some sail may this way shape its course,
With tidings of the human race—Oh! heav'ns!
Could I behold that dear, that wish'd for sight,
Could I but see some vestiges of man,
Some mark of social life, ev'n tho' the ship
Should shun this isle, and court propitious gales
Beneath some happier clime; yet still the view
Would chear my soul, and my heart bound
   with joy
At that faint prospect of my fellow creatures.
But not for me, such transport;—not for me—
Dear native land, I now no more must see thee,
Condemn'd in ever-during solitude to mourn,
From thy sweet joys, society, debarr'd!

SYLVIA.

But to your happiness what's wanting here?
Full many a time I've heard you praise the arts,
The polish'd manners, and gay scenes of bliss
Which Europe yields—yet ever and anon
I from your own discourse can gather too
That happiness is all unknown to Europe,
That envy there can dwell, and discontent;
The smile, that wakens at another's woe;
The heart, that sickens at another's praise;
The tongue, that carries the malignant tale;

      The

The little spirit, that subverts a friend;
Fraud, perfidy, ingratitude, and murder.
Now sure with reason I prefer these scenes
Of innocence, tranquillity and joy!

CONSTANTIA.

Alas! my child, 'tis easy to forego
Unknown delights —— pleasures we've never
    felt. ——

SYLVIA.

Are we not here what you yourself have told me
In Europe sovereigns are? — here we have fix'd
Our little sylvan reign. — The guileless race
Of animals, that roam the lawns and woods,
Are tractable and willing subjects; — pay
Passive obedience to us — and yon sea
Becomes our tributary; hither rolls
In each hoarse-murm'ring tide his various stores
Of dantiest shell-fish — the unbidden earth,
Of human toil all ignorant, pours forth
Whatever to the eye, or taste, can prove
Rare, exquisite, and good — at once the spring
Call forth its green delights, and summer's blush
Glows on each purple branch.   The seasons here
  On the same tree, with glad surprize,
  Behold each other's gifts arise:
  Spontaneous fruits around us grow;
  For ever here the Zephyrs blow:
      Shrubs ever flow'ring,
      Shades embow'ring;
      Heav'nly spots,
      Cooling grots,
           C   Verdant

Verdant mountains,
Falling fountains;
Pure limpid rills,
Adown the hills,
That wind their way
And o'er the meadows play,
Enamour'd of th' enchanted ground.

CONSTANTIA.

What is this waſte of beauty, all theſe charms
Of cold, inanimate, unconſcious nature,
Without the ſocial ſenſe ? thoſe joys, my Sylvia,
Thou can'ſt not miſs ; for thou haſt never
　　known 'em.

SYLVIA.

But ſtill thoſe beauteous tracts of Europe,
which you ſo much regret, are full of men ;
And men, you know, are animals of prey :
I'm ſure that you yourſelf have told me ſo
A thouſand times. ——————

CONSTANTIA.

And if I have, my child,
I told a diſmal truth. — Oh ! they are falſe,
Inexorable, cruel, fell deceivers ;
Their unrelenting hearts no harbour know
For honour, truth, humanity, or love.

SYLVIA.

Well then, in this lone iſle, this dear retreat
From them at leaſt we're free. ——————

CONSTAN•

CONSTANTIA.

Poor innocent!
I can't but grieve for her —— [*Bursts into tears,
aside.*

SYLVIA.

Why fall afresh
Those drops of sorrow? —— pray you, now give
o'er. ——

CONSTANTIA.

My heart will break—I do not grieve, my child—
I can't conceal my tears—they must have way—

SYLVIA.

Nay, if you love me, sure you will not thus
Make my heart ake within me! —

CONSTANTIA.

No, my sweet —
I will not weep — all will be well, my love —
Oh! misery! — I can't, — I can't contain ——
The black ingratitude! —— [*Weeps.*

SYLVIA.

Say, is there aught
That I can do, Mama, to give you comfort? —
If there is, tell me — shall I fetch my fawn?
Dry up your tears, and he is your's this moment
— I'll run and bring him to you. ——

CONSTANTIA.

Sylvia, no! ——

SYLVIA.

Nay do, Mama—I beg you will—you shall. [*Exit*
C 2　　　　Constan-

CONSTANTIA *alone*.

Alas! I fear my brain will turn — the fun
Full fixteen times has made his annual courfe,
Since here I've dragg'd a miferable being,
The victim of defpair; which long e'er now,
To phrenzy kindling, muft have forc'd me dafh
My brain in madnefs on yon flinty rocks,
And end my pangs at once; if the keen inftinct
Of ftrong maternal love had not reftrain'd
My wild diforder'd foul, and bade me live
To watch her tender infancy; to rear
Her blooming years; with fond delighted care
To tend each bloffom of her growing mind,
And fee light gradual dawning on her foul.
And yet to fee her thus, — to fee her here,
Cut off from ev'ry focial blifs; condemn'd
Like fome fair flow'r that in a defert grows,
To breathe its fweets into the paffing wind,
And wafte its bloom all unperceiv'd away!
It is enough to break a mother's heart.
Let me not think on't — let me fhun that thought.

[*Sits down and fings.*

I.

What tho' his guilt my heart hath torn,
    Yet lovely is his mien,
His eyes mild-op'ning as the morn,
    Round him each grace is feen.
But oh! ye nymphs, your loves ne'er let him win,
For oh! deceit and falfhood dwell within.

II, From

II.

From his red lip his accents ftole,
 Soft as kind vernal fnows;
Melting they came, and in the foul
 Defire and joy arofe.
But oh! ye nymphs, ne'er liften to his art,
For oh! bafe falfhood rancles in his heart.

III.

He left me in this lonely ftate!
 He fled, and left me here,
Another Ariadne's fate,
 To mourn the live-long year.
He fled — but oh! what pains the heart muft
  prove,
When we reveal the crimes of him we love!

Re-enter SYLVIA.

SYLVIA.

I cannot bring him now — in yonder ftream
That thro' its pebbled channel glides along
Soft-murm'ring to the fea, he ftands to cool
His beauteous form in the pure limpid rill.
But ftill he fhall be your's ——

CONSTANTIA.

To thee, my child,
To thee he caufes joy — but joy to me
There's nothing now can bring — left by my
  hufband!
By the falfe barb'rous man! ——

SYLVIA.

SYLVIA.

And yet this man
You ftill regret — you muft excufe me now —
I vow, I can't but think, 'midft all your grief,
All your reproaches, your complaints againft
  him,
That ftill this man, this cruel fell deceiver,
Has found, — I know not why — within your
  breaft
Some tender advocate, to plead his caufe.

CONSTANTIA.

No, Sylvia, no; my love is turn'd to hath! ——

SYLVIA.

Then dry your forrows and this day begin
A happier train of Years — and lo! the fun
Emerges from the fea — He lifts his orb
Above the purpled main, and ftreams abroad
His golden fluid o'er the world — the birds
Exulting wake their notes — all things rejoice,
And hills, and groves, and rocks, and vallies
  fmile.
Let me entreat you then forget your cares,
And fhare the general blifs. ——

    [The fun is feen to rife at a diftance, as it
                were out of the fea.

CONSTANTIA.

Once more all hail,
Thou radient power, who in your bright career
Or rifing or defcending, haft beheld
My never-ceafing woe! — again thou climb'ft

                                        In

In orient glory, and recall'ft the cares
And toils of man and beaft — but oh! in all
Your flaming courfe, your beams will never light
Upon a wretch fo loft, fo curft as I am.

SYLVIA.

And yet, my mother ——

CONSTANTIA.

Mine are pangs, my child,
Strokes of adverfity no time can cure,
No lenient arts can foften or affuage.
But I'll not grieve thee, Sylvia — I'll retire
To fome fequefter'd haunt — There, all forlorne,
I'll fit, and wear myfelf away in thought. [Exit.

SYLVIA, alone.

Alas! how obftinately bent on grief
Is her whole mind! — the votarift of care!
In vain I try to foften her afflictions,
And with each art beguile her from her woe.
I chide, intreat, carefs, and all in vain.
And what to me feems ftrange, perverfe, and
          wond'rous,
The more I ftrive, the more her forrows fwell;
Her tears the fafter fall, fall down her cheek
In ftreams fo copious, and fuch bitter anguifh,
That I myfelf at length, I know not how,
Catch the foft weaknefs, and o'erpow'r'd with
          grief,
Flow all diffolving in unbidden tears.
Affift her heav'n.—Her heart will break at laft—
                              I trem-

I tremble at the thought — I'll follow straight
And still implore, beseech, try evr'y way
To reconcile her to herself and me.
But see, look yonder! what a sight is there!
What can it mean, that huge enormous mass
That moves upon the bosom of the deep!
— A floating mountain! — no — a mountain
        never
Could change its place — for such a monstrous
        bulk
How light it urges on its way — how quick,
How rapid in its course! — What can it be ——
— I'll tow'rd the shore, and from the pointed
        rock
That juts into the waves, at leisure view
This wond'rous sight, and what it is explore.

END of the first ACT.

ACT II.

SCENE, *Another view of the Island, with an opening to the sea between several hills and rocks.*

Enter SYLVIA.

SYLVIA.

✳✳✳ TILL I behold it—still it glides along
✳ S ✳ Thro' the tumultuous sea—and lo!
✳✳✳   before it
    The waves divide! and now they
      close again,
Leaving a tract of angry foam behind.
It must be, sure, some monster of the deep;
For see!—upon its huge broad back it bears
Expanded wings, that, spreading to the wind,
Lie broad incumbent o'er the surge beneath—
—Ah! save me, save me!—what new forms
      appear!
What shapes of unknown being rise before me!
From yon huge monster's side they issue forth,
And bolt upon the shore!—behold, they stop,
And now with eager disconcerted pace
Precipitate rush forward on the isle, ——
Now 'mongst the rocks they wind their silent
      way.

         D   FERDI-

FERDINAND *and* HENRICO *appear.*

Protect me, heav'n! defend me! shield me!
    — ah!
Hide me, ye woods, within your deep recess;
Ne'er may these monsters penetrate your haunts;
Ne'er trace my footsteps thro' your darksome
    ways.
Behind the covert of this woodbine bow'r
Oh! let me rest conceal'd! —   [*She retires.*

FERDINAND *and* HENRICO *come forward.*

HENRICO.

No trace appears,
No vestige here is seen of human kind.
'Tis drear, 'tis waste, and unfrequented all.
And hark! — what noise? — from yonder toil-
    ing deep
How dreadful sounds the pealing roar! — my
    friend,
My valued Ferdinand, 'twere best retire.
This cannot be the place. ——

FERDINAND.

Oh! my Henrico,
This is the fatal shore — the well-known scene,
Yon bay, yon rocks, **yon** mountains, from
    whose brows
Th' imbow'ring forest over-hangs the deep,
Each well-remember'd object strikes my view,
Answers the image in my mind preserv'd,

                              Engraven

Engraven there by love's recording hand,
And never, but with life, to fade from thence.

HENRICO.

And yet thy love-enfeebled foul may form
Imaginary tokens of resemblance.
This foil unbeaten feems by mortal ftep.

FERDINAND.

No, my Henrico, no — this is the fpot ——
My heart in ev'ry pulfe confirms it to me.
This is the place, the very place, where fate
Began to weave the tiffue of my woes.
Oh! I was curft, abhorr'd of heav'n, or elfe
I ne'er had trufted the contentious waves,
But kept my ftore of happinefs at home.

HENRICO.

Repine not for an action that arofe
From filial piety, — a father's mandate
Requir'd obedience from you. ——

FERDINAND.

To his fummons
I paid a glad attention — yet, good heav'n!
Why in that early æra of my blifs
Should then his orders come, to dafh my joys?—
Oh! I was bleft with all that rareft beauty,
With all that ev'ry Venus of the mind,
The tender heart, and the enliven'd wit
Could pour delightful on the raptur'd fenfe
Of the young bridegroom, whofe admiring eyes
Still hung enamour'd on her ev'ry charm,

D 2   And

And thence drank long infpiring draughts of
        love,
Unfated ftill, — ftill kindling at the view.

HENRICO.

Thy fate indeed was hard ————

FERDINAND.

Heav'n knows it was ————
Each foft defire, each joy refin'd was mine —
The hours foft glided by, and as they pafs'd
Scatter'd new bleffings from their balmy wings;
They faw our ever new delight; they faw
A blooming offspring crown our mutual loves;
The mother's features, and her ev'ry grace
In this our daughter exquifitely trac'd.
But to be torn from that fupreme of blifs, —
My wife, — Conftantia, — and my beauteous
        babe,
Here to be left on this untravell'd ifle,
To pine in bitternefs of want! — their bed
The cold bare earth, while the inclement winds
From yonder main came howling round their
        heads,
Until at length the friendly hand of death
In pity threw his fhrowd upon their woes.

HENRICO.

Too fure, I fear, they're loft. ————

FERDINAND.

Perhaps, my friend,
Perhaps when gafping in the pangs of death, —
                                        — When

— When ev'ry beauty faded from her cheek,
— And her eye languifh'd motionlefs and dim,
Perhaps ev'n then, in that fad difmal hour,
My name ftill hover'd on her quiv'ring lips,
And nought but death could tear me from her
   heart.

HENRICO.

Her tend'reft thoughts no doubt were fix'd on
  thee.

FERDINAND.

Her tend'reft thoughts! oh! no — her utmoft
  rage ——
Who knows, Henrico, but fhe deem'd me falfe;
Deem'd me a vile deferter from her arms?
She did, — fhe muft — each ftrong appearance
   join'd
To mark me guilty — Oh! that thought ftrikes
  deep
It's fcorpion ftings into my very heart.
Could fhe but think me fo refin'd in guilt,
So exquifite a villain, as to caufe
A moment's anguifh in that tender breaft,
Where all the loves, where all the virtues dwelt,
— 'Twere mifery, — 'twere torture in th' ex-
  treme ——
And yet fhe thought me fuch — by heav'n fhe
  did —
Accus'd me of the worft, the blackeft treafon,
Of treafon to my love — ftung with th' idea
She roam'd this ifle, and to thefe defert wilds
      Pour'd

Pour'd forth her lamentable tale ;—who knows
But on fome craggy cliff whole nights fhe fat
Raving in madnefs to the moon's pale gleam ;
Until at length all kindling into phrenzy,
Clafping her infant clofer to her breaft,
With defperation wild from off the rock
Headlong fhe plung'd into the roaring waves,
While her laft accents murmur'd faithlefs Fer-
    dinand.

HENRICO.

Diftract not thus your foul with fancied woes.
She could not think thee faithlefs ; thee, whofe
    mind,
Whofe ev'ry virtue were fo well approv'd.

FERDINAND.

Still will I hope fhe did not.—Oh! fhe knew
I made that voyage in duty to a father.
A while we fteer'd a happy courfe, until
Beneath the burning line, from whence the fun
In ftreight direction pours his ardent blaze
On ev'ry fever'd fenfe, a ftorm arofe,
Sudden and wild ; as if a war of nature
Were thund'ring o'er our heads—full twenty
    days
It drove us headlong on the dafhing furge
Far from our deftin'd way, until at length
In evil hour we landed on this ifle.

SYLVIA.

SYLVIA *returns, and peeps from behind a hedge.*

SYLVIA.

Methought I heard a found, as if they both
Held mutual converfe —— yonder lo ! they
    ftand ——
They do not follow me —— what can they be ! ——

FERDINAND.

There is the fpot, juft where yon aged tree
Imbrowns the plain beneath, on which the
    villains,
The unrelenting band of pirates, feiz'd me —
There I receiv'd my wound, and there I fought
Till my fword fhiver'd in my hand — worn out,
Opprefs'd by numbers, pow'rlefs, and difarm'd,
They bore me headlong to the beach; in vain
Piercing the air with horrid cries; in vain
Back towr'd the cave, where poor Conftantia
    flept,
With her lov'd infant daughter in her arms,
Straining my ardent eyes — my eyes alone !
For oh ! their cruelty had bound my arms,
And tears and looks were all I then could ufe.

SYLVIA.

The voice but indiftinctly ftrikes my ear,
Would they would turn this way. ——

FERDINAND.

Fetter'd, ty'd down,
They dragg'd me to the veffel—bore me hence——

                    In

In vain our ship pursued — In vain gave chase —
Form'd with detested skill the guilty bark
In which they plung'd me, gliding oe'r the main
Outstripp'd their tardy course — they steer'd
    away
Far to their regions of accursed bondage,
Far from Constantia, far from ev'ry joy
A doating husband, and delighted father
Feels in mix'd rapture with his wife and child.
Oh! I could pour my plaints — but I'll not
    wound
Thy ear, my friend, with further lamentation.

HENRICO.

Would Heav'n I could remove the cause ——

FERDINAND.

Alas!
That cannot be — Thou can'st not bid return
The irrevocable flight of time; recall
The moments of our young delight; annul
And render void, what once the hand of fate
Hath from it's stores of woe, pour'd down upon
    me.

SYLVIA *(half concealed.)*

Why will they stand with looks averted thus?
I long to see their countenance and mein.

FERDINAND.

But yet, thou best of friends, yet grant me this;
Assist my search; — oh! let me roam around
This fatal shore — the isle's circumference

Circles

Circles a fcanty fpace — we cannot lofe
Each other here — do thou purfue that path
That leads due eaft — this way I'll bent my
　　courfe.

HENRICO.

By heav'n there is no tafk of hardihood
Of toil, or danger but I'll try for thee;
For thee, my friend; — to thee I owe my life,
And that more precious boon, my liberty:
Thou haft releas'd me from the falling chain,
From flav'ry's bitter prefure — 'twas thy fkill
That form'd the plan of freedom, feiz'd the
　　veffel,
And made your friends the partners of your
　　flight.
— For thee I'll roam around — but oh! I fear
Our fearch will prove in vain ——

FERDINAND.

Too fure it will ——
And yet it is the doom of love like mine
To dwell for ever on the fad idea
Of the dear object loft; to vifit oft
A lonely pilgrim ev'ry well known fcene,
Each haunted glade, where the lov'd object
　　·ftray'd;
To call each circumftance of pafs'd delight
Back to the foul; in fond excurfions feek
The dear lamented fhade — Then, oh! my
　　friend,
Then let me tafte that fad, that penfive comfort,
　　　　　　E　　　　　　　　Range

Range thro' thefe wilds; afcend each craggy
 fteep,
Try in each grotto, in each gloomy cave
If haply there remain fome veftige of Conftantia.
         [*Exit.*

HENRICO.

On yonder beach we'll meet again — farewell ! ——

SYLVIA.

Conceal thee Sylvia,—ah !—it comes this way !—
Then let me feek the covert of the woods,
Where nods the browneft horror; there lie fafe
From the unufual fight of thefe ftrange beings.
         [*Exit.*

HENRICO, *folus.*

How cruel is my friend's condition ! — doom'd
For ever to regret, yet never find
The object of his foul — his early love
He lavifh'd all on her — with her it goes
To the dank grave, and leaves him haplefs here
To die a lingering death. — Yet ftill I'll try
By ev'ry office friendfhip can perform
To heal the wound that preys upon his life.
         [*Exit.*

*The back scene closes, and presents a thick
    wood; then enter* SYLVIA.

SYLVIA.

What have my eyes beheld? — my flutt'ring
        heart
Beats quick in ftange emotions — from yon
        grove
Of tufted trees, I faw this namelefs being
Walk o'er the ruffet heath — it's face appear'd
Confefs'd to view — It cannot be a man ——
No lines of cruelty deform'd his vifage. ——
Were it a man, his untam'd favage foul
Would ftrongly fpeak in each diftorted fea-
        ture ——
This was all pleafing, amiable and mild:
A gentle forrow, bright'ning into fmiles,
Such as befpoke a calm, yet feeling fpirit,
Sat on it's peaceful brow, and oe'r it threw
A gentle gleam of fweetnefs and of pain.
— It cannot be a woman neither — no ——
The drefs accords not with that mode, which
        oft
My mother hath defcrib'd — Whate'er it be
Attraction dwells about it; winning fmiles;
Affuafive airs of tendernefs and joy.
I'll feek my mother — fhe perhaps may know
Thefe forms, to me unufual — By this row
Of darkfome pines, my fteps all unperceiv'd

May gain the place where with affiduous hand
She works, and teaches the rude rocks to tell
Her mournful elegy — what mean my feet?
— Why ftand they thus forgetful of their office?
— Why leaves th' involontary figh! — and
    why
Thus in quick pulfes beats my heart? — my
    eyes
A mifty dimnefs covers — In my ears
Strange murmurs found — my very breath is
    loft ——
What can it be? — I know thee fear! — 'tis thou
That caufeft this! — and yet it can't be fear —
Fear cannot thrill with pleafure thro' the veins;
Knows not this dubious joy — thefe grateful
    tremblings ——
I cannot guefs what thefe emotions mean,
Nor what this bufy thing my heart would want!
Let me feek fhelter in my mother's arms. [*Exit.*

Scene changes to the firft view of the ifland
where CONSTANTIA'S *infcription is feen*

Enter FERDINAND.

No — never more fhall thefe fond eyes behold
    her.
Loft, loft, my poor Conftantia loft! — In vain
I fearch thefe gloomy woods — In vain call out
Her honour'd name to ev'ry hill and dale.
                My

My eyes are falfe, or on the craggy bafe
Of yonder rock fome inftrument appears,
The mark of human kind ———   [*Takes it up.*
A broken fword!
Oh! all ye heav'nly pow'rs! — the very fame —
This once was mine — unfaithful to it's truft
It fail'd me at my utmoft need — I fee
The well known characters; the very words
That form'd it's motto — 'tis, it is the fame —
Oh! were Conftantia found! — what do I fee?
All o'er with hair the flinty rock beftrew'd! —
Thefe were her decent treffes — thefe in anguifh
She tore relentlefs from her beauteous head,
Up by the roots fhe tore, and fcatter'd wild
To all the paffing winds — fhe ftill may live! —
Conftantia? — my belov'd, — my life, return! —
Conftantia! — ha! — what myftic characters
Are hewn into the rock? — my name appears —
                                   [*He reads.*

STOP TRAVELLER.

HERE

CONSTANTIA,

WITH HER LITTLE INFANT,

SYLVIA,

WAS DESERTED BY HER HUSBAND,

THE PERFIDIOUS

FERDINAND;

WHO PRETENDING TO LAND HER

FOR REFRESHMENT

FROM

FROM THE DANGERS OF A STORMY SEA,
BARBAROUSLY LEFT HER
ON THIS UNHOSPITABLE ISLAND,
WHERE SHE ENDED HER DEPLORABLE LIFE.

Support me, heav'n! — ah! no — withold your
    aid,
Ye unrelenting pow'rs, and let me thus,
Each vital spark subsiding, thus expire.
                   [Leans against the rock.

Enter HENRICO.

HENRICO.

What hoa! — my Ferdinand! — this way the
    sound
Struck on my list'ning ear — what means my
    friend
Thus growing to the rock, transform'd to stone,
A breathing statue, 'midst these shapeless piles?—

FERDINAND.

Henrico there! — read there! ——

HENRICO.

Letters engrav'd! —   *[He reads to himself as
                           far as*
SHE ENDED HER DEPLORABLE LIFE.
Alas! my friend — *They gaze speechless at each
    other for some time, then Ferdinand falls.*
The storm of grief o'erpow'rs his feeble spirits.
                             Now

Now rouze thy ftrength, my Ferdinand, and
      bear
This load of forrow like a man. ———

FERDINAND.

I do ———
Thou fee'ft I do — I do not weep, my friend —
Thefe eyes are dry — their very fource is dry —
— I am her cruel hufband to the laft. ———

HENRICO.

Oh! thou wert ever kind and tender to her.

FERDINAND.

Tender and kind! — look there! — there ftands
      the black,
The horrid roll of guilt denounc'd againft me.
Lo! the dread characters! — let me perufe
The whole fad record; of this bitter woe
Still deeper drink, and gorge me with affliction.
                              [*He reads.*

FRIEND!
WHOE'ER THOU ART,
PITY MY WRONGS,
BUT AGAINST MY HUSBAND,
(FOR LOVE LIKE MINE CANNOT FORGET
WHERE ONCE WITH DELIGHT IT FIXED)
I CHARGE YOU NEVER MEDITATE R - - - -

Revenge, fhe meant to fay—the word's begun—
But death untimely ftopt her hand—oh! mifery!
She thought me falfe, and yet could love ftill—
                                          The

The wound now pierces deeper — had fhe loath'd
    me,
Abhorr'd me, curs'd me, 'twere not half the
    torture
This angel-goodnefs caufes — and to lofe her!
To lofe a mind like her's, that thus could pour
Such unexampled tendernefs and love,
Amidft the keeneft anguifh — on the earth
Meafure thy length, thou wretch accurft ! —
    there lie,
For ever lie, and to thefe woods and wilds
Howl out thy griefs in madnefs and defpair.

HENRICO.

I feel, I feel thy forrows — oh! my friend, ——
Cruel event ! — your tears alas ! are juft ——
Then let them flow, and let me mingle mine —
Your gufhing forrows may affuage your grief,
This ftorm of rage attemp'ring into peace.

FERDINAND.

Who talks of peace ? — let phrenzy feize my
    brain ——
Come, moon-ftruck madnefs, with thy glaring
    eye,
And clanking chain ; come, fhoot thy kindling
    fires
Into my utmoft foul ; — blaft ev'ry thinking
    pow'r ;
Raze each idea out ; — tear up at once
The feat of memory — no — leave me that ——
Still leave me memory, to picture forth

               Conftan-

Conſtantia's lovely form, that I may ſit
With unclad ſides, upon ſome blaſted heath
And gloat upon her image ; — ſee her ſtill,
See her whole days with fancy's guſhing eye,
And gaze on that alone ——

HENRICO.

Ariſe my friend,
And quit this fatal ſhore ——

FERDINAND.

And quit this ſhore!
But whither turn ? — ah! whither ſhall I go ? —
Where ſhelter me from miſery ? — this iſle
Shall be my journey's bound. ———

HENRICO.

What can'ſt thou mean ?

FERDINAND.

Never again to draw the vital air
But where my love expir'd — to feed my ſoul
With theſe ſad objects, this ſepulchral tale,
Ev'n to the height of yet unheard-of anguiſh :
To print my pious kiſſes on the rocks ;
To bathe the ground, which her dear footſteps
        preſs'd,
With the inceſſant tears of burning anguiſh ;
To make theſe wilds all vocal with her name,
Till this cold lifeleſs tongue ſhall move no more.

HENRICO.

By heav'n, you muſt not think ——

F   FERDI-

FERDINAND.

Farewell! — farewell! ——
Confult thy happinefs! — for ever here
By fate I'm doom'd to ftay —— alas! Con-
　　ftantia! ——
To perifh with thy infant here! — no friend
To clofe thy ghaftly orbs! — thy pale remains
On the bare earth expos'd, without the tribute
Of a fond hufband's tears o'er thy dead corfe; —
Without the laft fad obfequies — yet here,
I ftill will raife an empty fepulchre.
There fhall no cold unconfcious marble form
In mockery of imitated woe
Bend oe'r the fancy'd urn : myfelf will be
The fad, the penfive, monumental figure,
Diftilling real anguifh o'er the tomb ;
Till wafting by degrees I moulder down,
And fink to filent durft. ——

HENRICO.

What man could do,
Already youv'e perform'd ——

FERDINAND.

Prithee, no more ——
I will about it ftreight — this place affords
Materials for the work — Thither I'll bring
Whate'er can deck the fcene — Conftantia, yes
I will appeafe thy difcontented fhade,
Then follow thee to yonder realms of blifs.

　　　　　　　　　　　　　　　　　　[*Exit.*

HENRICO.

HENRICO *folus.*

His vehemence of grief bears down his reafon.
He muft not linger here — his ftay were fatal —
Force will be neceffary — to our boat
I'll haften back and call fome trufty friends
To drag him from this malancholy fhore.

END of the Second ACT.

ACT III.

The same scene continues.

Enter SYLVIA.

T HRO' the befriending gloom of arch=
ing bow'rs,
Thro' walks, where never fun-beam
pierc'd, at length
I've gain'd this deep-encircled vale — ah ! me !
I feel ftrange tremors ftill — fhe is not here ——
Mama ! — where can fhe be ? — her mournful
tafk
Waits for her ling'ring hand —— my deareft
mother —
She anfwers not — what noife is that ? — me-
thought
I heard fome fteps advancing — 'tis my fawn
That ruftles thro' the foreft glade — he ftops
And looks, then runs, and ftops again to take
A fearful gaze — he too perhaps has feen
Thefe unknown beings — yonder lo ! he ftands
In mute expreffive wonder — heav'n protect me !
— Thro' this clofe path, that gradual winding
up

Leads

Leads on to plains, to woods, and verdant lawns
Embofom'd in the rock, I'll journey up ——
The day now glows intenfe, but by the rills,
That thro' embow'ring groves come purling
  down,
I oft can lay me, and enjoy each breeze
That plays amid thofe craggy fcenes — a noife
From yonder interwoven branches — ha! ——
Ye guarding angels, fave me! — fee, fee there—
That thing again! ——

Enter HENRICO.

HENRICO.

What beauteous form in thefe forlorne abodes
Attracts my wond'ring eyes? ——

SYLVIA.

Ye heav'nly pow'rs!   [*Retiring from him.*

HENRICO.

It fwims before my fight — whate'er thou art,
Virgin, or goddefs — oh! a goddefs fure! ——
Thou goddefs of thefe manfions! — for thy looks
Beam heav'nly radiance, with propitious ears
Accept my fupplication ——

SYLVIA.

Ha! — it fpeaks ——
It fpeaks — what doft thou mean! ——

HENRICO.

Oh! fay what place,
What clime is this?—and what art thou that thus
Adorn'ft this lonely manfion? ——

SYLVIA.

SYLVIA.

Will you firſt
Promiſe to come no nearer?

HENRICO.

With devotion
As true as ever pilgrim offer'd up
In holy fervor to his ſaint, — I promiſe.

SYLVIA.

How gentle it's demeanor! — tell me now
What thing thou art?

HENRICO.

One born to miſery; ——
A man, whom fate ——

SYLVIA.

A man! — art thou a man?

HENRICO.

I am. ——

SYLVIA.

Oh! heav'ns! — a man! — protect me — ſave
me ——   [Runs away.

HENRICO.

Nay, fly me not — a ſudden impulſe here
Bids me perſue — forgive, thou unknown fair,
That with ſoft violence I thus preſume
To force thee meaſure back thy ſteps again.

                              [He brings her back.

SYLVIA.

Force me not thus, inhuman, barb'rous man —
What have I ſaid — Oh! worthy gen'rous man,
                                        Thus

Thus on my knees I beg, — have mercy on
 me ——
— I never did you harm — indeed I did not. —

HENRICO.

Arife, [*raifes her*] thou lonely tenant of thefe
 woods,
And let me thus, — thus as befits the man
Whofe mind runs o'er with rapture and furprize,
Whofe heart throbs wild with mingled doubt
  and joy,
Thus let me worfhip this celeftal form, ·
'This heav'nly brightnefs, to my wond'ring eyes
That fheds fuch influence, as when an angel
Breaks thro' a flood of glory to the fight,
Of fome expiring faint, and cheers his foul
With vifions of difclofing heav'n.

SYLVIA.

He kneels! —
He kneels to me! — how mild his very look —
How foft each word! — are you indeed a man? —

HENRICO.

I am, fweet faint — and one whofe heart is prone
To melt at each idea beauty prints
On his delighted fenfe; and fure fuch beauty,
Touch'd by the hand of harmony, adorn'd
With inexprefive graces, well may claim
My lowlieft adoration and my love.

SYLVIA.

This language all is new; — but ftill it has
I know not what of charming in't, that gains
        Upon

Upon the lift'ning ear — If this be falfhood ; —
Then falfhood can affume a pleafing look.

HENRICO.

Why thofe averted eyes?

SYLVIA.

What would you have?

HENRICO.

Oh! if thou art as gracious, as thou'rt fair,
Say have you feen Conftantia? when and where,
And how did fhe expire? ——

SYLVIA.

Conftantia lives ——
Why didft thou fay expire? — my mother lives,
Lives in thefe bleft abodes ——

HENRICO.

Ah! gentle Sylvia, ——
So I will call thee, — daughter of Conftantia,
Oh! fly and find her out — mean time I'll feek
Th'afflicted Ferdinand. ——

SYLVIA.

What doft thou fay? ——
Can he, can Ferdinand be here? — that falfe,
Perfidious, barb'rous man, — can he be here?

HENRICO.

He is, my fair; nor barbarous nor falfe.
Fortune that made him wretched, could no
     more.

ANOR

Anon you'll know the whole; to waste a mo-
    ment
In conf'rence now, and longer to suspend
The meeting of this pair, who now in agony
Bemoan their lot, were barbarous indeed.

SYLVIA.

But may I trust him? won't he do her harm?

HENRICO.

He won't, my beauteous fair. ——

SYLVIA.

Is he like you? ——

HENRICO.

His goodness far transcends me ——

SYLVIA.

Then I think
I'll venture to comply — let's go together. ——

HENRICO.

Oh! I could tend thy steps for ever; hear
Soft accents warbling from thy vermeil lip,
Watch thy mild-glancing eye; behold how
    grace,
Whate'er you do, which ever way you bend,
Guides each harmonious movement; but this
    hour
Is friendship's due; then let us instant fly
Thro' diff'rent paths — thou to seek out Con-
    stantia,
And I to find her husband — haply so

G   Their

Their meeting will be fpeedier — farewell!
I'll bring him to this very fpot — adieu!
For a fhort interval adieu, my love!

SYLVIA.

Farewell! — another word — pray what's your
    name?

HENRICO.

Fair excellence, Henrico I am call'd.

SYLVIA.

Pray do not tarry long, Henrico ——

HENRICO.

Why
That pleafing charge, my fweet?

SYLVIA.

I cannot tell;
But as you're leaving me, each ftep you move,
My fpirits fink; a melancholy gloom
Darkens the fcene around, and I methinks
Helplefs in folitude am left again
To wander all alone a dreary way.

HENRICO.

Oh! I will come again, thou angel fweetnefs!
Yes, I will come, and at that lovely fhrine
Pour out my adoration and my vows.
Yes, I will come, to part from thee no more;
A moment now farewell! —   [Exit.

SYLVIA.

SYLVIA, *alone.*

Farewell! — be sure you keep your word ——
  He's gone,
And yet is with me still — abfent I hear
And fee him in his abfence — ftill his looks
Beam with mild dignity, and ftill his voice
Sounds in my ear delightful — what it means,
This new-born fenfe this wonderful emotion,
Unfelt till now and mix'd of pain and joy,
I cannot guefs — how my heart flutters in me!
I'll not perplex myfelf with vain conjecture;
Whate'er the caufe, th'effect, I feel, is pleafing.
  [*Conftantia is heard finging within the fcenes.*
Oh! heav'ns! what noife! — it is my mother's
  Voice ——
Again fhe pours her melancholy forth,
As fweetly plaintive as when fad Philomel,
Beneath fome poplar fhade, bemoans her young,
And fitting penfive on the lonely bough,
Her eye with forrow dimm'd, fhe tunes her dirge,
Warbling the night away, while all around
The vocal woodland, and each hill and dale
Ring with her griefs harmonious — hark! —
  that way
It founds — all gracious powr's direct me to her.
    [*Exit.*

A fhort fong is heard within the fcenes,
  then enter CONSTANTIA.

From walk to walk, from glade to glade, o'er all
The fea-girt ifle, o'er ev'ry mountain's top,
   G 2   I roam

I roam from place to place; but oh; no place
Affords relief to me — the sun now leads
The sultry hours, and from his burning ray
Each living thing retires; yet I endue
His fierceft rage, The fever in my mind
Heeds not external circumftance, and time
Witholds his medicinal aid — the trees,
And rocks themfelves his pow'rful influence
        own;
— All but my grief — that, each fucceeding
        day
Sees in my heart frefh bleeding as at firft.
Delay not thus, ye cruel fates, but come
And wrap me in eternal reft. — Till then
Let me perfue my melancholy tafk.

                        [*Works at the infcription.*
            Enter FERDINAND.

                FERDINAND.
Away with their ill-tim'd, officious care.
I'll none of it — 'tis cruelty not friendfhip ——
'Tis mifery protracted, 'tis with art,
Inhuman art, to lengthen out the life
Of him who groans in torment — no — they
        never fhall
Compel me back to a bafe world again! ——
I've liv'd enough — my courfe is ended here —
For here Conftantia lies — ye heav'nly pow'rs!
What means upon yon confecrat d ground
That vifionary form, with lifted arm
And gleaming fteel, that feems in act to carve
The rugged ftone? ——

                            CONSTAN-

CONSTANTIA.

What is't I hear ! — a voice !
A groan ! — from whence — ha !

[*Seeing Ferdinand.*

FERDINAND.

'Tis, it is her ghost,
Her discontented shade that hovers still
About this place.

CONSTANTIA.

Avaunt, thou air-drawn shape
Of that Perfidious — ah ! —— [*She faints away.*

FERDINAND.

Leave me not thus ——
Oh ! ever gracious, ever gentle, say ——
'Tis gone — in sullen silence gone ! ——

Enter HENRICO.

HENRICO.

Quick let me find him, to his raptur'd ear
[*Laying hold of Ferdinand.*
Give the delightful tidings — ha !

FERDINAND.

And thus
I sink at once and follow my belov'd,
[*Falls into Henrico's arms.*

HENRICO.

He faints — He faints — the chilling dews of
death
Distil

Diſtil thro' ev'ry pore — my Ferdinand,
Awake, ariſe, and hear the joyful ſounds
Of happineſs reſtor'd — His eyes unfold
To ſeek fair day light, and now cloſe again
As if they ſicken'd at the view ——

FERDINAND.

Forbear,
And let me die! ——

HENRICO.

Conſtantia lives — ſhe lives
Once more to fold thee in her warm embrace.

FERDINAND.

I ſaw her fleeting ghoſt — ſullen and pale
It vaniſh'd from my ſight ——

CONSTANTIA.

Haunt me not thus
Thou cruel tyrant form! —   [Coming to herſelf.

HENRICO.

Whence is that voice?
Oh heav'ns — Conſtantia there! —— ſhe too
        entranc'd
Lies ſtretch'd upon the ground —

FERDINAND.

Where is Conſtantia?
Oh! let me fly to her embrace — 'tis ſhe —
                                            It

It is my wife! — it is Conſtantia! — ſtill,
— Oh! ecſtaſy of bliſs? — ſhe ſtill ſurvives —

CONSTANTIA.

'Tis mere illuſion all; — the falſe creation
Of ſome deceitful dream ——

FERDINAND.

'Tis real all ——
Again I fold her thus — the known embrace
Hath thrill'd it's wonted tranſport to my heart.
My life, my ſoul, thy Ferdinand is come,

CONSTANTIA.

And com'ſt thou then, inhuman as thou art,
Com'ſt thou again to wreak thy falſhood on me?

FERDINAND.

By heav'n I ne'er was falſe — daſh not my joys
With thy unkind ſuſpicion of my love,
While thus tranſported far above the lot
Of human bliſs, I preſs my lips to thine,
Inhaling balmy ſweets, and all my ſoul
Runs o'er with joy, with wonder and delight.

CONSTANTIA.

Did'ſt thou not meanly leave me here a prey?

FERDINAND.

And can Conſtantia deem me then ſo baſe?
Can ſhe believe me ſuch a vile betrayer?
— Can'ſt thou? ——

CONSTANTIA.

On this unhoſpitable ſhore
Left as I was ——

FERDI-

FERDINAND.

Oh! mifery! — thou we're
While I was dragg'd by an infidious band
Of pyrates, favage blood-hounds! into bondage
But witnefs heav'n — witnefs ye midnight hours
That heard my ceafelefs groans, how her dear
    image
Grew to my very heart! ——

CONSTANTIA.

And haft thou then
Been doom'd to flavery?

FERDINAND.

I have.

CONSTANTIA.

And groan'd
This long, long time beneath oppreffion's hand?

FERDINAND.

E'er fince thefe eyes have gaz'd delighted on
    thee,
The bitter draught of mifery was mine.

CONSTANTIA.

And wert thou true indeed?

FERDINAND.

By heav'n I was.

CONSTANTIA.

And have I then accus'd thee? — have I pour'd
A thoufand ftrong complaints againft thee? —
    called

High

High judging heav'n to witnefs to my wrongs,
Told all thefe wilds, thefe rocks, thefe wood-
  crown'd hills
Of injur'd truth and violated love?
Falfely I talk'd, unjuftly I complain'd
Of injur'd truth and violated love,
My Ferdinand was true — again 'tis giv'n
With his lov'd form to glad thefe eyes, to rufh
With eager tranfport to his fond embrace,
To cling around his neck, and growing to him
Pour the warm tears of rapture and of love.

       [They embrace.

Enter SYLVIA.

SYLVIA.

I heard my mother's voice — what do I fee?
In a man's arms! — embracing and embrac'd!

FERDINAND.

Is that my Sylvia? — oh! it muft be fo ———
My child, my child furvives! — furvives to take
A raptur'd father's blefling, and o'erpay
His fuff'rings paft by his excefs of joy,
This interview of mingled tears and kiffes.

       [Embraces her.

SYLVIA.

How gentle his deportment too! — I feel
A foft attraction bind my foul to his.
—Mama, are thefe the men, whom you defcrib'd
Inexorable, cruel, fell deceivers? ———

    H   CONSTAN-

CONSTANTIA.

I was deceiv'd myself, my child; for truth,
Honour, and love, and conftancy are theirs.
I now have proof of unexampled goodnefs

SYLVIA.

Indeed I ftrongly thought you wrong'd 'em
much,
When firft Henrico met my wond'ring eyes.

FERDINAND.

Henrico is my friend, my beft, Conftantia,
And thou hereafter fhalt know all his virtues.

SYLVIA.

And fhall I know him too? ——

HENRICO.

Thou fhalt; —and I
Will live thy flave, if thou wilt deign to love me.

SYLVIA.

Love you! — I know not what you mean by
love;
But if with pleafure to behold thee; if
To hang upon thy words; to mourn thy abfence;
With joy to meet again, and feel my heart
Form new defires, and wifh it knows not what,
If that be love — I do already love you ——
I love you better than my fawn.

HENRICO.

How fweet
The voice of innocence — oh! thou fhalt be, ——
— My

—My friend will smile consent,—yes, thou fair
   nymph,
Shalt be my bride ——

SYLVIA.

Your bride! — what's that?

HENRICO.

My wife. ——

SYLVIA.

No, sir, not that. — I crave your pardon there ——
— I beg to be excus'd — I do not chuse
To be left helpless on a desert island.

CONSTANTIA.

Thy father did not leave me, Sylvia; — no; —
He could not prove deliberately false.
His heart was unsusceptible of fraud. ——
— Anon you'll know it all. ——

HENRICO.

Mean time, my fair,
Banish thy fears; and let me with this kiss
On the white softness of this lovely hand,
For ever dedicate my heart.

SYLVIA.

Oh! heav'ns!
What must I do, Mama? ——

CONSTANTIA.

Requite his love
With fair return of thine, ——

SYLVIA.

SYLVIA.

Muft I do fo! ——
The tafk appears not undelightful — yes;
To thee I can refign myfelf.— but tell me;
Wilt thou ne'er leave me? wilt thou ever here
Fix thy abode? ——

HENRICO.

No;— we'll convey thee hence,
To the foft influence of a milder clime:
There, like a flow'r tranfplanted, thou fhalt
    flourifh,
And ne'er regret this warmer fouthern fky,
But thrive and ripen, to the wond'ring world
Unfolding all thy fweets to higher bloom

SYLVIA.

What place is that? — and whither will ye bear
    me?

FERDINAND.

To thy dear native foil — to England, love. —

SYLVIA.

To England!

HENRICO.

Yes! the land of beauteous dames;
'Mongft whom thy matchlefs excellence fhall
    fhine
With undiminifh'd radience, and exert
It's gentle pow'r, by innocence endear'd,
By virtue heighten'd, and by modeft truth
                            Attemper'd

Attemper'd to such sweetness, that each fair
With unrepining heart, and glad consent
Shall own thy rival claim; and ev'ry youth
Touch'd by the graces of thy native beauty,
Shall join to make thy form the public care.

SYLVIA.

I cannot quit this Island ; — cannot leave
These woods, these lawns, these hills and deep-
        ning vales,
These streams of-visited, each well known haunt
Where hand in hand with innocence I've stray'd,
And tasted joys serene as in the air,
That pants upon yon trembling leaves. ——

FERDINAND.

Such joys
For thee shall blossom in thy native land,
And new delights arise. — There cultur'd fields
Wave with the golden harvest ; commerce pours
Each delicacy forth ; there stately domes
Attract the wond'ring eye ; there cities swarm
With busy throngs intense, and smiles around
A scene of active, cheerful, social life.
Thither I'll lead thee, sweet ——

SYLVIA.

And yet my heart
Misgives me much : — does not contention there,
And civil discord render life a scene
Of care, and toil, and struggle ? — does not
        war
From foreign nations oft invade the land,
With all his train of misery and death ?

FERDI-

FERDINAND.

Thy lovely fears are groundlefs — ours the
                land
Where inward peace diffufes fmiles around,
And fcatters wide her bleffings — there a
        king, ——
(My friend comes later thence, and tells me all)
There reigns a happy venerable king
Difpenfing juftice and maintaining laws
That bind alike his people and himfelf.
From that fource liberty and ev'ry claim
A free-born people boaft, flow equal on
And harmonize the ftate; while in the eve
And calm decline of life our monarch fees
A royal grandfon ftill to higher luftre
Each day expanding; emulous to trace
His granfire's fteps, to copy out his actions;
And bid the ray of freedom onward ftretch
To ages yet unborn.

SYLVIA.

And do the people
Know their own happinefs?

FERDINAND.

They do, my fweet:
Pleas'd they behold their native rights fecur'd;
Their commerce guarded, and the ufeful arts,
That raife, that foften, and embellifh life,
All to perfection rifing. With a fenfe

Of

Of their own bleffing touch'd, with one confent
They pour their treafures, and exhauft their
    blood
In their king's righteous caufe; and Albion thus
Raifes her envied head; thus ev'ry threat
Of foreign force, each menace of invafion
From a vain, vanquifh'd, difappointed foe,
Like broken billows on her craggy cliffs,
Shall murmur at her feet in vain. ——

S Y L V I A.

Methinks
I long to fee this place ——

F E R D I N A N D.

My Sylvia, yes,
Thou fhalt return — propitious gales invite —
Come then, Conftantia — oh! what mix'd emo-
    tions
Heave in this bofom at the fight of thee? —

C O N S T A N T I A.

I too run o'er with ecftacy of joy,
And tears muft fpeak my happinefs — I long
To utter all my fond, fond thoughts; — to tell
The ftory of my woes, and hear of thine;
While at each word our hearts fhall melt within
    us,
And thrill with grief, with tendernefs, and love.

F E R D I N A N D.

The tale fhall ferve us in our future hours
Of tender intercourfe, to fweeten pain,

                                                To

To calm adversity, and teach our souls
To bend in love, in gratitude, and praise
To the All-good on high, who thus befriends
The cause of innocence; who thus rewards
Our suffering constancy; whose hand, tho' flow,
Thus leads to rapture thro' a train of woe.

FINIS.

www.ingramcontent.com/pod-product-compliance
Lightning Source LLC
Chambersburg PA
CBHW030923050726
47498CB00003BA/881